Heathens

A Vampire Mafia Romance

Thea Lawrence

Book One of the Blood and Bullets Duet

Edited by Kayla Morton and Ben Browning

Cover design by 3 Crows Book Author Services

https://linktr.ee/3crows.author.services

@3crows.author.services on Instagram

ISBN: 9781738881024

Print: 978-1-7388810-1-7

Kindle: B0BM74DTKK

AUTHOR'S NOTE

AND PLAYLIST

This book contains adult scenes and dangerous situations, including: Dismemberment, primal play/chase kink, praise kink, degradation and humiliation kink, gun play, knife play, choking, spit kink, masturbation with blood, guns/gun violence, slapping, discussions of drugs, frequent alcohol and tobacco use, blood drinking/blood play, discussions of grief, discussions of child loss, mentions of physical abuse and sexual assault, torture and mentions of torture, the aftermath of a pandemic, drugging, kidnapping, unprotected sex, misogyny, dubious consent.

Playlist

For those of us who love a walking red flag.

CONTENTS

Epigraph	1
1. DOMINIC	2
2. DOMINIC	9
3. SOFIE	17
4. SOFIE	24
5. DOMINIC	32
6. SOFIE	43
7. DOMINIC	55
8. SOFIE	62
9. SOFIE	71
10. DOMINIC	77
11. DOMINIC	85
12. SOFIE	93
13. DOMINIC	100
14. DOMINIC	106
15. DOMINIC	113
16. SOFIE	122
17. DOMINIC	131

18. SOFIE   141

19. SOFIE   152

20. SOFIE   160

21. DOMINIC   172

22. SOFIE   180

23. SOFIE   188

24. DOMINIC   198

25. SOFIE   206

26. DOMINIC   213

27. DOMINIC   218

28. SOFIE   224

29. SOFIE   233

30. DOMINIC   240

31. DOMINIC   247

32. SOFIE   259

33. DOMINIC   268

Thank You   276

About the Author   277

The Prince of Darkness is a gentleman.
- William Shakespeare, King Lear (Act 3, Scene 4)

DOMINIC

SANTA CRUZ, CALIFORNIA, 1987

MY FOOT'S ON THE gas as we leave the city behind us – not that there's much to leave behind. It's mostly desolate after the plague, the riots, and our not-so-subtle takeover.

The Ferris wheel's been toppled over for years, and the roller coaster tracks are home to juvenile vampires who use them to ambush any humans who may walk by at night.

Once chipper-looking storefronts have punched out windows; shards of broken glass still stuck in the frames that resemble jagged teeth, waiting to devour anything that walks past.

Through the winding roads, I see a white building reflecting the moonlight that pours down like liquid silver. I slow the car down and turn off the headlights so as not to give away our position.

"Okay. We have two hours to get this done before the sun rises and we turn into little piles of goo."

"Dominic, this is insane."

I kill the engine and smile.

"It is, but that's what makes it so brilliant."

Theo's hands are twitching more than usual as he glowers at the building, and I can't help but grin even wider. He has one of the most formidable faces I've ever seen, like someone chiseled his furrowed brow out of granite. The guy always looks like he's trying to figure out a math equation that's *really* pissing him off.

He lets out a heavy sigh, shaking his head as he picks at the skin around his claw-like nails.

He's always been the more uptight of the two of us, though I'm sure he'd call himself calculated. Careful. But me? To my face he'd say I'm reckless, but I know he thinks I'm a fuckin' idiot.

Personally, I prefer passionate.

I fix my hair in the side mirror, making sure that the streak of silver is fully visible among the dark strands. The reflection always throws people off at first, but I'm glad that aspect is little more than folklore. I'm not sure if I could deal with not knowing every line on my face, every speck of bright green hidden in my blue eyes. I've been working with the same reflection for over a century, and I never fail to craft my image with purpose.

Benefits of a less than mystical vampirism, I suppose.

"This plan's not just insane, it's really fuckin' stupid," he mutters.

He's sure not to face me, but we both know I heard it.

"You've been saying that the entire drive over. Wouldn't shut up about it."

"Dom, it's just a fuckin' warehouse! Why does this place even matter to you?"

He knows why.

"If it's *just a warehouse*, why is he keeping it so hidden? Why is it off the books?"

He has his own little nightclub up near the mountains, very exclusive and guarded by a small army of vampires and human goons. Only those who are invited get to party there. Anything he wants, goes. Murder, mayhem, you name it. If he wants you gone at the end of the night, you're *gone*.

But this? I at least expected one of his men to be standing outside with a gun in his hand. Instead, it's totally barren. There are some windows that are boarded up, and the door is chained and locked from the outside. That wouldn't even keep raiders out, let alone someone like me.

"How do you know this place even belongs to Rene? What if the human was just lying to you?"

I snort.

"Nobody lies to you while you're pulling their teeth out."

Getting him to talk was easy. It always is when you're as good as I am. You could call it a passion of mine.

"Just think about it Theo, none of this makes any sense. Why does he even own this building? Why is it out in the middle of nowhere? Why is he keeping it hidden but leaving it completely unguarded?"

"Because he's a power hungry, arrogant fuckin' maniac? Who the fuck knows with Rene?" Theo reaches into his pocket and stuffs a cigarette between his lips. "You know, we could be doing something fun right now, or, hey, even something boring! Literally anything other than walking into this potential death trap."

"Yeah, like what?" I ask. "What's a guy like you want to get up to in a hole like Santa Cruz?"

"Get laid, get drunk, eat someone? Remember when we used to drive up to San Fran and party all night? How come we never do that shit anymore?"

"Revenge."

Theo scoffs, straightening himself and lowering his voice in mockery..

"*Revenge*. Fuck, you sound like such a dick."

"I *am* a dick, and wait, that was supposed to sound like me?"

"So, revenge for what?" he asks, ignoring me completely. "He hasn't done anything to you in forever. Fuck, he practically lets you run wild."

I shake my head, affording him a soft chuckle.

"You still don't get it? This isn't about some recent sleight. This is about getting what's mine, about getting what he promised me."

Before he can bite back, headlights shine into the rearview mirror. The disappointment in Theo's eyes might have crushed me if I could still bring myself to care.

"Dom, tell me you didn't call them."

I pat him on the shoulder.

"It's a team effort, Tierney."

Theo and I step out of the car while Luke and Mateo prepare their weapons. They're both dressed in black suits with matching dress shirts and ties. It's a bit much, but who am I to ruin their fun?

Mateo's conventionally attractive, shorter than me by a few inches, and packs a hell of a lot of muscle onto his frame. If he weren't so pale, he'd almost look like your typical California boy, with long blond hair and a slightly crooked nose from one too many breaks, all topped off with gray eyes that remind me of storm clouds.

Luke is the polar opposite, with short dark hair and brown eyes. He has a slightly rounder, chubbier face, and thick dark brows that always make him look like he's scowling, unless he's grinning like an idiot, which is often. His thin frame doesn't quite fill out his suits, and he almost looks like he's swimming in them at the worst of times.

I lean in and kiss Mateo on the forehead, patting his cheek as he unloads some gas cans from the trunk, one for each of us.

"You're a good man, Mateo. Have I told you that?"

He flinches, fear in his eyes.

"No, sir, this would be the first time."

I chuckle as I grab one of the cans and thrust it into the air.

"Let's go, boys! Let's see what big, bad Rene Deschamps has squirreled away in his warehouse. Maybe it's a gorgeous woman. You've been looking for one of those, huh, Theo? Now that I think of it, how long's it been since Debbie left you?"

"Shut up," Theo mutters. "Asshole."

Luke and Mateo chuckle as the four of us head toward the building, climbing through brush and dead branches to reach an overgrown staircase.

"Dom, you have to know this could be a trap." Theo's voice is quiet, barely audible over the sound of Mateo kicking away dried twigs and leaves.

"Sure, but so what if it is?" I shrug. "We've got guns."

"Great," Theo mutters. "You thought of everything."

I clap him on the back. He's been there for me since we were young, always my right-hand man, and through it all I can't think of a single time he's put up with my shit. More important than that, though, he's never really had much of a sense of humor.

"Come on, lighten up for once, huh? You said you wanted to have fun. This is fun!"

I hear something crack around the side of the building as Theo rolls his eyes. Luke has already wandered off and the three of us leap over the railing, heading straight for the noise. We spot him tossing decayed plywood behind him as he clears away jagged pieces of glass with his foot.

"See, it's great news! We don't even need to blow up the front door," I boast, puffing out my chest.

As we crawl through the window, my eyes quickly adjust to the dark, taking in the scene and assessing for any potential threats. It's the most benign place in the world, maybe a little distressing for humans, but not for us. The only mildly notable aspect is the pungent stench of bleach.

So it turns out Rene's hidden gem is an old hospital. There's graffiti on the walls and floors, a wheelchair abandoned near a stairwell and some gurneys that have been toppled over as though everyone here left in a hurry. I spot bloody handprints on the wall that wouldn't seem out of place in a horror attraction, and the underlying smell of piss and shit, unfortunately, explains the bleach.

"Where'd the kid say to go?" Theo asks.

"Up," I reply curtly.

Dark stains look to be nearly consuming the peeling white paint on the ceiling. It looks like blood, but it's too old to tell from a look.

"Up. That's all you got?" Theo scoffs.

I light up a cigarette and take a long drag.

"Well, the building only has two floors, Theo. It's up or down– and give the kid a break. You think you could communicate complex ideas with half your teeth missing?" I grin. "I was quite happy with simple answers at that point."

"You didn't *have* to pull out his teeth, we would have gotten it out of him."

I shrug.

"I know, but it's so much *fun* when they scream. Gives me a little..." I shiver, exaggerating the motion.

Theo lets out a heavy sigh. I can tell he's already tired of my theatrics.

But that's only the half of it. I get a kick out of killing Rene's lap dogs whenever I can find them. I'd take down every single one of them if I could get away with it, but he's been especially quiet lately. Some people are saying he's skipped town, but I don't buy that for a second. He's got nothing to gain from leaving, and everything to lose. He's planning something. I just don't know what it is.

"Found a stairwell!" Luke calls from the end of the hall.

Not yet, at least.

Luke reaches the top of the stairs first, listening at a door before signaling the all-clear. He tries the handle, but it's locked, so he leans back and kicks the entire thing off of its hinges.

"Atta boy, Lukie!" I shout, stepping through the threshold into an expansive, and surprisingly clean laboratory.

There are notes scattered around the counters, formulas written in chalk on the walls, and some kind of dark liquid in beakers and small vials. Scanning the rest of the room, I quickly spot a large black bag on the floor and freeze.

"Dom, I fuckin' told you, it's a trap!"

Looks like Theo's seen it too.

"You don't know what it is," I snap back.

"I don't? Because that looks like a bomb to me. How about you?"

I shrug.

"And we're immortal, so it's no big deal."

"Not technically immortal, though." Mateo counters.

Luke points at his best friend, nodding, with big puppy dog eyes.

"Immortal or not, I don't want to spend the next three days looking like someone ran over a Big Mac with a tractor!" Theo exclaims.

I ignore Theo, turning to Luke and giving him a quick nod.

"Alright, open it."

"Me? Why should I have to–"

I drop my can of gasoline on the ground, rip my pistol out of my jacket and fire at his feet. A deafening *crack* echoes through the room and Luke leaps into the air, hissing at me.

Bullets might not mean much to us, but they're still a bitch to deal with in high enough volume, and like Theo, very few of us enjoy the prospect of being a bloody pulp while we slowly heal. The more serious among us, however, come prepared. My bullets are made of silver, with essence-of-garlic packed into the hollow point for good measure. Like so many things, humans figured it out first and we get to take full advantage of it.

Sure, there are the classics like decapitation or direct sunlight. Those are still effective, but there's something to be said for the elegance of a bullet.

"*Open it,*" I snarl through clenched teeth.

Theo takes a step forward, but I stop him, placing a hand on his chest.

"Very kind of you to offer, but it's not your job."

Luke glances between us, clearly panicking as I level the gun at his head.

"One more chance, Lukie: be a good boy, and open the bag."

DOMINIC

RENE'S LAB

MY SHOE TAPS OUT an impatient rhythm against the tile as everyone stares at Luke crouching in front of the bag, psyching himself up. He reaches for the zipper and slowly starts the unveiling. His hand is trembling. It's so quiet that I can hear the wind rustling the trees outside.

I rub the back of my neck, trying to rid myself of the icy feeling that's shooting down my spine. This could be a trap, and I could have just fucked us over. Big time. I glance at Theo, whose eyes are fixed on that bag as the slow sound of the zipper opening gets louder and louder. He looks like he wants to scream as he runs his hand through his hair.

The moment of tension is short-lived, however. As the bag opens, Luke lets out a relieved sigh, holding up a small vial of red liquid.

The others look to be a mix of relieved and confused. I'm immediately transfixed.

"What the fuck is that?"

"Don't know, don't care." Luke murmurs.

I stride over to him and take the vial from his hands.

"Dom, be careful," Theo warns.

"Thank you for your concern, it's noted."

Theo's always ready for the worst, but if I listened to him, we'd never get anything done. I unscrew the cap while the other three watch on with bated breath. Theo has his hand on his gun while Luke backs away, eyeing me with trepidation. Mateo hasn't stopped chewing his fingernails.

I close my eyes and sniff at the liquid: copper and iron.

I grin.

"It's blood," I whisper, my mouth beginning to water as I raise my voice. "Just blood, boys. You can relax."

"You don't know that," Theo hisses. "Put it down. We need to figure out what this place is for."

I take another whiff. There's the copper, and the iron again... but there's something else, something chemical that I can't quite place.

Theo is already walking around rifling through papers and looking up at the formulas on the chalkboard.

"So what's the report, Einstein?"

"I don't know," Theo replies. "But I have a feeling *that* shit is the whole point."

"Yeah, you think they're producing it or something?" He ignores me as he rustles more papers.

I raise the vial to my lips. This is boring, and there's no time like the present.

"Dom!" Mateo's eyes go wide as they meet mine. "What are you–"

Theo whips around, a pad of paper clutched in his fist, as I drain the mystery liquid. The second it hits my tongue, I can't help but let out a groan. Exquisite. It's hard to imagine it was brewed in a lab. It tastes almost exactly the same as the real thing.

"Dom, stop!" Theo shouts.

I toss the vial on the ground, savoring the appealing sound of shattered glass as I drop to my knees. I want more. There has to be more in the bag. Sure enough, it's full of them. But no, these are different: clear liquids labeled with names I could never hope to pronounce. I lick my lips as I rifle through the rest of the bag's contents for more finished vials.

"It's blood, Theo, like I said."

"No, it's not, you idiot!" I can practically feel Matteo and Luke tense up as he berates me. They rarely see me let things slide, but Theo's a special case. "It's some sort of synthetic concoction. There's something else in there. It's not pure!"

He thrusts out a pad of paper covered with calculations into my chest.

"The fuck am I supposed to do with this?"

Theo points at an equation, holding my gaze with his icy stare.

"It's *almost* vampire blood, but not quite. They've either done something to a real batch, or somehow made it themselves from scratch." He glances at the boys and back at me, lowering his voice. "We don't know what we're dealing with here. There's no talk about this anywhere right now, so what do you think Rene's gonna do when he finds out we know about this shit?"

Vampire blood is extremely valuable, but obviously in relatively short supply. For humans it's an inoculant against almost any disease, but it also has some... side effects. They experience euphoria and temporarily heightened senses. It's like ecstasy, except it doesn't fuck with your brain chemistry. At least not long term. For us, it's usually just a great vintage. Obviously a little frowned upon, but mostly fine if you don't get hooked.

"So what's this?" I ask, shaking the pad of paper. "The recipe?"

Theo sighs, rubbing his eyes.

"It's called a formula, genius."

He paces around the room, taking quick glances at some of the scrawled equations and other haphazardly placed notes.

"It looks like this is the one they've been using, maybe the final version."

"How do you know?" Mateo pipes in. Poor fool looks like he has even less of a clue than the rest of us.

"Because the other papers only have half of this. Whatever Rene is trying to make, whatever this is supposed to be, it's some sort of mix. The base is clearly blood, either vampire or human, but it gets combined with some other stuff. Probably those other vials," Theo explains.

"The clear shit? So what is it, and what's he making all this for? He owns the goddamn city. What, he wants a drug racket on the side?" I chime in.

Theo pinches the bridge of his nose.

"Does it look like 'my secret plan' is written anywhere on the page?"

I frown, ready to retort, but Theo moves in close, lowering his voice again.

"If Deschamps is making this, he's doing it for a reason. It can't just be to sell to humans, can it?"

"Maybe he just wants to make some really tasty blood?" Luke offers.

Theo's barely holding himself together, and I can't help but grin whenever Luke riles him up. I may just have to thank Rene personally for this stupid lab after all.

"You know what? I've decided. Everyone's got a vice, and why not help them out by providing the best possible experience? More importantly, we get to screw Deschamps out of whatever he's got planned, and *I* get fucking rich in the process. Boys, grab what's left of the bag and let's get the fuck out of here. And don't forget the gas, we're torching the place along the–"

"Not so fast!" A voice barks from the door.

Shit.

I quickly stow my gun in my coat, ensuring it's hidden before turning to face our new guest.

A blonde woman in a black leather jacket with dark eyes points a crossbow at us. Well, mostly at me. I can hear her heartbeat from here, clearly human. She has mottled, nearly ashen skin, and dark circles underneath her eyes. I can smell the sweat on her body before it even forms on her forehead, and I spot the puncture wounds on her neck just as Rene's stench wafts toward me. I can barely hold back the urge to gag.

"I see Rene's sent his best and brightest to guard the place."

"Put the formula down!" She shouts. "There are more of us coming. You'd better leave while you can!"

I chuckle.

"Somehow, I doubt that."

I take a step forward, and her whole body straightens, aiming the crossbow vaguely at my chest. Sure, if that thing hits just right I'm toast, but she's far from a marksman.

"Take one more step and you're dead!"

I grin and look around at Theo and the rest of the boys. They all have their hands in the air, half in mockery. Mateo is already licking his chops. He hasn't eaten well in a few days. Hell, neither have I.

As she cranes her neck to get a full view of what she's up against, I spot Rene's brand on her neck. A deep "R" burned roughly into her skin to let everyone know where her loyalties lie. I can't judge, there's one burnt right into my chest, and it's a lot harder to make them stick when your body naturally heals. At one point I might have even taken it as a mark of pride, but now it's a secret shame, buried under a stretch of tattoos.

Rene loves to do this shit, to brand people like they're cattle. He gives them food and shelter and they get to live in relative luxury while he feeds off of them. When they've outlived their usefulness, they get that coveted invite to his private place up in the mountains. I sometimes wonder how many go knowing what's coming, and how many others still trust him up to the very end.

She doesn't look like she's too much longer for this world, but even if she's not next on the chopping block, a failure like this will be her end. At least I can offer her a less gruesome exit. At least a little.

"Put the crossbow down, dollface."

She bares her teeth and tightens her aim on my chest. While I admire the tenacity of humans, it can get dull to deal with, and there's nothing I hate more than being bored.

"Okay," I shrug. "We'll do this the hard way, then."

Her eyes narrow as I reach for my hidden gun, and I can see her fingers almost grasp the trigger, but I just barely beat her to the punch. A single shot rings out, echoing through the room as the hole her bolt tore through my jacket compliments the gushing wound in the center of her chest. She hits the ground with a thud, her body trying to process the shock.

There's blood everywhere, and I can already feel myself losing control. Luke and Mateo creep toward her, slow and silent, hissing softly. I can feel their hunger matching my own. My jaw tingles, fists clenched, as the smell of her fresh blood begins to overwhelm me.

I take a step forward.

"You boys hungry?"

Mateo rumbles like a beast waiting to strike, but Theo lurches past the others without a word, grabbing the woman by her hair and slamming her up against the wall. The longer I stare at her, the less human she becomes. She's just the blood dripping from her mouth. Pouring from her chest. Just food.

But it's impossible to ignore that smile. It's vicious; completely overwhelming every other part of her even as she slowly loses consciousness.

"You had a chance. He won't stop. You know he won't."

She thinks I'm afraid of him. It'd be worth a laugh if I wasn't so fucking hungry.

The four of us descend on her like vultures on a corpse. I tear into her flesh, savoring the squelching wet sounds as I go. Her still-warm blood quickly coats my throat and my eyes roll back in blissful ecstasy as she screams.

I didn't realize how hungry I was.

Theo groans, sucking on her neck and tearing until her jugular bursts. Blood spurts from the wound like a grotesque fountain. Luke and Mateo take a wrist each as her body convulses, her head slamming against a wall accompanied by a gurgling groan. In moments, the entire room stinks of the most exquisite scent, and in another minute her heart is stopped for good.

We drink until she's dry, and by the time I manage to pull myself away, she's less than a husk. I back up, panting as I wipe my mouth on the sleeve of my jacket while the others come up for air.

Mateo's eyes are wide, dancing around for another food source. When he spots the pool of blood on the floor, he rushes for it. I grab him by the back of his suit like a mother cat would grab a kitten.

I can sense his hunger, his desperation. He's still young and having difficulty controlling his bloodlust. The dwindling human population hasn't made things easier.

Mateo gnashes his teeth at me as I grip his chin as hard as I can, feeling the bone almost give way beneath my fingertips.

"We're. Not. Animals."

"But boss, I'm *starving*!" He looks pathetic, like a child begging for dessert.

My jaw clenches as Theo and Luke wipe their mouths, both licking the blood from their fingers. Theo walks past me, grabbing the black bag and tucking the formula inside of it.

"I'm guessing you still want this?"

"Yeah, we're taking it with us." I turn to Mateo. "Do whatever you need to in here, but pour the gas over everything once you're finished. I don't want a trace of a formula left for Rene to work with. This blood, drug, whatever it is, it's *mine*. Understood?"

"Yes, boss," Mateo almost sobs with joy. "Thank you."

The second I release him he dives for the floor, his tongue sliding against the tile as he laps up the pool of coagulating blood. He even grabs the dead woman's fingers and sucks on them like candy.

Theo lets out a disgusted groan as he retrieves his own gas can.

"Christ, Mateo. Show some fuckin' decorum."

"He's young. Let him be," I mutter. "Mateo, you have five minutes! Do *not* make me come back up here."

As we reach the door, I motion to the opposite ends of the hallway. The boys head off without another word as I pop a cigarette into my mouth. Theo's gas can is the first to empty, but it's not too long before Luke saunters back toward me and I check my watch.

"Mateo! Your five minutes are up!"

A pathetic yelp rings out from beyond the doorway and moments later he's barreling down the stairs, draining his can behind him. Gasoline cascades down the steps as he finishes emptying it, tossing it into the corner before turning to look at me, expectantly. There's blood on his chin, all down his neck, his hands... it's even in his hair.

"You get everything?" I ask.

He nods, and I wrap an arm around his shoulder.

"Well then, I think we can call this a successful outing. Let's go, boys."

Back outside, Theo stands beside me as I light a cigarette. I take a good long drag as we stare up at the soon-to-be inferno in silence. Across the street Luke and Mateo struggle to load everything into their car, still a little blood-drunk in the afterglow.

Theo releases his longest sigh of the night and I raise a brow.

"Rene's gonna hunt us down, you know. There's no coming back from this."

I smirk, taking one last drag before flicking the cigarette onto the gas-trail at my feet. Within a minute or two, the whole thing will be up in flames.

"Let him try."

SOFIE

Nox Nightclub

I HATE IT HERE.

Okay, maybe hate is a strong word, but it's hard to feel *good* about finally becoming a business owner when it's during the goddamn apocalypse.

I used to be a lab tech at Santa Cruz Blood Bank. I worked hard, and I loved my job. Eventually, I wanted to be a doctor. I wanted to help people. Now, I run a vampire bar. The upside to all of this is that my ass looks great in latex dresses.

Ruby and I opened Nox in '86, a few years after everything went to shit. In the beginning, it was just to survive, but soon we realized we could take some power back from the vamps who took our city for their own. We couldn't give them the satisfaction, the right to obliterate us, so we carved out our own little corner of the city. A year later, we're thriving. Nox is a key pillar of the community, and the buffer between them and us.

In the early days, when we still had the resources, some of us ran tests on the few vampires we managed to kill. We quickly discovered that their blood had healing capabilities, not just for them but for us. It helps with smaller wounds, bolsters the immune system, and acts as a kind of inoculant against the plague that was killing us.

So, we used that knowledge to our advantage. Early negotiations led to the realization that both groups had something to offer; trading in blood only made sense, in a sick sort of way. But we had to convince their leaders that population control was good for them, that they couldn't just go on a feeding frenzy. It didn't happen overnight, but even the most stubborn vamp started to realize that all of us dying in a few years wasn't the best of plans.

Now we get booster shots every six months, and in return we provide a continuous food source. We donate blood to the blood bank to keep them fed and they don't run rampant and kill all of us. The goal is to live together in some kind of harmony. Sure, some of them want nothing more than to drain us until we're dry, but the more reasonable vampires understand the delicate balance that has to be maintained.

I balance my arm on the desk as I lean over the tiny, nearly shattered compact that I've had since I was sixteen. All I can see is a green eye surrounded by glittery copper shadow and strawberry blonde lashes. I've successfully covered my dark circles with powder, but as the night wears on, they'll rear their ugly head again. I don't even have much of this shit left.

Makeup and perfume are hot commodities these days, given production is effectively non-existent, at least in Santa Cruz. I give a vamp some extra blood, or an enterprising human a stack of cash, and they give me a few tubes of lipstick and some powder. Sometimes I wonder if things are as fucked in the other cities.

As I'm dragging the eyeliner across my lid to make a wing, a knock on the door makes me jump out of my skin.

"Shit!"

Close to five years of disease, famine, and spending practically every night in hiding made me more than a little nervous. There's not a day that goes by where I don't dream of dying, each time in some increasingly horrific way.

Luckily, when I gather my nerves to look up, all that's in the doorway is my business partner, Ruby. She's pulled her long dark hair into a high ponytail, and she's sporting a black spandex dress that's so short I can see her underwear from this angle.

The sluttier we dress, the more the vamps like it. Sure, the world's practically come to an end, but some things never change.

"Sofie, you've got to loosen up. You look like a mess!" She laughs.

"And you've gotta learn to knock quieter."

"Yeah, sure, it's my fault you're so on-edge knocking on a door gives you a heart attack."

I flip her off and she cackles, sauntering toward me as I pick up the eyeliner pen and finish my wing.

"You need me out there? Another fight?"

"Nah. We're fine on that front. But we *are* almost out of A negative. O negative, too."

"Again?" I sigh. "We opened like two hours ago."

"That last batch you got is popular. I don't know what's different, but they're going fucking crazy over it. Greg tried to suck it off of my goddamn fingers."

She shudders and I follow suit. Some of them are disgusting enough to make the money seem less enticing.

"Well, there should be more in the fridge in the back. We always have extra stock."

Ruby shakes her head.

"Checked it. Nothing."

"Basement?" I ask with a wince, already knowing the answer.

"Gone," she replies, reaching into my desk drawer and pulling out a pile of papers to get at the pack of cigarettes she knows I'm hiding.

She drops the papers on my desk as she lights up a smoke. I glance down at them, and can't help but feel nostalgic. My dissertation, abandoned before I could even get started on it. Sometimes I still rifle through it and wonder what I could have been if everything hadn't come crashing down around us. Usually I just hide shit underneath it.

Ruby takes a drag, a look of calm rolling across her face. I wouldn't have survived any of this without her. She's like liquid sunshine, or she would be if sunshine had the foulest mouth on earth. She's sweet with customers, but she's got the kind of bite that lets people know not to fuck with her. Hell, just last week I saw her shove a gun down a vamp's throat. No mercy.

"Hey, save some for me, you leech."

She strikes a playful pose, lazily gesturing with the cigarette in her hand.

"You know, Sof, you shouldn't smoke so much. It's bad for your health."

"Says the asthmatic. Gimme that."

I make a quick grab for it, but she easily steps aside.

"Fuck you!" She laughs, her dark blue eyes shining in the low light. "I'm stressed out, this is my therapy!"

"The blood problem? Can't we just offer them something else? Since when did these fuckers get so picky?"

"Nah, that's just it. We're running out of pretty much everything. I don't know about you, but a vamp bar running out of blood doesn't sound like a great time to me, especially with sunrise 6 hours out."

I take a deep breath, cracking my neck as I stand.

"I'll call the bank, see if they can run something over in a pinch."

"Great! I'll get the cash out of the vault."

"Double," I remind her. "Remember, delivery's extra at night."

She's already nodding as she heads for the door.

"So, what, five grand?"

"Maybe seven?" I call. "Make it worth the driver's while."

She stops and throws out a quick salute with two fingers.

"On it, boss."

"We're both the boss, Ruby. You can do this stuff too!" I yell after her, but she's already long gone.

Ruby's always been better at the whole bar-part of the operation, but I'm the one with the connections. She's never liked negotiating with the blood bank, says there's too much technical speak, and it all gives her flashbacks to her days as an ER nurse. I think she just doesn't enjoy doing the legwork, but who can blame her? Blood is finicky and has to be transported carefully. If it gets too warm, it's virtually unsellable. The vamps say it doesn't taste the same.

The bass from the music out front rattles the walls as I pull out a cigarette of my own and dial the blood bank. It rings and rings and rings, and I grow bored within seconds. My eyes fall to the polaroid on my desk, lingering a little longer than I'd like. Me and my baby boy Charlie. He's got that fiery red hair, just like mine, and a big smile that practically splits his face in half. I reach out and trace the outline of that smile. There's so much joy in his eyes, in his little arms that stretch out toward the camera while I push him on the swing. This picture is the only thing I have left of him – that and the memories. He died during the first wave of the plague, right along with Sam.

I blink away the threat of tears and suck a little harder on my cigarette. Most days, I try not to think about Charlie too much. It's hard to hold on to that grief. There's been so little time to mourn the ones we lost, and now, with this newfound stability, I'm too tired to do it. Sometimes I worry I wouldn't know how anymore.

We always share a few words of comfort when someone brings up the unending waves of death we've faced. There are always a few pats on the back, and some *I'm so sorry*'s, but nobody's really *there* for you. Who wants to sit here and listen to me cry over my dead son and husband? Everyone has a dead spouse, a dead child, a dead parent, a dead friend. I can't hold it against them, but it weighs on me all the same.

They haunt every room I'm in.

So I swallow it, every last bit along with shots of whiskey at the bar. Most nights, it's easier to be drunk. Even if I pretend to be okay, it comes out in nightmares, bursts of anger that seem to sprout up like weeds at the most innocuous things, or racing thoughts that keep me awake while I lie in bed.

I'm so tired of this anguish, but it seems like it's not tired of me.

Ruby's heels click against the floor, and suddenly, there's a rolled up bundle of cash in front of me. She grins and hops up onto the desk beside me, kicking her feet like she's a kid at the doctor's office.

Finally, the phone line clicks and someone picks up.

"Santa Cruz Blood Bank."

I turn on my best customer service voice and exhale smoke and grief all at once.

"Hey Avery! It's Sofie Fournier at Nox. We need another delivery–"

Avery laughs and I can hear the "no" already. It's in the way her tongue clicks.

"Can't do that. We're short-staffed."

"Come on, Avery," I whine, immediately losing my professional tone. "Don't do this to me."

Ruby raises an eyebrow.

"I'm sorry, but this is the third order in two weeks. I told you, we're short-staffed and we've got our donations coming up soon." Avery sounds exhausted. *"If you want more blood, you're going to have to come and pick it up."*

My eyes fall on the clock in front of me. It's only 11:00 pm. We need this blood to get us through the night.

"Fine," I groan. "I need 150 units of... god, just everything you can spare. It should tide us over for tonight."

"Business that good, huh?" Avery chuckles over the other line.

"Booming." I take a spin in my chair. "You should come and work here. I know you make a mean margarita."

"Nah, I like my workplace fang-free," she laughs. *"But hey, speaking of, you know you're always welcome back here, right? Any reason you're risking it all night after night?"*

"Because you don't pay enough."

"Sofie, you know all of that money goes–"

"Back into operations. I know, I know."

Avery would never admit it, but working at a blood bank is easily one of the most dangerous jobs in this city. The vampires monitor it like nothing I've ever seen before. Every shipment is a risk, and donation weeks are like bringing cattle into a slaughterhouse. Symbiotic relationship or no, not every vampire is out for the good of their kin. Some of them are starving, and others just don't care who or what they hurt.

"I'll get it ready. Just come through the back alley. The front's... well, it's just not a good idea right now."

"Great," I reply. "Thanks, Avery."

"See you in a bit, Sof."

I hang up the phone and put my head in my hands, groaning loudly. Ruby begins to rub my shoulders, and I already know what's coming next.

"You want help? I can put Kirby in charge while we're gone. She'll rule this joint with an iron fist."

"Yeah, until the blood runs out and she punches a vampire in the face," I murmur. "It's fine. I can go by myself."

"You know damn well that it's dangerous to go out on your own. *At night.* I'm coming with you." Her blue eyes are narrowed and hardened. "Don't be so proud, Sof. It makes you look like an idiot."

I relax my shoulders as she digs into them, cutting through the tension like butter.

"There's no getting you out of my hair, huh?"

"You're stuck with me," Ruby replies, giving me a quick slap on the back. "Now get your coat and let's go."

SOFIE

THE SANTA CRUZ BLOOD BANK

MY EYES SCAN THE street as I drive, raking over puddles covered with rainbow slicks of oil, flattened cardboard, smashed bottles, and plastic cups left abandoned on the ground. Everything near the old Santa Cruz Boardwalk lies in ruins.

Ruby's focused on the clock. The timing has to be exact. We don't want to wait outside of the bank for too long, or we're vulnerable. She exhales a cloud of smoke and chews on her lip.

There's reinforced glass on the van, and guns in the glove compartment loaded with silver bullets.

"I forgot how intense this shit is."

"Yeah," I mumble as I make a left-hand turn. "It's no wonder they hire those big dudes in those armored trucks to deliver this stuff."

"Yeah, and even *that's* not safe," Ruby mutters. "Remember what happened to Bill?"

"Poor bastard."

I draw a deep breath as the building comes into view. Humans guard the back doors in full riot gear with massive guns. I flash my lights three times to get their attention; the signal for a pickup. A while back, some vamps caught on to this little method of communication and tried to swarm them. Now, the Bank hires big burly dudes who can hold their own. They're armed to the teeth. I've seen these guys take on a group of vamps all at once like it's nothing.

The second I park the van, we're on the move. Ruby and I grab our weapons, looking straight ahead as we head for the back door. My muscles are coiled like springs, ready to run or fight. It's become my regular state of being.

As we approach, one of the guards lifts his helmet and I immediately recognize Jesse, with his warm brown eyes. He's massive, probably somewhere around 6'5", and at least 300 lbs of muscle. I smile reflexively. Jesse is a bright light, even on the darkest of nights.

"Avery said you were back on pickup duty!" He calls with a playful smile. "Good to see you both!"

"I wish it were under better circumstances!" I laugh as Jesse opens the door for us and ushers us inside.

The moment we step through the doors I find myself struggling to adjust to the extremely bright light, rooting through my bag for my sunglasses. The blood bank uses UV lights inside the hallways, so even if a vampire gets in, they're blistered and screaming within a minute or two; easy enough for the guards to pick off. I don't know how anyone works here without having a constant headache, though. Avery always said sunglasses are a life-saver, but my head kills me regardless.

"A's got the delivery for you up front," Jesse announces. "She's on her dinner break, doesn't want to be disturbed, otherwise she'd say hi."

"No, she wouldn't," I laugh.

Beside me, Ruby groans, covering her eyes with one hand. If she weren't wearing 40 pounds of eyeliner, she'd probably be rubbing it all off.

"Forgot my fuckin' glasses," she mutters.

Jesse chuckles as I hand mine to her.

"Are you sure?"

"Positive. You get migraines, I'm good, babe."

Ruby leans over and kisses me on the temple as we walk.

"Thanks."

The entire building smells like disinfectant and I can barely hear a goddamn sound as we move through the halls. I miss this place. It was quiet and simple work, and I loved my co-workers. I enjoyed testing blood, getting to learn a little something about each person who donated. The blood bank helped me pay my way through medical school, and it provided for my son. Then the world as I knew it ended, and so did my life.

Things were going too well, I guess.

"Business is good, I assume?" Jesse asks.

"It's great over there! You should come by for a drink, Jess," Ruby offers.

"Yeah, I'll put on my finest kevlar," he laughs. "I don't know how you run that place with all of those vamps. They have to be a couple seconds away from ripping out your throat at any given moment."

"Most of them are chill," Ruby replies. "Some of them are jerks, but the rules say we get to shoot them if they try to kill us, so... not too different from here!"

"Guess we're both livin' the dream, huh?" Jesse laughs.

We turn a corner and head toward the front of the building. There are more guards and a petite, mousy-looking girl with short blonde hair sitting at a desk. She's dressed in a dark red blouse with matching red lipstick. She reminds me of a pixie with a little upturned nose and full cheeks dusted with freckles. Her head whips up when she hears us approach and I can see her brows knit together, even underneath her sunglasses.

"The boss has a delivery for them," Jesse informs her. "Should be prepped."

"For Nox?" She asks.

"That's us," I confirm, digging into my pocket.

I pull out the wad of cash while the girl hands me a form confirming my order. I sign the dotted line at the bottom and hand her the money.

"There's about two grand extra in there. For your trouble."

"It's no trouble," she replies as she unrolls it and counts the cash so fast I can barely see her hands moving. "I just wish we had another driver. I'm sorry you had to come all the way down here."

"Well, you can use that to help with hiring some more," I tell her.

Even with everything being so transactional, we try to look out for each other. You never know when you're going to see someone again, if at all. People disappear so fast. Things go wrong so quickly.

Ruby grabs the case and turns to me, brows raised as I finish the transaction.

"You ready?"

I nod.

"I'll walk you out," Jesse says softly. He turns to me as we head for the exit. "We miss you here."

"Yeah, Avery said the same thing."

"You sure? That doesn't sound like her."

Ruby chuckles and I shake my head.

"Hey, so... you guys have really tightened up your operations since the last time I made a pickup."

"Yeah, A's been expanding on the deal with Deschamps. He wasn't too keen on the UV lights or hiring more guards, but she convinced him somehow. If this place is gonna run like clockwork, we need all the help we can get."

This operation really has changed a lot, far from the humble facility it was before the chaos took hold. It's basically a military outpost at this point. I miss the old days. Even if being locked in a lab for 10 hours a day is most peoples' idea of hell, it was important work. We saved a lot of lives. I guess they still do, in their own way.

Gotta keep the vampires fed.

"Well, you're doing a hell of a job," Ruby remarks.

"It's all Avery," Jesse chuckles. "This place would fall apart without her, or the suckheads would have taken it over."

All I can see are spots and bright lights when we hit the doors and step into the night. I rub my eyes and Ruby opens the back door of the van. We toss the bag inside while Jesse and the other guards keep watch, their guns at the ready and shields out. It's amazing how quickly the tone shifts when your lives are back on the line.

"I'll drive," Ruby offers.

"Thanks." I turn back to Jesse. "And hey, thanks for..."

"Doing my job?" He asks.

"Yeah," I chuckle. "Sure."

"Be safe on the drive back."

As I go to open the passenger side door I catch a car down the street out of the corner of my eye, with two men gathered around the trunk. One of them looks agitated, and both of them are covered in crimson. A third man climbs out of the car. It's hard to see exactly what he looks like outside of a few details as he leans against a streetlight, his long dark hair pushed back and out of his face and a cigarette stuffed between his lips.

Vampires, obviously. I can tell by the way they move as the first two head for the building. It's so fluid, every step, every reach, is like ballet. It's beautiful, and a little haunting. One of those things that you just can't help but be mesmerized by.

"Sof!" Ruby calls from inside the van, snapping me back to the moment. "Let's go!"

As I turn to grasp the door handle, the man with the cigarette in his mouth locks eyes with me, looking me up and down. My heart hammers against my ribs. Every alarm bell is going off. I'm not safe here.

As he exhales a gigantic cloud of smoke, I climb into the van and lock the door behind me.

"What was that?" Ruby hisses. "Are you trying to get yourself killed?"

"Sorry." I shake my head, trying to rid my mind of him. "It's nothing."

The man is still standing outside as we drive past. Staring at us. At me. I swear I can see him smirk as Ruby turns the corner.

"You know him or something?" She asks.

"No," I murmur. "Probably just a hungry vamp looking for blood."

She makes another right hand turn back toward the bar and I check the side mirror. Nobody's following us. I take a deep breath and relax into the seat a little more.

"Hey, so... thanks for coming with me."

"No problem. You and I both know you couldn't have done this alone."

I snort.

"Sure, whatever you say."

"You would have gotten halfway down the street, turned around and asked for my help anyway, Sof. You're stubborn as hell but you always come crawling back."

"Fuck you."

"Fuck you back," Ruby laughs.

She's the person I feel the safest with, and the person I can lean on for pretty much everything, and I know she feels the same.

I met Ruby during the riots, back when this all started. I had just lost Charlie and Sam, and I was filled with nothing but rage. Something needed to be done, but I didn't know what. I was angry at everyone for letting the plague get out of control, and at myself for being helpless to stop it.

I didn't know what to do with it all, didn't know who it was for or where to put it. So, I decided it was for everyone. I just wanted to smash something, so when I heard that a massive swarm of people were taking to the streets to protest what little government was left, I was all in.

First, we were just fighting cops, but they didn't stay in the streets for long. I'm still not sure if they knew what was coming, or just gave up their posts, but that was the night the vamps came out looking for blood and power. These days they say they've been around for centuries, and who can say if it's true, but what's certain is they picked a perfect day to take the reins.

No one knew what was happening at first, but as member after member of the crowd got torn into, we scattered. I nearly died, cornered in a dark building after being chased for what felt like hours, before Ruby pulled me into her apartment and barricaded us in. With so much free food still in the wild, the vamps gave up pretty quickly, and we weathered the storm. We've been roommates ever since.

I found a family with Ruby, and then a new purpose when we finally opened Nox. In so many ways, the club gave me a reason to live again, but I'll never forget or forgive the powers that *were* for what we lost.

Ruby pulls around the back of the bar, the headlights cranked up all the way. We hop out of the van and she takes a step back, keeping watch for me while I grab the case of blood with a grunt. Most jobs in the old world "require" you to lift 50 pounds, but at this one you have to balance that along with a chambered pistol. Never a dull moment.

Ruby lets out a long breath as I slide my key into the lock.

"Hey, so you wanna keep moping in your office, or do you want to get out there and sling some drinks?"

We also serve alcohol at Nox. Turns out vampires like to get drunk and dance their asses off as much as humans do.

"I wasn't moping, I was doing payroll."

"You were moping." Her expression suddenly becomes soft and serious. My heart drops to my stomach, knowing exactly what comes next. "Charlie's birthday's coming up, isn't it? Next month?"

"I've been trying to forget," I whisper.

He would have been eight this year.

Ruby wraps an arm around me, pulling me close and kissing my forehead.

"Let's have a drink to take your mind off it. We'll make some money, and then go home and eat macaroni and cheese right out of the pot."

I smile sadly, my chest tight as she holds me. I watched my baby die behind a clear fucking shower curtain while I was in a full hazmat suit. Sam ripped his own suit off so that he could hold our son one last time.

I lost them both within three days.

My grief isn't unique, I know that. Generations of parents before me have lived through it and continued on despite the dull ache. Still, parents shouldn't have to bury their children. Hell, I didn't even get that. They burned the infected bodies to slow the spread. Charlie doesn't even have a proper resting place. I think that's the part that cuts me up the most.

Ruby's touch is calming, and I breathe in the smell of her cinnamon shampoo. These moments are rare, but she's always been there for me. Tears form in my eyes and she squeezes me tighter. She's all I have.

"You in there, babe?" She asks after a few minutes of silence.

"I'm here. And yeah, a drink sounds great right about now."

She beams at me as she pulls away.

"Good. Let's go make some money and get our asses home."

DOMINIC

DUNCAN TOWERS

I NEED HER.

I know it's dramatic, but so am I.

She was made for me, a perfect concoction of everything I've ever wanted, all wrapped up in a pretty little package. I haven't even tasted her, but the smell of her fear mixed with her perfume weighs heavily on my mind, making my head swim.

It might as well be Christmas morning.

As the van peels away, she cranes her neck to look back at me and I smile, the most exquisite rush of warmth and adrenaline pulsing through me like wildfire. She's beautiful, long red hair, rich olive green eyes, soft freckles; the gun in her hand makes her even more appealing.

I have to follow her.

"Dom!" Theo calls from the door. "The fuck are you lookin' at? Come on!"

"Who *was* that?" I ask.

"The humans?" Theo replies, clearly annoyed. "Who gives a shit? They're just doing a blood run, you still hungry or something?"

I want her, and not just in a 'I want to bite down on her throat and drain her dry' kind of way. I want to touch her, to feel her lips crushed up against mine. I want to listen to her moan in my ear as I break her.

My cock strains. Sex and blood go hand in hand, after all. Feeding on someone is an extremely sensual experience for both partners, when we're not ripping their throats out, at least.

"I'm serious, Theo. Who was that?"

"You think I know everyone in this town?"

"I think you're a big fuckin' gossip," I mutter.

Theo finds dirt on everyone. He's got a such silver tongue, even Rene's men somehow manage to fuck up and tell him their secrets on the regular.

"You want me to find out, Boss?" Luke offers, his eyes blown out and his face still smeared with blood.

He's always eager to please, like a puppy. I toss him my keys.

"Nothing physical, just get me a name and report back."

Luke salutes me and hops back into his car, the wheels screeching against the asphalt as he rushes to complete his new mission.

Theo sighs behind me.

"Dom, we don't have time to get you laid tonight. We have to figure out what the fuck we just stole, and then how to keep it from Deschamps."

I'm not worried about Rene. We have a mutual understanding. He quietly holds onto his power, slowly but surely expanding, and I provoke him into striking out once in a while. We fight, people die, rinse and repeat. I realize that makes me look like the bad guy, but there's something that has to be understood about Rene. He's far worse, far more dangerous than I am.

We were supposed to be partners. Rene promised me a little slice of the city when everything went to shit. But when the time came to divvy it up, he flipped it all sideways. Said it was too complicated, and that he needed someone he could trust to help him handle it all. And that was me. He could always trust me to help when things got tough.

Until he couldn't.

It's mostly been a stalemate ever since I broke away, but the war we wage isn't always so balanced. The city has paid the price.

But soon it won't matter, Deschamps will be gone from here, or better yet, dead, and I'll take what is rightfully mine. All of it.

"Dom!" Theo snaps his fingers. "Come on!"

"Yeah, yeah," I mutter, following Mateo and him inside.

This building was supposed to be an apartment complex, filled to the brim with our kind. The humans have been extremely vocal about the fact that a bunch of bloodsuckers were setting up shop next to their main source of income wouldn't be the most neighborly thing to do, especially when that income comes in the form of their sweet red. So, now it's just the head of my operations in the city. I live up at the top, but the rest is practically empty, mostly just storage and a few offices throughout. It's a decent compromise, one that Rene was vocal in his distaste for.

It's a shame, really. Fully furnished suites, high vaulted ceilings, dark windows, and beautiful black and gold marble floors, all of it empty and unused. Hell, even the front desk goes unmanned, but I still got a big golden DUNCAN TOWERS sign built into the wall. There are some things you can't skimp on.

"We have to hide this shit," Theo mumbles.

"You know, Theodore, sometimes I think you're the one in charge and not me."

"Maybe that's because half the time you act like an uninvited kid at a birthday party. What the hell were you thinking burning that lab down?"

"I told you–"

"Revenge. Yeah," Theo grumbles. "Still fucking stupid. Who cares if he's working on some kind of blood substitute, drug or not?"

"Drugs mean money, Theo, and money means power," I sigh. "Have you learned nothing over the last five years? We're going to make this shit right under Rene's nose, and it's going to make me rich. I'll buy this fucking city out from under him. Every one of his men will work for me before long."

"We."

"What?"

Theo turns his head, his expression stony.

"*We're* going to be rich."

"Theo, there's no 'I' in team. Of course I meant we. It's always the two of us! Now I need you to get that head of yours out of your ass. We have work to do."

We step into the elevator and he presses the button for the penthouse. 30th floor. Mateo nibbles nervously on his claw, still covered in blood. He never knows what to do when we fight.

"Wait, boss, doesn't Rene already have a deal with the humans and the blood bank?" Mateo asks, his eyes bouncing between us.

"So do we. What's your point?" I growl.

"Well, if he's got this on the side now... isn't he doing better than us?"

Theo snorts and hangs his head, his shoulders trembling as he laughs silently. The elevator opens and I turn to Mateo, tilting my head to the side and looking him up and down. He's young, hasn't learned his place in all of this. I turned him a year ago, and he's got a hell of a long way to go when it comes to respect. With one hand, I grip his throat and squeeze as Theo lets out an exasperated groan.

"Cut it out, man."

I lean in close, digging my claws into Mateo's skin while he struggles, wincing in pain.

"You speak to me like that again, and I'll toss you out into the sunlight without even an ounce of regret."

His eyes are back to being filled with fear, just the way I like it.

"Y– yes, sir."

"That's how much you're worth to me, Mateo. A couple seconds of sunlight, you understand?"

He nods, choking as he struggles to breathe.

"Good boy."

I release him and he stumbles backward, wheezing and straightening out his suit as Theo and I step into the penthouse. This is my fortress, even though I rarely spend much time here other than sleeping through the day. I may always be on the move, but I love it here.

The entire apartment is open concept save for my bedroom and a spacious bathroom, both tucked off to the side. There's a black velvet couch sitting in the center of the room, flanked by all the art that I've collected over the years — mostly

Renaissance. I'm not so big on modern art, despite the big price tags. I prefer the classics I wasn't around for.

Theo places the bag on a coffee table before heading to the bar cart to pour himself a drink. Mateo perches himself on the edge of the couch, unsure exactly what to do as I linger by the window, staring down at the city.

I could make this place better, happier. Humans and vampires living and working side by side. For me, of course, but for a reasonable cut.

Rene makes alliances, sure, but there's always a catch. Some hidden little clause that'll ruin you when you least expect it. He only plays by the rules with the humans because he's the one that makes those rules.

And now everything is under his control: the blood bank where humans go to make monthly donations, the vaccine clinics, food, weapons, drugs. He doesn't respect them, he just wants to drain them dry as he keeps them in line. It's a blind spot, one of the only ones he has.

I dig my cigarettes out of my jacket pocket and light one, the smoke swirling around my head in delicate ribbons. Theo and Mateo have struck up a conversation that's already fading into the background as my mind swims, slowly being overtaken by visions of fiery red hair. As obsessed as I am with Rene, I can't get her out of my mind.

Even from across the street, I could see her pulse racing in her neck. When she looked back at me as they drove by, could I have been imagining a little smile? No, it was there.

I should have just gotten back into my car and followed her.

She's a temptress.

"So what's your big plan, hotshot?" Theo asks, nudging me as he hands me a drink.

I shrug.

"Don't know yet."

He scoffs.

"What do you mean you don't know?" He knocks on my skull and I swat him away. "You burn his lab down, steal a formula for a drug you know nothing about, and then you tell me you don't know? *Again*?! You're too reactive, Dominic. What about when he finds out this time, huh? What're we going to do then? We still haven't recovered from the last big clash. Motherfucker, what if Rene finds out we're low on men? You think he's just going to wait for us to get back on our feet?!"

"We'll figure it out, get ahead of him. You have a degree, right? Chemistry?"

He stares at me like my face is melting.

"Yeah, Dom, yeah I do, but that doesn't mean I know how to make this shit! I didn't exactly keep up with modern scientific literature. Do you even remember how long ago that was?"

I turn to him and cock my head to the side.

"You're the brains of this operation, aren't you?"

He raises his middle finger as he plops down next to Mateo on the couch. I let out a long sigh. Sure, I've thought it through. We can sit on this formula for a while, maybe dangle it over Rene's head, kidnap a few of his minions to see if they know how to make it. It's all so dull, so rote; planning always takes the theater out of life. Besides, right now, all I want to do is bask in this victory, and maybe fuck some of this adrenaline out of my system.

That little redhead could help with that.

"Someone can make this, can't they? I mean, Rene found people." Mateo leans forward and unzips the bag, pulling out some of the supplies. Small vials of clear liquid, empty containers, syringes. What it's for is anyone's guess. "He must have just started making it recently, right?"

"The rest of the formulas looked like trials," Theo replies. "Shit was all crossed out on the other notepads and notebooks, so we don't even know how long it's been in the works." He turns to me. "We would have a better handle on this if our Fearless Fuckwit hadn't burned the entire lab down."

"Yeah, why'd you do that?" Mateo asks, his brows knitting together as if he was struggling to find the answer to a deep philosophical question.

"Why not?" I shrug. "We've done it before."

"Before, we knew what we were dealing with," Theo replies. "Before, we had a plan. This time you flew in there like a bat out of hell–"

"Nice metaphor," Mateo chimes in.

"Little on the nose," I mutter.

"Go fuck yourself!"

Theo takes a moment, sighing and pinching the bridge of his nose.

"Look, I'll sniff around, see if I can find another vampire who knows enough to help us make this shit, one who *doesn't* already work for Deschamps, but we're going to have to find a secure place to do it, and equipment."

"Set up a lab in the office downstairs," I tell him. "Get whatever you need, pay whoever you need to. We're making this stuff, and we're going to get it pushed through all the bars and the nightclubs. Hell, we can ship it to other cities and use it as a foothold to grab more territory. Expand."

It's a dangerous idea, but the rewards for success are massive.

"Why don't you just kidnap one of Rene's people?" Mateo asks. "Make them do it all for you."

"Well, first off, we'd have to figure out which one of them knows how to make this shit, and people can lie," Theo replies.

"Not if you–"

"You gotta stop with the teeth pulling, man!" Theo exclaims. "Anyway, he might not even realize what's happened yet, or who did it, but the moment some of his people go missing, especially ones with very specific skill-sets, he's going to put two and two together."

Mateo looks like he's pushing a boulder uphill right behind his eyes, when suddenly a loud ring echoes through the apartment.

I cringe, moving quickly to hit the button for the intercom.

"Yeah?"

"Boss! I found her," Luke shouts on the other end of the line.

I can feel my blood burn.

"Where?"

"Nox. They went in through the back door with the blood. Now she's behind the bar. She must work there."

Nox is one of the most popular bars in the city, and the only one that was officially greenlit by Rene. The... extra services they provide there have made it the main haunt of some of the most wealthy vampires around.

Tonight is my lucky night.

"I'll be down in a minute. Keep the car ready."

I've never set foot in Nox, despite all the positive buzz. Human-owned and run out of a large abandoned church near the Boardwalk. After Rene made his big show of endorsing the place, I sent Theo in to make our own little deal: we don't cause trouble, and they won't "unleash hell" upon us. It's the closest thing to neutral ground we're going to get.

"Theo, I'm going out on the town. Don't wait up!"

He gets to his feet, clearly at the end of his rope.

"Dom, you're covered in blood, dressed like absolute shit, and we've still got all this whole formula thing to figure out!"

I ignore him, walking to the kitchen to wet a towel as he stays right on my heels. He groans as I wipe down my face and neck.

"How do I look? Be honest with me, Theodore."

"Dom, this is serious." He leans over the counter, his Irish accent coming through a little stronger than usual. It always does when he's stressed. "You don't *really* know what that formula is or even what it does. Be honest with *me* here. You just took it to give Rene the middle finger, yeah?"

"I told you, Theo, all I need is for you to find me someone who can figure this formula shit out. We'll build the lab, make the drug, and sell it. Easy money for us, and the first steps to taking Rene for everything he's worth. We'll carve up this motherfucking town any way we like. You and me." I toss him the towel as he shakes his head to himself. "But first, clean yourself up would ya? You look like shit."

They've painted the church black and violet, and hung a gigantic neon sign out front. There's even a bell tower at the top that rings when it's last call. They sure went all-in with the theme, I'll give them that.

"It's a feeding night," Luke tells me as I let the engine die, watching vamps trickle in and out of the front doors.

"Feeding night, like...?"

"Private rooms, and if you pay good money, you get fresh blood, right from the source." He turns to me, a big smile on his face. "And sex."

"Of course," I mutter.

"Well, not always sex, but you don't have to drink blood out of those dinky little shot glasses. That's the most important thing. You know how much it is for a shot in there?"

I sigh, eager to get going as I unbuckle my seatbelt. I've barely thought about this place since we all made our deals about a year back. Now I kind of wish I had come myself knowing that cute redhead might have been manning the bar. After what happened tonight, I'm itching to blow off some steam.

I climb out of the car, and Luke follows, bouncing at my side like an excitable puppy.

"You're chasing that girl, aren't you?"

"I'm chasing a fucking drink," I bite. "Cool it."

I should have brought Theo with me. Luke is going to be hard to control, and I don't want to waste all of my time babysitting him.

As we head through the doors, I'm immediately hit by an intoxicating mixture of cigarette smoke, iron, and alcohol. Music booms through the speakers, so loud that it rattles my skull.

I'm surprised to find the interior of the bar is exquisite, with stained glass windows peppering the walls and century-old brick locking it all in place. All the pews have been ripped out and replaced by tables. There are open "confessional booths" that act as VIP areas for guests to sit and drink without being disturbed. I expected a gaudy mess, but they really pulled it all together.

A DJ stands at the back of the room on a pulpit, headphones on as he spins records. There are humans in old Gogo cages hanging from the ceiling, gyrating to the music as they overlook a sea of my kin, all grinding up against each other on the dance floor. Dozens of vampires pulse like a vein while they pour shots of blood down each other's bodies and lick it off.

How the fuck haven't I been here before?

Humans move through the crowds with ease as they serve out their drinks, both blood and alcohol. A few of them seem to recognize me, but say nothing as I continue to take everything in. For serving staff, they're all surprisingly well armed.

Finally my eyes land on the redhead at the bar, and time seems to stop. She's even more beautiful up close. A tight black dress hugs her in all the right places. Her eyes are the most mesmerizing shade of green, offsetting the fake smile she flashes as she takes orders.

I drift through the crowd, staring only at her. Everything else is background noise. The closer I get, the more intoxicating I find her. When she catches my eye, I can see her give a moment's pause before recognition hits her like a bolt of lightning. I tilt my head with curiosity. Does she recognize me, or does she *know* me?

Luke taps me on the shoulder. I was so caught up in her that I didn't even notice him bouncing along beside me. I have to resist the urge to push him away.

"Boss, you got money?" He asks with a big smile. "I wanna head for the feeding rooms."

I dig into my wallet and casually hand him a few thousand dollars in cash. That should get him out of my hair for a while.

"Knock yourself out, kiddo."

"Thanks, Dom – Er, Boss! Thanks Boss!"

He bolts for the heavily guarded back rooms and doesn't look back.

I make my move toward the bar, her eyes darting back to me as I approach. Just as I'm about to take a seat, another vampire slides into the stool in front of me. Right in front of my cute redhead.

He's got silver hair and a bone white suit. Even from the back of his head I recognize him as one of Rene's little goons.

But most importantly, he's sitting in my seat.

Staring at *my* girl.

SOFIE

Nox Nightclub

"Your drink is on the counter." Ruby pats my shoulder while I work on hooking up the last blood bag to the dispenser.

"Thanks, babe."

Once I'm finished, I get to my feet and am immediately confronted with a sea of customers. No rest for the wicked, I suppose.

But I'm here to sling drinks and look damn good doing it.

I jump right into the action and start taking orders. It doesn't take me long to get back into the swing of things in all the soft chaos of the bar. Honestly, I'm grateful for any distraction. After a while, I'm greeted by a breathtakingly beautiful couple holding hands leaning up against the counter. The man has a square jaw and prominent cheekbones that are his most defining facial feature, along with slightly sunken eyes and thick brows.

His girlfriend has golden hair, a sculpted face, and a long straight nose with full lips. She's wearing a tight sapphire dress made of shiny latex, and minimal makeup. She smiles at me and I return the gesture, my cheeks heating up. Some of these vampires are so good looking that one glance from them can make my knees knock together.

"What can I get you?" I ask.

"Two shots, O negative for her and B positive for me," the man replies.

It all tastes different, or so I've been told. These vamps are wealthy enough that they can afford to have a preference. It's like the difference between the people that are happy with 10 dollar wine, and the ones that don't break a sweat popping corks on bottles worth thousands.

"Coming right up." I fill each shot glass with their respective blood type until it's nearly to the rim before sliding them across the counter with an empty smile. "Eighty for both."

The man gives me a hundred and I tuck the change into the tip jar beneath the bar as he and his girlfriend sniff at their drinks. They almost always double check to make sure that they've gotten what they asked for. I used to be a fucking hematologist, but you think they believe me when I tell them I know my shit? Of course not. It's been an entire year, with some of these vamps here almost every night, and they still don't trust us to get it right.

I watch them walk to a back booth as I move to serve a few more patrons. The place is really filling up quickly, and Ruby grabs another bartender to help on the other end, quickly pouring shot after shot. Soon I get lost in the mayhem of the night, dragged away in the undertow of a familiar chaos. It's kind of nice.

As I'm cleaning small droplets of spilled blood off of the table, a gust of cool air rushes in from the front door. When I glance up, my heart nearly skips a beat.

It's the vampire from the bank run. I'm almost certain of it. He's dressed impeccably in a black suit with a turtleneck underneath, and what's worse is that he looks even better up close.

I'm temporarily distracted by another customer, but my eyes keep getting drawn back to him. His gaze feels like a set of claws digging into the back of my neck. He's standing in the middle of the dance floor while everyone else moves around him like an ocean.

Shit.

I've fucked my share of vampires since I started working here. What goes on in the feeding rooms stays in the feeding rooms. It's like Vegas, but with a little more blood and a lot less gambling.

I try to look away, busying myself with polishing a glass, when suddenly, a shadow looms over me. As I glance up my eyes meet Drake, an older vampire dressed in a white suit with long silver hair. He winks, and I force a smile.

Drake is a creep. He's always trying to grab our asses when we wear skirts. He thinks his species' distinction makes him special, entitled to human beings. I don't even like the fact that I know his name.

"Hiya, sugar."

The nickname, combined with the sound of his voice, always makes my skin bristle. It's gravelly, but there's something about it that's equally demanding and weaselly, like a pitch from a used car salesman. He works for Rene Deschamps, and spends most of his money here, so it's hard to refuse him... even if we all loathe him.

I think Ruby spits in his drinks.

"What can I get you, Drake?" I ask with a sigh.

He grins and licks his yellowed fangs like a hungry dog. The tooth beside his left fang is gold, *pure* gold he'll tell you, as if it matters. His eyes crinkle at the edges, but the smile doesn't quite touch them. Even over the music, I can hear the disgusting sounds he makes as he slurps up his drink. It makes me want to throw up.

"Don't look so pleased to see me," he purrs. "How about five minutes alone with you in that feeding room?"

The world may have changed, but men haven't. If anything, they're worse.

"Five? You got a stamina issue or something?"

"Why are you such a cunt?"

"Why are you so persistent?" I fire back. "It's pathetic. Anyway, I'm not working the rooms tonight."

"You've never even given me a shot."

Ruby pulls her gun out of her holster and lays it on the counter.

"Watch yourself. Unless you wanna suck on this all night."

He ignores her.

"Come on, sugar. Just five minutes. We could even go to the alley."

I chuckle, leaning over and giving him a tiny view of the breasts he'll never be able to touch.

"I got a proposition for you."

"Yeah?" He rumbles, his eyes glued to my tits.

"Yeah. How about you take your dick, stick it in the doorframe, and I slam it in there as hard as I can?"

He frowns, readying what's certainly going to be another great comeback, but...

"Drake Kingston, right?"

A hand is already on his shoulder. I didn't even see him walk up, but a pair of icy blue eyes are staring down at Drake. The man's voice is rough, raspy, and deep.

"Who wants to know?"

My stranger leans in.

"I do, and I want you to leave this pretty gal alone so she can do her job."

"This *is* her job, asshole," Drake spits.

I practically feel the grip on his shoulder as it tightens, until the unmistakable sound of bone crunching cuts through the cacophony of noise. Drake's body crumples, and he hisses as his eyes flash amber. I slide his regular order toward him. The last thing I need to deal with is a goddamn bar fight.

"It's on the house. Keep your fuckin' nose clean."

He lets out a dismissive snort.

"I was just–"

"Leaving," the new arrival croons, extending his words in a sing-song tone. "Goodbye, Drake."

"This is my seat, asshole!"

Drake tries to remove the man's hand, but within half a second, his arm is being twisted so hard that his whole body goes limp. He lets out a scream, collapsing fprward onto the bar as his face contorts in pain.

I gag at the horrible crunching sounds, it's like someone twisting a plastic bottle in their hands. His fractured bone pierces the sleeve of his suit, already soaked in blood.

"And now it's my seat. Leave the lady alone and keep it moving, *Drake*."

The newcomer shoves him off of his bar stool, taking his place as Drake's limp body topples to the ground. I'd say vampires are dramatic, but I'd be wailing too if someone snapped my bone like a fucking tree branch.

He turns to me, smiling the whole time as Drake gets to his feet and stumbles into the crowd. Anger swirls in my gut. This is my bar, and I can handle these things. I don't need this... *goon* stepping in for me.

Even if he's drop dead gorgeous.

"We have security for that," I grind out through clenched teeth.

"Don't seem to be doing their jobs," he replies, a sly smirk tugging at the corners of his mouth.

"I could have handled him."

"I'm sure you could." His icy eyes shimmering, flashing yellow for a brief second. It happens when they want to feed, or they're angry, or if they're just horny. It scared me at first, but you get used to it. "You look like a tough guy. It's nice to see you up close."

I shake my head, cleaning the blood up that Drake left on the counter. This guy is flirting with me, or trying to.

"You followed me here?"

"Just a happy coincidence," he replies.

He taps his claws against the bar, and I pull out my standard smile.

"What can I get you?"

"A shot of whiskey, and another of O negative."

"Any preference for whiskey?"

"Johnny Walker Blue," he rumbles. There's a hint of an Irish accent that makes my stomach flutter.

I hate myself for showing any kind of weakness. I know he can see it, it's written all over his fucking face. Vampires aren't exactly subtle when they're looking at prey. But it's hard to tell if he wants to fuck me or eat me.

As I grab the shot glasses and line them up beneath the tap. I can see him watching me, and I can't stop myself from stealing a glance at him. He lights a cigarette and wraps his plump lips around it. For a split second, I wonder what they might feel like against my–

Nope. Stop it. You don't need to go there.

"You're spilling," he informs me.

"Wh–Shit!" I hiss as I realize there's blood dripping down my knuckles.

Ruby snorts and tosses me a towel. He picks it up before I can reach it, holding it up for me.

"Sorry, just let me wash my hands."

"Not a problem."

I turn my back, rushing for the sink to grab a brush and get under my fingernails. I don't need any of these vamps trying to lick dried blood off me.

When I glance back over my shoulder, it's clear he hasn't taken his eyes off of me. He winks and gestures with a 'come hither' motion.

I swear, it's getting hotter in here by the second.

"You gonna be able to pour me that whiskey?" He teases.

I glare at him and he smirks, tilting his head to the side as I abandon the towel. I grab the bottle and tilt it upside down and dramatically pour a perfect shot before flipping it in the air, slamming it back down on the counter. He snickers.

"You wanna make fun of my skills?"

He shrugs.

"The bottle flipping was excellent. I'm just curious why you had such a hard time with the blood."

God, his *voice*. It's like honey.

"Just a busy night," I reply.

"Of course."

I scan the bar as he drinks. Other vampires seem to be avoiding the surrounding area completely. Ruby's laughing with a few of her regulars, and her tip jar is already full while mine looks like a tumbleweed just rolled through it.

This guy sucks blood *and* my income.

"You're really killing my tips tonight."

"Oh?" He mutters. "Why's that?"

"You're scaring all my customers away."

He places a hand on his chest, eyes wide.

"Me?"

"You," I reply flatly.

He might be cute, but I need to make money.

He takes out his wallet and pulls out a small handful of bills, his eyes devouring me whole.

"Does that cover it?" He asks, his voice a gentle purr. "The tips you might have made tonight, I mean."

My knees wobble. He's holding at least three grand.

"I..."

"I owe you for those drinks, too, hmm?" He pulls out more money. Another thousand. "How's this?"

"That's... a lot," I choke out.

There isn't a whole lot left to the economy these days, and Vampires tend to hang on to their money. It's why we overcharge for pretty much everything here. Not this guy, though. He throws it away with a smile.

"Can I stay now?"

"What for?" I laugh. "You could buy half the bar with that stack."

"I like what I'm looking at," he replies, his eyes sliding down my body.

I don't know why, but I like the attention more tonight than ever before.

"Why don't you have a drink with me?" He asks.

I chuckle. If we were in a private feeding room, things would be different, but I don't drink with patrons at the bar. I prefer to keep some level of distance between me and the customers who want to tear out my heart and bite into it like a pomegranate. But this guy is making things very difficult. It's the way he's looking at me, his eyes lingering for just a little too long on my lips, my neck, my tits. I'm used to it, but coming from him, it's different.

Is it because of what he did to Drake? No, it has to be more than that.

"I don't drink at work," I reply curtly, but part of me aches as I cut off the possibility.

He gestures to the drink sitting behind the bar, the rim stained with my lipstick. "Then what's that?"

I nibble on the inside of my cheek.

"That's not mine."

"I see. Well–"

"Dom!" A voice calls over the music, a man pushing through the crowd to reach him. "We gotta go, dude."

"Why?"

The brunette vamp leans in close and whispers something in Dom's ear. He looks over his shoulder toward the feeding room, and his face breaks out into a malicious smile that makes the hairs on the back of my neck stand up. Thankfully, his friend holds him back.

"Bad idea. We don't have any backup."

Just as my eyes follow theirs, I notice the alarm for the feeding rooms go off. It's a red blinking light carefully hidden behind the bar so we can deal with any problems quickly and quietly.

A vamp in the back has gone too far.

"Sof! We gotta go!" Ruby calls, jumping the bar and heading straight for the feeding rooms with her gun in hand.

I stare back at the two vampires, my eyes narrowing.

"What did you do?" I growl at Dom's friend.

"It wasn't me!" He throws his hands up. "I swear, I left that dude *plenty* satisfied. And alive."

"Pretty quick, though," Dom replies with a smirk.

His friend sighs.

"It was a handjob, dude, I–" He shakes his head. "Look we've *got* to go! It's gonna get ugly."

What the fuck is this guy talking about?

Dom turns to me with a smile.

"It's a shame we have to cut this short."

"Yeah, I'm real broken up about it," I mumble, watching security head into the feeding rooms.

Fuck.

Dom smirks and drains his drink, slamming the glass down on the counter. His eyes meet mine a final time, and he holds my gaze as long as he can as he slides a business card across the counter.

"See you tomorrow night. We'll get that drink."

With that, he slides off the bar stool and disappears, swallowed up by the crowd.

"Sofie," a voice growls. It's Ares, one of our security guards. "You've gotta get back there. It's bad."

"Dead?"

"No, but he got her close. Seemed to be on purpose, too."

I shove the card into my apron and sprint to the back, Ares at my heels.

"Who was it?" I ask over my shoulder.

"Deschamps."

It's my lucky fucking night, one of the biggest egos in Santa Cruz in *my* goddamn bar.

"Jesus, when did he get here?!"

"When you and Ruby were on your run," Ares replies, ushering me inside. "He promised to be on his best behavior. I should have shot the fucker at the front door."

"Sure, if you were in the market to buy matching tombstones for all of us. Look, just make sure the door stays open in case the shit hits the fan."

I'm not trapping myself in a room with a vamp like Rene Deschamps.

Ruby's standing at the end of the hall, her gun already pointed at Rene. He's grinning ear-to-ear, his hands lazily stretched in the air. There's no fear in his eyes. He's clearly only in this position because he wants to be.

Ares takes Ruby's place as I pull her aside, eyeing Rene up and down as the vampire tilts his head quizzically. I rest my hands on her shoulders, forcing her to look directly at me. She's pale, blinking rapidly as her chin trembles.

"Talk to me, babe," I whisper.

"He drained Kirby," she stammers. "She's stable, I think. Bobby took her into another room. He's got a shock blanket, and he's giving her fluids."

Dread makes its home in the pit of my stomach, adrenaline preparing me for the worst. She might be alive now, but that could change.

I steal a quick glance at Rene and find him looking straight back at me, a wall of muscle in a dark red suit. His ashy blond hair is slicked back, almost plastered to his head. He reminds me of one of those old gangsters from the '40s, or at least the movies, with deep scars on his cheeks and a sunken face. His nose is slightly crooked from far too many breaks, likely before he was turned. His brow has a permanent crease in it, making him look serious even when he's grinning like a fucking clown.

My fingers wrap around the gun at my side and I draw it instantly, aiming it at Rene's head as I storm toward him. He chuckles, staring at me like I'm some kind of pathetic animal.

"Watch where you're pointing that thing, little girl."

The glib comment only fuels my rage. I could just pull this fucking thing and end this right now.

"You knew the rules when you entered the feeding room, correct? I'm here to run a bar, not a goddamn mortuary, Deschamps."

He shrugs his shoulders, as remorseful as a child who got caught with his hand in the cookie jar.

"I'm *so* sorry miss, guess I just got a little overzealous. But is it really my fault? You know, your establishment doesn't offer much in those drinks you serve. You should reconsider your business model, turn a much bigger profit with only a couple changes. I could help–"

I cock the gun and grit my teeth.

"We offer plenty. I don't give a fuck who you are, Deschamps. Get the hell out of my club and don't come back."

Rene reaches out, grasping my arm as he presses my gun to his forehead, his face just inches from mine. He's daring me to pull the trigger with one silent look. My heart is thundering in my chest. It's not lost on me that I'm standing face to face with one of the most powerful men in the city.

He studies my face for a moment more, his little smile twitching ever so slightly.

"I'm willing to bet you don't have the guts."

"Try me, asshole."

His voice is dry and emotionless; despite his smile, there's no joy in it. The only thing I can read is pure boredom.

"I'll have my crew in this club in seconds, and they'll rip you and your little friends apart. They're everywhere." He turns his head as though he's daring me to look toward the open door, but I keep my eyes on him, my heart hammering at the base of my throat. Kirby's blood is still staining his mouth. "So go ahead. Do it. It's your policy, isn't it?"

"Get the *fuck* out of my club," I repeat. "Don't make me tell you again."

He releases my arm and pushes me backward into Ares, who catches me before struggling to level his gun again. Deschamps doesn't even move, but I'm sure he could have had us all on the ground in a second.

And he knows I know it.

"Don't worry, my lovely hosts, I'll be taking my leave," he chuckles as he walks toward the open door.

A few vampires glancing inside scatter like mice as he strides out of the room, with Ares in close pursuit to ensure he makes a quick and complete exit. Ruby slides her gun back into her holster as I slump against the wall.

"I'm gonna check on Kirby. We should close the rooms down for the rest of the night."

"Maybe the rest of the club, too," I sigh, head in my hands.

"I'll... let you know what shape she's in," she rasps.

I hold myself together as Ruby makes her exit, but the second she's out the door I can feel myself breaking down. I don't even know what to do, nervously pulling at my hair for a moment before jamming my hands back into my apron. My mind runs wildly through every possible outcome of the night's events.

Almost none of them are good.

As I fiddle around nervously, my fingers brush against crumpled paper at the bottom of my apron pocket. Dom's business card. I shake my head as I flatten it out, giving it a quick glance before sitting up completely straight.

DOMINIC DUNCAN
CEO OF DUNCAN ENTERPRISES

My heart drops into my stomach. Two in one day?

"You've got to be fucking kidding me."

DOMINIC

NOX NIGHTCLUB

SHE MARCHED RIGHT BACK there and stuck her gun in Deschamps' face, bold as brass. The way she moves when she's angry, the fire in her eyes, and the way her muscles tremble with rage beneath that dress? I'm getting harder just thinking about it.

I linger on the dancefloor, eyes fixed on the feeding rooms while music pounds all around me and Luke tugs at my sleeve.

"Come on, man," Luke whispers. "He's gonna come out here. We don't need to deal with that shit right now."

Luke's right. There's no way Rene's figured out what's happened yet, and we don't want to do anything that'll draw his attention. He'll find out soon enough, but I don't give a shit about that right now. The only thing I'm focused on is that gorgeous fucking redhead with her gun in Rene's face.

Luke is practically bouncing beside me, silently begging me to give this up and leave. I just want one last look at her. I have to come back here, have her tell me about the whole thing. Fuck her while she describes what she did to him.

"Dom–"

I grab him by his hair and yank him toward me. He lets out a pathetic whimper.

"Stop your whining, you're going to draw attention to us."

"We kind of already did," Luke winces.

I glance around and realize there are eyes all over us.

All over me.

A few of Deschamps' men are sitting in booths, flanking either side of the dance floor, including Drake Kingston who's still nursing that broken arm. His eyes are piercing, staring me down, but he's not what really catches my attention. Off in the back, I catch another glance of Rene and my little redhead. He's leaned in close, purposely pressing the barrel of her gun to his forehead. She's holding steady against the second most dangerous man in the city.

Good girl.

As much as I want to see how this ends, Rene's men are already shifting in their seats, eager to start something I'd rather not have to finish. Look at me, making sensible decisions. Maybe finding the right woman really *does* change a man.

I grab Luke and we head for the exit. The warm, humid air feels suffocating, and I can't help the pang of regret that echoes through my body, already losing a bit of my newfound cool. I want to turn around and rip Deschamps' heart out with my teeth. I want his blood running down my throat while I fuck that redhead from behind until she screams for me.

The only thing I can think about as I start up the engine and peel away is my little redhead and the fiery look in her eyes. Jesus, I need to fuck her. Hard and brutal. Blood. Bruises. Maybe even break some bones. I light a cigarette and take a long drag.

I think I'd come in my fucking pants if I saw her blow Rene's head off.

"They're following us," Luke's panic slices right through my thoughts.

I glance in the rearview mirror. Drake's at the wheel of some unmarked black car with a couple of goons along for the ride. Could this guy be any more pathetic?

"The fuck's he gonna do?" I snort.

Suddenly, the sound of screeching and twisted metal fills the air, accompanied by a sharp jolt as he rams straight into us. This is not how I wanted to end the night.

I turn back to Luke, ready to dole out instructions, but he's already leaping into action. He may be an idiot, but when it comes to not so random acts of violence, he's always ready to go.

He opens the sunroof, his gun in his hand as he climbs to his feet, a little unsteady on the leather seats. I make a sharp right as gunshots consume the quiet night, accompanied by a chorus of squealing tires. Drake rams us again and I'm forced to crank the wheel, making a blisteringly sharp turn as I step on the gas. Lucky for me, Nox isn't too far from the wharf, territory that I gained from Rene last month. All the twists and turns are fresh in my mind as I keep my foot on the gas.

It comes together as if I had planned it, swerving just in time to force Drake off the main road and toward one of the loading docks. Luke fires a bullet right through the driver's side window and it nearly hits him as they sail on by. By the time Drake's straightened out his car, he's fallen behind enough that the shots he's firing have little chance of hitting much of anything. He's tenacious though, I'll give him that, as he tries to match my swerve toward the wharf.

After a couple minutes of trailing further and further behind, he seems to give up, slowing down and preparing to turn back toward the city.

"Not so fast, motherfucker," I purr.

I slam on the brakes and flip us into reverse, crushing the gas pedal as hard as I can as we careen backwards and close the gap between us. I can see Drake struggling with the gearshift, his tires squealing on the asphalt as he realizes what's happening.

"Shoot the tires!" I bellow. "I don't want him getting away!"

"I'm trying, man!" Luke roars.

It's only a few more shots before the tires deflate, and Drake and his cronies wrench the doors open. Two of them pop off a few ineffectual shots, but it's too late. Drake breaks into a run just in time for me to swerve into his path, plowing him straight back into his own vehicle with a wet crunch.

Luke glances down at me from the sunroof, gesturing to the other two vamps who were smart enough to keep running. I shake my head, and he slams himself back into his seat with a contented sigh. It'll be nice to have someone alive to tell Rene what I did.

"Man, I gotta work on my aim."

"You're fucking right you do. I would have had that done in two seconds," I scoff.

"Then why didn't you, asshole?!" He pauses for a moment, clearly terrified he'd gone too far. "Because I– I sucked out there. I'm no good at this stuff!"

Looks like he still knows his place. Good boy.

The sky is transforming, beautiful yellows and oranges that bathe Santa Cruz in a gorgeous glow. I find myself drifting into a smile as I make a loop back to the penthouse. It all reminds me of her, of her blazing red hair. I want to be wrapped up in it. In her.

Beside me, I can feel Luke getting nervous, and for once, I can't blame him. This is the most sunlight either of us has ever got to see in years. You can't help but to fear it, but I'm in awe at the same time. There's a deep craving, one that comes from missing the simplicity of a warm summer's day; existing without all these complications and rules. But those days are long behind me now, and that craving only leads to a quick and fiery end.

My car pulls up to Luke's apartment and he darts inside. Within another few minutes, I'm back home, pulling my jacket over my head to make sure I don't get scorched on the short run from my car to the penthouse. I really should get some sort of awning put in, or a fucking umbrella. Anything. But I have more pressing matters to attend to. The formula, Rene, and...

I'm going to see her again. I have to.

———⊰✦⊱———

I take the bag out of the safe in my bedroom, listening to the little vials clink together before I toss it on the coffee table. Theo said I needed a plan, but I can barely think. So, I head into the kitchen and find myself staring at an open fridge; at the bags and bags of blood that we stole from a shipment last week. Poor motherfucker didn't even see it coming.

He didn't just have blood, though. A quick search of the vehicle told me he was working for Rene on the side, smuggling weapons, ammo, and all kinds of shit.

I pull out a bag of A negative, fill a glass about halfway and take a sip, scowling slightly at the flavor as I head back into the living room. It's a little sour and bitter, but I'll get used to it.

My shirt is suddenly suffocating, so I strip it and my jacket off, tossing both on the couch before I sink into it. I'm exhausted, and I should be asleep, but my mind won't stop spinning.

"Plan, I need a plan..."

It's so antithetical to everything I know. I lean over and rifle through the bag, shaking one of the bottles out of sheer frustration. I wouldn't even know where to start with any of this shit. It's like I've got the ingredients to make a cake, but I can't read the goddamn recipe.

I wonder if Theo and Mateo have had any luck on their end.

It's nearly sunrise, probably only a few minutes until every single vampire still in the streets has to scatter for shelter. Theo likes to go to bed early, and he doesn't like to be disturbed, which means I can't call him to talk this shit out.

My eyes slide closed and I tilt my head back, the glass resting on my thigh. My mind wanders back to Nox, to her, and that gun shoved in Rene Deschamps' face. My oldest obsession and newest obsessions gather like a storm cloud in the back of my mind until I'm fucking aching. I'm dreaming of all the ways she could have killed him and I don't want to stop. My cock throbs as my mind twists the other way, running through all the things I want to do to her; all the ways I want to make her scream out in bliss, all the ways to make her hurt.

I wish she was here right now, on her knees in front of me with those big green eyes gazing up at me like I'm a fucking god. I'd give anything to have my hand in her hair while she takes me all the way down her throat.

I groan at the thought of it and palm my cock.

"Fuck."

Those full lips would look so pretty wrapped around me, leaving big smears of red lipstick behind. I can almost feel her mouth engulfing me, taking me as deep as she can, all the way down until she chokes. I squeeze my cock through my pants to relieve some of the pressure. The next time I see her, I'm taking what's mine.

She's definitely into me. I could see it in her eyes as I teased and prodded at her. It's hard for humans to hide that kind of shit. Their pupils dilate, their cheeks flush, and they make really intense eye contact. She was doing all of that and more, all while telling me I was losing her money.

I like the ones who play hard to get.

I abandon my drink on the coffee table and unzip my pants, tugging them down my hips a little as I tease myself over my briefs. I'm tortured by lust, ready to push myself until I can't take it anymore.

I need something brutal and raw. I want to fuck her as I slowly suck down on her neck, but all I've got is my hand and some second-hand blood in a glass. My eyes pop open and I reach over, snatching the crystal off of the table, tipping it over and letting a pool of crimson fill my palm. I shove my hand back into my briefs and wrap my fingers around my cock, squeezing hard before my hips buck into my hand. I can't wait until it's her pussy surrounding me.

I don't even know her name, but I want her bent over my couch, my fangs lodged in the side of her neck while I fuck her hard and deep. I want those tits in my mouth, my tongue swirling over her perfect little nipples. I want to feel that warm pussy quiver around my cock. I want her fiery hair wrapped around my knuckles like a rope while she begs me to fuck harder. Faster.

My strokes speed up and the heat inside me builds. I pull my cock right out of my briefs and stare down at it, slick and covered in blood and a bit of precum leaking from the tip. I let my eyes fall shut again, and I can see her on her knees, taking me all the way down her throat like a good girl, licking the blood off of me.

"That's it," I groan. "Fuck, princess, just like that. Such a good girl taking every inch."

I thank god for my extremely vivid imagination. The fantasy is so intense, I can hear her moans.

It all feels so real, my cock getting slicker and slicker as I push myself closer to the edge. My muscles clench and heat spreads all down my legs and up into my chest. I wonder what she'd look like with my hand around her throat and my claws digging into her skin. I wonder what that snarky voice would *really* sound like as she desperately moaned my name. Thankfully, I'm going back tomorrow to find out.

Suddenly, the knot in my belly slips loose, and I'm coming so fucking hard my body arches right off of the goddamn couch. One hand slams into the cushion and my claws sink into velvet. Liquid fire rushes through me, forcing my back to arch as my heels dig into the floor, and I let out a ragged grunt.

"Fuck!"

Ropes of cum land on my chest, some of it dripping down my knuckles. What the fuck has this woman reduced me to in a single night? My strokes slow down and I open my eyes, losing sight of my imaginary vixen as I take in the scene in front of me. I'm fucking covered in cum and blood. Little aftershocks of pleasure shoot through me as I swipe my thumb over the head of my cock, shivering a little.

The sudden absence of my intense fantasies gives way to a deep and solemn loneliness. It couldn't even wait for me to come down before it stabbed into me. It's been a long time since someone has captivated me the way she does.

I sigh and reach behind me, grabbing my turtleneck to wipe myself clean. Exhaustion overtakes me as I reach for my drink, downing the rest in one go before I drag myself up.

I need a fucking shower and some sleep.

Tomorrow's gonna be a busy night.

SOFIE

Nox Nightclub

"Is your lover boy here yet?" Ruby teases.

I roll my eyes as I slide two shot glasses toward Hunter, one of our regulars.

We've been a little more paranoid since Rene nearly killed Kirby. Ruby and I shut down for a couple of nights so that she and the other staff could recover. We almost lost her, and I don't want that to happen again.

"Oh, who's her lover boy?" He asks with a smirk. "I thought your pussy closed up shop."

"Just for you, babe," I purr.

He chuckles and pulls more money out of his wallet.

"Come on, tell me. I'll make it worth your while."

Hunter reminds me of a Ken doll and a motorcycle club reject smashed into one. Blue-green eyes with a sharp jaw and hair that's teased to high heaven. He's got a mesh shirt on, and a bullet belt to bring attention to the fact that he wears pants that are so tight, he might as well just walk around naked for all they leave to the imagination.

I yank the bills from his hand and shove them into my bra before he can take them back.

"Nobody is my lover boy, Hunter. Just like nobody invited you to this conversation." I lean over the counter and lick my lips. His eyes glaze over with lust. "Tell me something, *Hunter*. Is that even your real name? Seems pretty on the nose for a vamp."

"I'll tell you if you tell me, are those your real tits?" He fires back. "Never seen 'em up close."

He reaches out, but I'm faster, grabbing the shot of bourbon he ordered and pouring it over his head. Ruby claps and drums on the table, laughing as liquor drips down his face.

I can see his fists clenching as he growls.

"Down boy," I purr. "One wrong move and you're out. Permanently."

I grin as Ruby tosses me a damp rag and I wipe up the mess that I've made.

"You know, these pants were 800 bucks."

"You got ripped off. They look like shit."

"You're such a bitch," he chuckles. "And yeah, Hunter's my real name."

"Might as well be named Dracula."

Hunter snorts, shaking his head, and just like that it's as if nothing happened. He takes another shot and glances around, spotting a woman who's been sitting alone at the end of the bar all night.

"I'll see you gorgeous gals later. I've gotta dish out the charm to someone worthy of my attention."

He heads toward the woman at the end of the bar, who already looks less than impressed to see him.

Ruby sighs.

"She's gonna need a puke bucket to deal with him."

"Or a body bag," I reply, taking the empty shot glasses and tossing them in the dirty dish bin beneath the bar.

"So long as she kills him outside, I don't give a shit."

"Admit it, you'd miss him a little."

Ruby shoots me a toothy grin.

"The only thing I'd miss is the outline of his dick in those pants."

I roll my eyes and spray some cleaner onto the counter, scrubbing hard as I take the chance to do a quick look around the room.

It *really* bugs me that I haven't been able to get Dominic out of my mind. I wonder if he was scoping the place out, trying to get a handle on how we operate so that he could run off and open up some competition. It wouldn't surprise me. He's one of the two most powerful men in Santa Cruz, and we've got to be one of the most successful nightlife spots for vamps; maybe he wants to run us out of business.

"Hey, space case," Ruby whispers, knocking gently on my skull. "You in there?"

I frown and glance sidelong at her.

"What?"

"You've been cleaning the same tiny spot on that counter for a whole minute now. I think you're gonna scrub right through the varnish." She cocks her head. "Could you... actually be waiting for someone special?"

She's been teasing me about him non-stop tonight. There's no way I'd tell her about the business card that's sitting on my nightstand, or the fact that I've been having trouble sleeping. He's buried in my brain like a splinter I can't pry out.

"I don't know what you're talking about."

Ruby cackles.

"The fuck you don't! You're so on-edge I could see it from a mile away, or is dumping a drink over a customer's head part of our new business model?"

"It's the apocalypse, baby." I shrug. "Times are a-changin'."

I need to get outside and feel some fresh air on my face, and there probably won't be a better time than now. It's not a scheduled feeding night, so things are pretty slow with just a couple tables filled here and there.

"I'm going for a smoke," I tell her, patting my apron. I quickly feel out my gun, cigs, and a lighter.

"Sof, we make the rules. You can just smoke in the back," Ruby laughs.

The employee lounge has too many people going in and out. It's hard to think in there, much less take a breather without the next disaster being dropped right in your lap. Perks of being management, I guess.

"I'm going to take the trash out. Two birds, one stone." Ruby arches a brow, and I roll my eyes. "Bobby's guarding the back door. If I get in trouble, I'll scream."

She doesn't seem convinced. I must look like a kid begging to be let out of their room after being grounded.

"I'll be fine, Ruby. I promise."

"You want me to come with?"

"I'm armed, and I'll take the walkie-talkie."

"Sure, but how about you *actually* take it this time?" She insists.

We use them in case one of us needs to go out alone and the bar is slammed. Or, if it's a feeding night and someone's acting fishy. We take every precaution that we can, but if I'm being honest, I miss the luxury of just being able to escape outside at night and have a smoke all by myself.

"Happy now?" I ask with a sneer, waving it in her face.

"Very. Keep it on."

"Why, you wanna listen to me smoke and bitch about you under my breath?"

I pour myself a gin and tonic with extra mint leaves. Then I grab the trash and dramatically sling it over my shoulder, giving her a brief salute with the glass in my hand.

"I'll be back in 15, and if I'm not, send in the army."

"I am the army, bitch," Ruby shouts as I head toward the staff room. I make it all the way to the exit before I bump right into Bobby, my last obstacle to some peace and quiet.

"Where do you think you're going, Sof?"

Bobby always looks like he's about two seconds away from punching someone's lights out, which makes him perfect for the job. The fact that he was a Navy SEAL who can plug a vamp in the head from across a room is just a bonus. I've never seen this dude smile the whole year.

"I'm taking out the trash and having a cigarette, if that's alright with you."

"By yourself?"

He always sounds like he's being inconvenienced.

"Yup. Got a walkie talkie to communicate with the bar, a gun, *and* you'll be right here." I beam up at him. "Right?"

He looks down at his watch.

"You've got fifteen minutes before I haul your ass back inside. Clear?"

"Crystal."

All I can see is my reflection looking back at me through his sunglasses, but I know he's glaring at me, his lip curling as he slowly pushes the door open.

"Fifteen minutes."

"You got it, Private."

"It was Lieutenant."

I wince. He's gonna hold that against me forever.

As I slip out into the humid summer evening, the first thing I notice is the smell of trash and piss lingering in the air. It's less refreshing than I'd hoped, but it beats the gossip in the employee lounge. Probably.

I set my drink down on a rickety wooden crate, making my way to the trash bin as beads of sweat already begin to form on my hairline and upper lip. Even the few seconds of the open lid is enough for the rancid garbage stench to overwhelm me, and I gag as I slam it shut and double back. Before I have a chance to get comfortable with my drink, the walkie beeps and crackles, Ruby's voice too muffled to really make out on the other end.

"Mission complete. The egg is in the eagle's nest, over."

There's a brief pause before her voice crackles up again.

"The egg is– what the fuck does that mean?"

"It means I took the trash out, genius." I pull my cigarettes out of my apron and grab one with my teeth, dragging it out and lighting up. "Bobby's giving me fifteen minutes, saintly as he is."

"Hey, take all the time you need." There's another brief pause, and I cringe as I can practically feel her trying not to be overbearing, and failing. Miserably. *"But you're standing by the door, right? Not too far out?"*

"Yes, mom. I'm being good."

"Actually I prefer dad– Oh! Or daddy!"

Ruby's witch-cackle on the other end makes me smile.

"You're such a shithead," I chuckle along with her.

"I know, I know. Remember, just yell if you need backup."

"Got it, boss."

I sit down on the crate and take a sip of my drink, resting my gun beside me. The alleyway is shrouded in darkness, with only a slice of moonlight illuminating everything. I lean back against the wall. A wave of relaxation fills me all at once as a light breeze brushes against my cheek.

Silence gives way to old memories; an ache shooting through my chest as I think about the way things used to be. Sam and I would take Charlie down to the Boardwalk every Saturday and watch him stuff his face with mini donuts and cotton candy until he got sick. I always scolded him for it, but deep down, I loved it. He was gonna get the childhood I never had.

The gentle click of footsteps at the mouth of the alley pulls me from the past. My muscles coil and I grab my gun, aiming it at the darkness. My heart is in my throat and my hand trembles as I try to steady my breathing.

"You can relax. I came looking for you, but you weren't in the club."

That voice, somehow soft and rough at the same time. It sends a chill down my spine.

His footsteps get closer and I spot the red glow of a lit cigarette floating in the darkness before the moonlight cascades over him for a moment, illuminating him perfectly. His bright blue eyes are even more intense than I remember, before being lost again as he dips back into the shadows.

Dominic.

"And you just happened to find me out here?" I ask.

"I can smell your perfume, actually." I can hear the smile in his voice before I see it. "Normally it wouldn't be that useful, but yours is unique. Lavender, cinnamon, bergamot, and a pinch of vanilla, I think? You were wearing it the other night."

I raise an eyebrow, taking a whiff of my wrist. He's right.

"I'll take your word for it. All I can smell is blood, whiskey, and sweat." I glance off toward the dumpsters. "And of course, whatever else the alley has to offer."

I turn back and he's just a few feet away from me, smirking.

"That's in there too," he replies. "Really though, your friend said you were outside. Made me promise I wouldn't hurt you or she'd," He mimes cocking a gun. "I believe she said she'd blow my dick off."

"Yeah, that sounds like Ruby."

My eyes glide up and down his body. I tell myself I'm checking for weapons, that I'm not looking at *him*. I'm not very convincing.

He's dressed in a black dress shirt with the sleeves rolled up, slightly unbuttoned to expose a chest full of tattoos. An upside down gold cross dangles from his neck and his pants hang low on his hips, the shirt just barely tucked into them. His whole vibe is a lot less professional tonight. I can't help but like the change.

"It's more fun back in the bar, you know. That's where the action is."

"A matter of perspective. I'm interested in a very specific kind of action."

He puffs on his cigarette and an uncomfortable silence nestles between us. I look down at my watch.

"Sun rises soon, and last call is in thirty minutes. You'll turn into a pumpkin if you stay out here for too long."

"More like a pile of goo," he chuckles. "But, sadly, I can't simply flee with the sunrise just yet. I still owe you that drink."

"Well, that's a shame for you, because I don't give up my cigarette breaks for anyone. Not even Dominic Duncan."

The flippant remark seems to ignite something in him, as though he sees it as a challenge. Dominic tilts his head as the fading moonlight carves out his features, making them even more intense. Those cheekbones are so sharp, I can practically feel them cutting into my thighs. He'd look beautiful with his head between my legs.

I force myself to push the thought out of my head as he takes another step toward me.

"Look, what you do is your business, so long as you don't bring that shit into my club, but if you keep this up, we're gonna have trouble."

"Ah," he chuckles, taking a step back and blowing a smoke ring into the air. "I was going to buy you a drink for what you did to Deschamps the other night, but I suppose if you don't *care*..."

I quirk a brow.

"What I did?"

He can't stop the big smile from tugging at the corners of his mouth.

"Shoved a gun right in his face. That's a big move. I wish I could have done it myself."

"So, what, you let me do your dirty work for you?"

"Seems like you had everything under control. I wouldn't want to disrespect your club. The rules are sacred, right?"

"You broke a man's arm to take his seat," I scoff. "You're lucky I didn't put a bullet in *you* before I moved on to Deschamps."

"Right." He closes the gap between us as he takes a final drag from his cigarette before tossing it to the ground. "Because you're *such* a tough guy."

Every step he takes makes me question whether I want to jam my gun in his mouth just to shut him up, or beg him to slam me against the wall. It's not one thing, but everything about him; the way his jaw slopes, the way his lips curl into a malicious smile, the danger in his eyes. His entire being radiates menace and hunger, and I'm only a few steps away from being devoured. I crave the very idea of it.

"That's right," I whisper, lowering my gun and letting it hang loosely at my side. "You better watch yourself."

He backs me up against the wall, one arm stretched out to cage me in, but pauses, as my walkie-talkie clatters to the ground.

"And what's that for?"

"Backup," I mutter.

"Yeah?" He purrs. "And what do you need backup for?"

"You."

I can smell his cologne, woodsy and spicy, as it fills my nostrils. His fingertips trail delicately up the side of my hip, sending a shiver down my spine. He pushes even closer, his weight pressing me into the brickwork as his lips ghost delicately past my ear.

"You like to play games, don't you, little dove?"

SOFIE

Nox Nightclub

"What games?" I breathe.

"Hard to get."

I can't help but smirk.

"You barely tried the other night," I whisper. "You have to play to win."

He tugs at the hem of my skirt.

"What would I find underneath this?" He breathes. "A little pair of panties? Do you even wear any?"

There's a fire in his eyes that's simultaneously exciting and dangerous. I saw a small flicker of it the other night when he snapped Drake's arm. He likes power; being in control. I tilt my head away slightly as he continues to play with the fabric, rubbing it between his fingers.

"If you wanted some time alone with me, you should have been here on a feeding night."

"I'm alone with you right now, love."

I take one final drag of my cigarette and toss it on the ground, blowing the smoke in his face. He ignores it, his fingers sliding up my skirt as he leans in closer. When his lips brush against my earlobe, I get a whiff of his cologne and my head spins. He teases my clit through my panties, forcing a moan to spring from the depths of my throat.

"And you have no one to protect you," he practically sings.

I raise my gun and press it to the oleander tattoo at the base of his throat.

"You think I go anywhere without this?" I breathe.

Dominic's low chuckle ripples through me like a wave as he continues to test my limits, his smile as wicked as ever as he studies my face.

"If I kissed you right now, would you pull that trigger?"

I press the barrel harder against his throat and he growls. I can't tell exactly how far I can push this, but the excitement that's pumping through me is a brand new high I want to chase.

"You want a kiss?" I whisper. "So soft for a vampire."

"You're an awfully big tease for a woman who's aching to be fucked," he purrs. "I can smell it all over you."

I slowly drag the gun down to his chest, stopping right above his heart.

"Mm, seems like you've got a filthy mouth, too."

"Well, it feels like my filthy mouth turns you on," He whispers, finally sliding his fingers past my panties and thrusting them inside me.

I swallow a moan, not wanting to draw attention from a certain security guard on the other side of the door. Dominic's fingers feel fucking incredible, curling and thrusting deep inside of me. I expected to feel pain from his claws, but I'm greeted with softness as he strokes my G-spot. My hips roll against his hand and my eyelids flutter. He must have retracted them for me. It's kind of sweet.

He grins.

"Something tells me I'm on the right track."

His other hand wraps around my throat, *those* claws sinking into my skin. Dominic gives me a few more teasing strokes before he withdraws his fingers from my pussy and shoves them between my parted lips. It's the same motion, thrusting them in and out like I'm sucking his cock.

"Would you like it if I told you what I *really* wanted to do to you the first night I saw you?" Dominic rumbles.

It's been so long since I've felt this kind of instantaneous attraction to someone else, human or vampire. Maybe this is good. Maybe we just need to fuck this tension out. He pulls his fingers out of my mouth, waiting for me to answer.

"Why don't you show me?" I rasp, catching my breath.

"Oh, I'm not sure you realize how dangerous that request could be."

"Why do you give a shit?" I whisper. "I have about ten minutes left on my break and there's a big, bad security guard who would *love* to fuck you up just through that door, so make up your mind."

"Oh, really?"

He wrenches the gun from my grasp, sliding the barrel between my thighs.

"Ride it," he commands. "I want it soaked."

I'm trembling, staring at him unblinking. Dominic tilts his head.

"Did you hear what I just said?"

I nod, and he smiles.

The barrel is cold, even through my panties, and I'm fully aware that this gun could go off at any second, but it's the danger that's getting me off. Dominic's gaze is intense. I can see that bright, beautiful golden color beginning to eclipse his blue iris as he stares me down.

His hand slides down to my hips and he rocks me back and forth across the barrel.

"Feels like you might need some instruction."

The ridges on the gun are hitting me just right, lighting up every nerve ending. It feels incredible, the lace from my panties only adding to the friction. Dominic guides me with a steady hand as my head thunks gently against the wall and I let out a moan. He pushes my underwear to the side and slides the gun up inside of me. I bite down so hard on the inside of my cheek that I taste blood. The second I exhale, I realize my mistake. He smells it, his lips ghosting over mine.

The moment of panic passes quickly as I see in his eyes that he's still in control. I lick the wound and stick my tongue out as an offering. He wants to take the bait. I can see it in the way his face twitches.

"Such a fucking tease," he growls.

"Takes one to know one."

Dominic grunts and continues to fuck me with the barrel of the gun. Each thrust lights up my brain like nothing I've ever felt before. The physical sensation blending perfectly with my fear and excitement becomes a whirlwind that threatens to consume me.

There's no chance that he hasn't noticed.

"How many bullets?" He whispers.

"Two," I grunt.

"Mmm. Even if you wanted to kill me, it wouldn't be enough. Your arm was shaking so much that your aim was way off."

"Fuck you," I growl.

He laughs, clearly knowing how close he's brought me to the edge. My clit throbs and heat cascades through my body, wildfire devouring me from the inside out. I wiggle my hips and reach up to squeeze my breast, running my thumb over a pebbled nipple.

My breathing quickens, my mouth dropping open in a silent scream. I'm about to come, but Dominic doesn't waste time, his mouth colliding with mine in a fiery kiss. This is what he's been wanting since the moment he first sat down across the bar from me.

His fangs are razors, slicing the edge of my tongue, groaning as he sucks on it. Sparks shoot down my spine as he tightens his grip around my throat. I whimper against his mouth, the barrel of my gun now hitting my G-spot with each thrust. The experience is dizzying, and the danger intoxicating.

And then, just as everything is about to explode, he pulls it out of me and steps away. I stumble forward, catching myself before I hit the ground, my breath ragged as I let out a desperate cry.

"Motherfucker!"

He laughs. He *fucking* laughs as he tosses the gun to the ground and tears my panties off of my body, shoving them between my teeth before I have another moment to respond. The next thing I know, he's unzipping his pants and pushing himself inside of me, stretching me to the point of the most exquisite pain.

"Tonight, the only thing you're coming on is my cock."

I can barely speak, my eyes rolling back as his hips move at a vicious pace.

"Oh, what happened? You were so tough a couple minutes ago." He laughs again as I let out a muffled moan. "I'm going to make you fucking *scream* for me."

Every stroke feels like an equal split of heaven and hell, bliss laced with barbed wire slamming right up against me. He buries himself deep inside of me and lets me grind my hips against his until my clit is swollen and my body aches for more. He sucks on my neck, his fangs a constant threat as they drag along my skin. It's like he's riling himself up; teasing himself as he fucks me.

The burn of his stubble against my skin, the way he smells, the way he tastes like whiskey, cigarettes, and copper, and the feeling of his rough hand clamped around my throat... it's overwhelming. I whimper as I listen to the guttural moans that spill from his lips.

"I want your blood dripping down those perfect tits. I want to lick that pretty pussy until you're crying; *begging me* to let you come."

I moan through the fabric again, unable to stop myself as my eyelids flutter.

"I'm going to mark you up so that when another vampire sees you, he'll know that you're *mine*."

I want to tell him that I don't belong to anyone, but the very idea of being *his* is pushing me closer and closer to the edge.

"And you're going to be a good little girl and sing for me, aren't you?"

He's not even talking about feeding on me. When's the last time this dude got laid? I nod my head and he fucks me harder, stroking my G-spot with every thrust. I'm so fucking close I can feel it. Just a few more–

A knock at the door causes both of us to freeze. I can't tell if my heart is racing even faster because I'm teetering right on the edge, or because Bobby could burst through that door at any second and catch us both in the act.

"Time's up!" Bobby's gruff voice calls through the door.

I turn back to Dominic and he pulls my panties out of my mouth, placing a delicate kiss to my lips.

"Please," I rasp. "I'm so close."

He pulls out of me and I groan at the hollowness.

"Patience is a virtue, little dove," he purrs as he tucks my panties into his pocket. "I'll be back for that drink tomorrow."

"What the fuck? You're just gonna leave me like this?!"

Dominic chuckles, cupping my face with one hand as I tremble in place. My cheeks are red and my chest tightens as he flashes me a shit-eating grin.

"Maybe we both like to play games."

"Sofie!" Bobby bellows. "I'm coming out there!"

Dominic is already halfway down the alley, walking backwards as he tucks my panties into his pocket. His eyes stay fixed on me.

"I'm here!" I shout at the door between heaving breaths. "Gimme a second!"

"I'll be back tomorrow," Dominic croons as he reaches the mouth of the alley, disappearing into the dark.

I yank my skirt down, steadying myself as I pick up my stuff. My legs are still shaking from my denied orgasm. I angrily shove the walkie talkie into my apron, along with my gun that's soaked with... me.

Cocky asshole. He's probably got a big fucking smile on his face, too. And he thinks he gets to just saunter back here tomorrow and get whatever he wants?

Yeah right.

DOMINIC

Nox Nightclub

Sofie. Beautiful name.

It was one of the last things I caught before I slipped into the shadows.

I hated being away the few days after our very first meeting, but Theo needed my help setting up the lab. Under the cover of night, we scrounged up all the supplies that we could, all while trying to stay under the radar. It was exhausting work, but seeing Sofie last night was the reward.

She was even better than the fantasies that had been brewing inside of my head. She's cold and abrasive, exactly what keeps me coming back. I like a woman who pushes my buttons. Some might say it's a character flaw, but I know what gets me off.

Everything about her was intoxicating, from the way she moved to the way she whined when I fucked her with her own gun. Maybe I should have taken that instead of her panties that are now wrapped around my knuckles. I wonder if that gun is resting against her thigh right now.

And after a taste like that? Nothing could keep me away from her.

I need her.

I need more.

And so I'm back at Nox all over again.

Small crowds of people move around me, but I don't pay much attention to them. My eyes are on her and the gorgeous hair that flows all the way down her back. And those eyes? So heavenly, I can see them clear as day through darkness.

She's the kind of beautiful that makes my legs wobble and wish that my heart could flutter. Instead, all I feel is a pull in the center of my chest, like a magnet. My fists clench as desire pumps through me, my claws digging into my palms as blood pools beneath them.

What the fuck is happening to me?

Vampires have a natural magnetism, but it's nothing like in the movies. We're expert hunters, excellent at charming people, and obviously skilled in using sex to our advantage. Unsurprisingly, everyone tastes better when you're making them come.

I stride toward the bar, making my way through a thick crowd of vampires on the dance floor. Some of them catch my eye, backing up a little to make room. There's an empty seat right in front of her, with no Drake-replacement to remove.

Perfect. Things are already going my way.

She slides a shot and a glass of whiskey to another patron, looking up as I hop onto the stool. She's dressed in a tight red latex dress that leaves nothing to the imagination. The fine hairs on her arm stand on end the second our eyes meet. She's giving herself away.

"You're back."

The sound of her voice is nearly swallowed up by the rhythmically thumping music. Her co-worker slips behind her, dark hair with a black leather jacket and a lace bra. I sort of remember her from the other night. She has a disarmingly bright smile that makes me smile right back at her.

"Sorry, Sof, I need another bag of O negative," she announces, resting a hand on Sofie's hip.

Sofie moves out of the way, staring straight at me as her friend grabs a couple of large bags from below the bar, and moves back to her station.

I return her gaze, refusing to take my eyes off of her the entire time.

I wonder if that's her real name, or just something she uses for work.

"I promised I'd be back, didn't I?"

She leans over the bar, a little smirk spreading across her face. I get a better look at the tattoos on her chest. A delicate lily near her shoulder with the name *Charlie* beneath it, the 'e' just barely obscured by the strap of her dress. She's got birds, and another large ornate flower that stops just at the base of her throat. Just like mine.

"Sure. Kinda late though, isn't it?"

"I'm a very busy man."

"And why should I care?"

Her mouth twitches, and I pull out another small bundle of bills from my wallet, sliding them across the table. It's much more than the cost of a couple of drinks. She raises a brow.

"This is for...?"

"For a shot of A-positive, a bourbon, and the rest of the night on this barstool."

I can tell she's already annoyed. Maybe things didn't quite go the way she expected last night.

"It's only $80 for the drinks."

"Think of it as an apology, Sofie."

Her jaw ticks the moment she hears me use her name, but she's silent as she collects the money and tucks it into her bra, only speaking up when it's safely hidden away.

"An apology, huh?"

"That's right."

She pours my bourbon and a shot of blood, plunking both down in front of me. I take the blood first, dipping my pinky finger into it and gently sucking on it. It's exquisite, much to my surprise, almost as good as getting it straight from the source. It reminds me of the old days when I was content with only drinking wine; I can taste and smell so much of the history behind the donor. This one, for instance: an avid runner. They eat their vegetables, but sometimes they like to indulge– whiskey, cigars, sex, even a bit of cocaine. That's what gives it an extra kick.

I can't help but wonder what *she* tastes like.

"So, you think you can just buy your way out of leaving me high and dry last night?"

I take the shot of blood and toss the entire thing back, running my tongue over my fangs as I swallow.

"Have a drink with me," I urge. "I'm buying, regardless."

She puts a hand on her hip. I spot chipped nail polish and fingernails bitten down to the quick, skin still raw from where she's torn it off.

"I told you last night, I don't drink at work."

So I can fuck her with her own gun outside of the club on her smoke break, but she won't have a drink with me? How the fuck does *that* make sense?

"You don't drink at work, or you don't drink with patrons?"

"You don't give up, do you?"

Her attention is dragged away by another patron who slides up next to me, ordering a shot of B positive and a vodka tonic. Sofie is all business as she grabs glassware. Both of us get a good view of her ass as she turns around to grab a bottle of cheap vodka off the middle shelf. The vampire next to me grins and a snarl rumbles in my throat.

"Back off, motherfucker."

He clears his throat and I casually sip my bourbon while she slides the drinks over. The newcomer is trembling a little as he hands her the cash, leaving a shitty tip as he walks away.

"If I have a drink with you, does it mean you'll stop coming in and I can work in peace?"

Her voice is a little throaty, with a sultry and flirtatious edge to it. Every time she talks, I feel the hairs on the back of my neck stand up, and my cock gets a little harder.

I dig another hundred-dollar bill out of my wallet and stuff it into her cup. She stares at me, like she's trying to figure me out.

"Is that what you want?" I ask.

"What, the tip?" She fires back. "Thought you gave that to me the other night."

Her eyes shine with a glint of cruelty as she takes my empty shot glass and tucks it beneath the bar.

"For me to stop coming in," I clarify with a grin. "Is that what you want?"

"Do you think giving me more money is going to get you that drink?"

"Well, money talks, and if you can't tell, I've got a gift for the gab."

She scoffs and shakes her head.

"You're tenacious."

"Have to be in my line of work."

"Good point. What line of work was that again, Mr. Duncan? I mean, we've all seen your highrise, but what exactly is it you do?"

"Anything I want," I reply as she pours herself a drink with the hint of a sour expression on her face.

I get the feeling she puts up this front for her own protection. She's a little cold and defensive. She should be. It's a dangerous world outside these doors — hell, even inside of them.

She holds up the glass, and I smirk.

"Atta girl," I praise, relishing the deep crimson on her cheeks.

There's only the smallest threat of a smile, nothing ever fully forming on her face. It must be hard to fake it. Vampires can be civil, but we flip like a light switch. I wouldn't trust us if I were human.

The air hangs thick between us, like a cloud carrying a month's worth of rain, aching for release. Her pulse isn't slowing, and her skin looks like it would be scorching to the touch. I ache to slide my hand between her thighs and listen to her whimper for me all over again. The way she throbbed beneath my touch was fucking heaven.

I can hear her breath hitch, even over the music, as she lifts her drink to her lips. I shake my head and hold out my glass, signaling for her to clink hers with mine. She obliges me and a thrill shoots through my veins.

"Was that so bad?" I tease.

She swallows her whiskey.

"The drink is amazing. Everything else... It's been fine so far."

She pours another drink and slams it back, probably an effort to calm her nerves. It doesn't look like it's doing much good. Her hand is shaking as she sets the glass back down onto the counter and stares at me.

For a moment, everything and everyone else melts away, and it feels like it's just the two of us here.

"You look nervous," I observe.

"I'm not afraid of you."

A lie.

Humans are so bad at this shit. I can smell her fear from where I'm standing, mixed perfectly with her perfume. It's different today. Fresh oranges, bergamot, and a hint of something earthy, like petrichor. I wonder who she buys from. The back of my neck tingles along with my jaw, and I reach back, rubbing at the skin.

"Oh, you're not?"

"No."

"And why not? You don't think I'm dangerous?"

"Because I know if any vamp tries anything in here, they'd be eating silver in less than a minute, even Dominic *Fucking* Duncan."

I grin and lick my bottom lip. Her eyes trace my tongue every step of the way.

"I like that. Maybe it'll be my new middle name?"

"Don't let it inflate your ego. I just thought it packed some punch."

"It does. I'd like to hear it in a more intimate setting." She pours me another drink and slides it toward me, probably trying to justify the massive tip I gave her. "Speaking of names, Sofie, is that your real one?"

"Why the fuck do you care?" She leans over the bar, wiping it down with a small black rag, getting close, but not so close that we actually touch.

"Well, if I'm gonna sit in front of a pretty girl every night, I'd like to know what to call her – you know, other than gorgeous, angel, princess..."

For the first time, I get a genuine laugh. It's mocking, but I'll take what I can get. For now.

"God, that's terrible. Do any of those usually work for you?"

"You're honest," I chuckle. "I like that."

Her eyes dig into mine and her smile falls away.

"You have to be in my line of work."

Gorgeous, sharp, and she doesn't take any bullshit. I love it.

"Are you going to answer my question?" I sip my drink. "Because I can come up with far worse nicknames for you all night."

She worries at her lip with her teeth, like she's debating whether to tell me something extremely important. Finally, she lets out a long sigh.

"Yeah, Sofie's my real name."

Her eyes light up just a little, like telling me had taken some weight off her shoulders, or set her free.

"It's lovely, I–"

Suddenly, there's a crash and a yelp from behind me. I turn to see a tall blond vampire tussling with a brunette, while a woman tries to break the two of them up.

"Son of a bitch," her friend spits, pulling her gun out of her apron. "Hey! Hunter! You know the fucking rules. None of that shit in here!"

"You good, Ruby?" Sofie pulls out her own weapon and her friend holds out a hand to stop her.

"Yeah, I got this. We need someone to sling the drinks."

Ruby hops over the bar and storms toward the action. I chuckle and sip at my bourbon as I watch her go, but it's only a couple of seconds before I hear another crash, this time behind the bar. When I turn back to Sofie, she's already staring right at me, a coy look lingering on her face while chaos continues to erupt behind me.

"I'm so clumsy," she mutters to no one in particular. "I'm heading to the back, gotta get a broom."

Her fingers trail along the counter as she walks to the end of the bar and takes one last look at me, daring me to follow, before disappearing around the corner.

She's taking a risk, and I know it. But this attraction between us that's been building is quickly bordering on obsession. I dreamed about her this morning. We were walking in the sunshine along the beach. Her hair was flowing behind her and her hand was woven in mine. I haven't seen the sun in over a century, but somehow it's burned perfectly into my memory. For the first time in years, I jolted from sleep, aching for my humanity.

I glance behind me to see two security guards hauling the rambunctious vamps toward the door. All eyes are on them, the perfect distraction.

I finish my drink, abandoning the empty glass on the counter before sliding behind the bar and into the back. They've done so much work on this place that you could swear it was never actually hallowed ground. The only hints are the stained glass windows, the heavy church doors, and the fact that this place somehow still smells like communion wine.

There's a sliver of light coming from a room at the end of the hall. Behind it I can hear her heavy breath, her heart pounding, her blood roaring. It drowns out everything else.

Sofie is leaning up against the wall as I enter, twirling a strand of red hair around one finger. It's a little storage closet, filled with boxes of supplies, glasses, syrups to make cocktails, and some old vestments still hanging in clear garment bags.

"Sir, this is for employees only," she scolds.

Without a word, I shut the door and close the gap between us, pressing my palms against the concrete wall to cage her in all over again. Her eyes burn into mine as her cheeks flush, making her freckles stand out even more. The smell of her perfume makes me want to drop to my knees and worship her; devour her. I wish we had more than just a handful of minutes.

I dip my head and listen to the sound of her breath rushing in and out of her chest like a raging river. Emboldened by the knowledge that I'm the reason heat is practically radiating from her body. She gasps as I run my tongue along the side of her throat.

"Sorry miss, but I've come to pay a debt."

DOMINIC

NOX NIGHTCLUB

"YOU LEFT ME HIGH and dry last time," she breathes. "Had to go home and take care of myself."

"Did you now?" I whisper.

My fingertips dance up her bare thigh, tugging gently at the hem of her skirt as I hum. Somehow I'm already addicted, and I haven't even tasted her yet.

"My removable shower head was *very* understanding."

"Oh," I chuckle. "I see I've been replaced already."

"Maybe," she teases. "We'll see how you manage tonight."

My fangs glide along her skin, an offer to cut into her like a hot knife through butter. It would be so easy to lift her up, pin her against the wall, and fuck her senseless while I drained her dry.

She places a hand on my chest, her fingertips fiddling with the buttons on my shirt.

"It's not a feeding night." She pops a few of them open and plays with the gold chain dangling from my neck. "You've gotta pay a lot more for that privilege."

"Do I?"

She pulls back, those crimson lips smirking at me, daring me to take what I need.

"Everyone has to choose sometime. You wanna eat me, or fuck me?"

I can practically hear the electricity crackling between us.

"Maybe someday I'll have to choose, but for now I think I'll take both."

She tilts her head, giving me no sign she's surprised.

I move in, capturing her lips in a fiery kiss as my claws extend, dragging carefully along her thigh. She lets out a soft groan that spills like honey from the base of her throat as my tongue plays against hers. I taste mint, nicotine, and whiskey. I can smell her soap, her shampoo, even the specific latex that was used to make her dress. It all mingles together to drive me fucking crazy.

She makes me feel like I'm spiraling. Every time I touch her, it's like I'm transported to a different time, a different place. There's something about her that feels familiar. Alive.

My hand slips between her thighs as she lifts her leg and hooks it around my waist. She's already soaked. The whimper that drips from her lips is so addicting, I wish I could bottle it. I want her broken, screaming for me. I want to know what she tastes like in every conceivable way.

Fuck, I'm losing my mind over this girl.

I grasp her tightly by the waist and turn her around, slamming her up against the wall. I pull her skirt up, and she yelps as I suck on the pulsing vein in the side of her neck.

"No biting," she growls, but it sounds more like a taunt, pulling me dangerously close to something I can't have. I have trouble taking no for an answer.

I have to be a very good boy today, at least if I'm planning to leave alive.

"Then tell me what you want, and you'll get it," I purr.

"I need you to fuck me," she groans.

The begging unlocks something primal and vicious in me.

"Say my name."

"Fuck me, Dominic. Please!"

It's a sweet, almost harmonious moan, like a choir of angels.

"Good girl."

She nearly falls to pieces at the praise. I'll keep that in mind for later.

My cock grinds against her ass, and every second I'm not inside of her is torturous. With one claw, I slice through her panties, ripping them from her body and tossing them aside. I don't know why she bothers to wear them anymore.

Sofie's clawing at the wall with those chipped fingernails. If she were mine, she could get those nails done whenever she wanted. She'd be my Queen, bathed in jewels and gowns. She wouldn't have to lift a fucking finger.

I kick her feet apart and unbuckle my belt, pulling my cock out of my pants and teasing her with the tip. Music pounds, vibrating the walls and her bones.

"You want this?"

She lets out another throaty groan, and goosebumps rush down my spine. I can't get enough of this woman; the way she smells, the way she moans, the way she writhes just for me.

"Yes, I need it."

I wind her hair around my knuckles and pull back as hard as I can.

She's an ocean, and I want to drown myself in her.

"Beg for it."

She smirks at me over her shoulder, her eyes full of fire.

"What would you do if I asked *you* to beg?"

"Play your cards right and you might find out." I flick my tongue against her ear. "But I wasn't asking."

She shivers, her pussy clenching around the tip of my cock as I push it a little deeper inside of her.

"Fuck me, Dominic." She draws in a long shaky breath. "Please."

Working women up to the point of incoherent babbling and tears gets me off. Sometimes, the foreplay is even better than the sex.

"That's pathetic," I grunt. "*Really* beg for it. I want to know you'd die without my cock inside you."

She exhales softly, followed by the sweetest whimper I've ever heard.

"I'm sorry, Mr. Duncan. Would you prefer it if I leaned over the bar and shoved my tits in your face like you have to pay for it?"

I smack her ass hard enough to leave a bruise and pull out of her completely. The crack echoes through the small space and I can hear her swallow a moan.

"Are you trying to piss me off?"

Her laugh is vibrant and mischievous.

"Why don't you find out?"

I tug harder on her hair, forcing her body to arch. Her fingernails scrape against concrete and she lets out a loud, high-pitched wail, almost singing for me.

"Do what I tell you and *beg*." I let out a soft hiss. The warmth of her body calls out to mine. I'm starved for her. "I could rip you apart, little dove."

"Please, Dominic!" Her voice cracks. "Fuck!"

"That's more like it," I whisper. "Tell me what you want."

"I want you to fuck me. I want to feel you inside of me." She looks over her shoulder at me. "Hold me down and take everything you want from me."

"I think you and I are going to have a lot of fun together, Sofie."

She whines as I bottom out, feeling her stretch for me. Her voice seems to get swallowed up by the sound of the music that's shaking the walls.

Her hand slams into the wall as I continue to fuck her, harder and deeper. This isn't how I wanted this to go. I wanted hours with her, something slow where I can tease her to my heart's content and watch tears stream down her face. I want *everything*.

I make a small cut in the back of her neck and my lips attach to the wound as she takes me deeper; her moans bleeding out between ragged breaths. I release her hair and place one hand on her hip while the other reaches up to cup her breasts, teasing her nipples through the cheap latex. She's rolling her hips backward into mine as her blood stains my tongue. She's so fucking sweet. I have to crush the urge to feed from her. It's almost instinctual at this point.

Her moan pulls me from my reverie and grounds me in the present. Her sweetness and the way she trembles and quivers for me. It's everything I've been missing.

It's been a while since I've fucked a human. I forgot just how perfectly soft they can be. I love a vampire who can take the brunt of my strength, but there's something about human fragility that makes me even harder.

"Fuck, you're gorgeous," I praise.

She's pulsing around me, and judging by the way her clit throbs against my fingers, she's getting fucking close.

I lean in and nip her ear before deciding to pull out. She whines at my absence, but I quickly turn her around, gripping her waist and slamming her up against the wall before lifting her off of the ground. She looks a little dazed, eyelids drooping like she's drunk on nothing but me. The thing I love the most about humans is that they stroke your ego without even trying, especially the ones that look at you like you're a fucking god.

"Wrap your legs around my waist, sweet thing. I want to see the look in your eyes when I make you come."

She obeys without question and I sink back into her, picking up the pace quickly and fucking her even deeper. Her head rolls to one side, beautiful moans slipping from her lips like prayers she's never spoken before. Just watching her makes me feral.

I need to come back here every single day for the rest of my life.

My cock throbs inside of her and I drink everything in – the sight of her, the smell of her perfume, and the way she bends and twists just for me. Electricity gathers at the base of my spine as the sounds of her moans and my desperate grunts filling the room.

"I'm–"

"Come for me," I whisper as my lips crash against hers.

Everything about this feels rough and ragged like a car crash. She's clawing at my suit, digging her fingernails into the back of my neck as I slam her against the wall repeatedly, trying to take some care not to shatter her completely.

I can feel the fabric of my pants dampen and she rips her mouth away from mine, letting out a loud moan when she finally comes. Just as she closes her eyes, I grip her chin tightly, still holding her up effortlessly.

"Look at me," I snarl.

She nods as I fuck her harder and harder, the knot in my stomach tightening until I think I'm going to burst into flames. My mouth attaches to her throat, and that big vein that throbs against my lips as she comes around me one more time. I like to test my own limits, to see just how much I can take before I give in and bite her, but I don't get to find out. Just before I'm about to *really* break the rules, she grips my hair and forces my head back.

"Don't think just because you're stronger than me that you can outsmart me," she grunts.

Before I even have the chance to chuckle, that knot in my stomach explodes, spreading heat throughout my body. I'm coming so fucking hard that I almost sink my teeth into her. She lets out another cry, squeezing me one last time as I'm reduced to groans and quivering muscle.

Her mouth finds mine, and the kiss is surprisingly sweet. She's got an edge to her, but when push comes to shove, there's a softness that I can't ignore. I can still taste the whiskey she drank mixed with her blood. Her fingers run through my hair, playing with it and scratching my neck, and for just a moment, I feel cared for.

When she breaks the kiss, she looks up at me with those big doe eyes that make my knees weak. Coppery hair falls down her shoulders, a few strands obscuring her face. I push it away, and instantly, I know I'm fucked.

"I have to see you again," I whisper.

"Keep paying and you can see me as much as you want."

I pull out of her and set her down, tucking my cock back into my pants. She turns away from me and smooths out her skirt, her eyes fixed on the floor, almost as though she's ashamed of what she's just done. The silence is awkward enough that I glance around the room until my eyes fall on something of interest: a Santa Cruz Blood Bank ID card with her photo.

Well, that complicates things a bit.

When I look back at her, she's tracing the back of her neck, feeling out the cut that I made there. In an instant, I watch her expression shift, and she's staring daggers at me. If looks could kill, she'd have me gutted by now.

"Dude, I said you couldn't bite me!"

Trust me, if *I* bit you, you'd know. I just nicked you, you can relax."

I can see frustration in her eyes brewing like a storm.

"I can't go out there like this!"

"Why? Is it part of your contract that you remain a pure, innocent maiden? I'm guessing it's a bit too late for that."

"Fix it, asshole," she seethes through clenched teeth. "You wanna start a feeding frenzy?!"

I like the attitude, but I can't tell if it stems from shame or paranoia. Slowly, I drag my tongue across my fang until I taste blood. I grasp her by the waist and pull her toward me, relishing the way her breath catches in her chest.

"You need to learn to watch your mouth. You know I kill people for speaking to me like that..."

"I–"

I dip my head and lap at the wound. It knits in an instant, and I gently suck on her skin, forcing a light groan to spill from her lips. I pull back and stare at her.

"Happy now?"

"Yes," she chokes.

"Good girl."

A knock at the door startles her and I spot another bartender staring at the two of us with wide eyes, her mouth dropped open. She has long blonde hair and wide set blue eyes that look perpetually shocked. She's a petite little thing with spindly limbs, dressed in a pair of denim shorts, thigh-high boots, and a red tube top that just barely covers her tits.

Sofie's heart thumps violently against me and I release her, watching as she tries to regain her balance. I try to bite back a smile, but it's nearly impossible. There are deep red splotches on her chest and I can smell her fear even from a foot away.

"H– hey, Kirby," she mutters. "I was just–"

"Ruby's looking for you. I assume you went looking for a broom and fell on something hard?" Sofie rubs the back of her neck and Kirby chuckles. "It's cool, Sof, I'll tell her you're fine."

The door shuts, and Sofie sighs as I straighten my suit.

"Are you working tomorrow?"

She nods.

"The feeding room."

"Perfect. I'll be here the second the doors open. We can do this right."

She says nothing, grabbing a broom as I head for the door.

I don't even need a response. I know she's hooked on me now. The tricky thing, though, is I might have fallen even harder.

SOFIE

Nox Nightclub

I STAND IN THE closet clutching the broom so hard I feel like the handle is going to snap. His cum drips down my thighs and I quickly grab a cloth from the shelf, wiping it up and tossing it into the trash. In the year that we've been running this bar, not *once* have I dragged a vampire into a supply closet and begged them to fuck me.

Another sharp knock rips me from my little spiral.

"I said I was coming!" I bark.

Ruby leans up against the door, looking me up and down as a playful smirk spreads across her face.

"I think you already did."

"Jesus Christ, you scared the shit out of me!"

"That was the goal. Fight's cleared up, by the way."

I nod and try to bring myself back down to earth as she sniffs at the air and takes a single step past the threshold.

"You get some new perfume? Or is that *someone's* cologne?"

"Shut. The fuck. *Up*," I hiss, stomping past her with the broom clenched tightly in my hand.

Ruby snorts as she follows me back to the bar, letting the door shut behind us.

I'm worried people will find out I'm just a *little* attracted to Dominic. Hooking up with the customers is unsurprisingly pretty normal at this place. The issue is the fact that every time he walks into this bar, I can't control myself. It's hard to breathe, hard to think, hard to have a conversation when he's staring at me. I hate feeling that out of control.

The moment I reach the bar, Kirby's already grinning at me, sipping on a soda. "So, how was it?"

I move to sweep up what's left of my broken glass, not listening and *definitely* not responding. Ruby takes a step in front of me, and I poke at her feet with the bristles of the broom.

"Move. You might have some glass under your shoes."

She remains still, challenging me.

"You like him."

I can feel a little frustrated snarl bubble up from my throat.

"We've had this conversation before."

"I know. I just like to bug you, but–"

"Uh... guys?"

Kirby's pinched voice makes my head snap up as she gestures to the front of the bar with a flick of her head.

There's no way. Rene *fucking* Deschamps. Again.

"Well, I'll be goddamned," Ruby mutters, her fingers brushing against the gun holstered on her thigh.

"I thought you told him to never come back," Kirby murmurs.

"I did. This fucker doesn't listen," I reply with a venom-coated tongue.

I watch him as he saunters through the room, flanked by four vampires who look big and burly enough to tear this place to shreds, along with everyone in it. Fucking great.

What's more interesting to me, though, is the young woman on his arm. She has dark circles under her eyes and pale, almost sickly looking skin. Her arms are twig-like with little to no muscle definition, and her face is sunken and sallow. She clings to Rene, swaying slightly as she stares up at him with adoration. I don't see fangs when she smiles, and the liquor in my stomach threatens to crawl right back up my throat.

"Jesus, is that a human with him?" Kirby squeaks.

"I think so," Ruby whispers. "Looks like she might be his own personal feeder."

This is a vampire only bar. If there are other humans in here besides the staff, it fucks with our bottom line. He's poking at my boundaries, flaunting his power. I continue to track him as he moves through the crowd. Vamps stumble backward to move out of his way. I can see the arrogance flooding his body as he struts toward a table and motions for a group to vacate it.

"Motherfucker," Kirby spits. "The fuck does he think he's doing?"

"I don't know," I sigh. "But I'm gonna find out."

I throw the broom on the floor and grab my gun from under the bar, heading straight for him. The only thing I can feel is scorching rage. I want to make him pay for what he did to Kirby.

If he wants to eat, I'll feed him silver all night.

One of Rene's men alerts him to my approach and he looks up, lips curling into a smile that's clearly rehearsed. My jaw ticks, but I try not to let my anger show. He's not going to get to me tonight.

"Good evening, pet," Rene drawls. "What can I do for you?"

I grit my teeth as he looks me up and down before turning to his friends.

"Pretty little thing, wouldn't you say?"

"You were told not to come back, and then you waltz in like nothing happened? *And* break another house rule?"

He takes another brazen lick of the woman's wrist, crimson on his tongue.

"Oh, I'm so sorry. I was unaware of these rules."

I clench my jaw so hard my teeth nearly turn to powder.

"The rules that were given to you by the bouncer when you first came in. Now, I know Ares is great at his job, so he would have told you that you are to *only* purchase blood from the bar, and I know you've got two working ears, so there's no chance you didn't hear it. What I *don't know* is how you got back in after the shit you pulled last time. "

"You seem to know a lot." Rene grins, showing me long, yellowed fangs. "Did you know your man is foolish enough to take a bribe, too?"

I'm not buying it. He's not the kind of guy to fold easily. I look to the front door, spotting a petrified Ares staring right back at me. What could they have threatened him with?

Rene digs into his jacket pocket and pulls out a thick roll of cash, tossing it at me. It bounces off of my chest and falls onto the ground.

"There, to show my contrition for my blunder the other night. You can keep the change. It looks like you might need a new skirt."

I don't even glance down to see whatever damage Dominic must have done. I know Deschamps just wants to keep riling me up.

"I'm asking you to leave, Mr. Deschamps. For the last time."

"And I'm *telling* you to get me a drink." He snarls, his calm demeanor slipping for just a second before he pulls it back together with a smile. "Let's see what else your fine establishment has to offer. Hell, if I'm so inclined, I might just buy the place from you."

"Not a chance," I growl.

His eyes rake up and down my body, clearly irritated by my resistance.

"It would be unwise to upset me, pet." The girl next to him drags her tongue along the side of his neck. I can almost hear it scraping against his stubble. "In fact, it would be in your best interests to *behave*."

I have to bite down on my tongue as he gestures to the bar with a flick of his head. Dominic is an asshole, but Rene is something else entirely. I want to take my heel off and jam it right in his fucking eye socket.

I thrust a finger out at him, leaning forward until I'm right in his face. His goons shift in their seats, but Rene doesn't even flinch.

"You get *one drink* and you're out of my fucking bar. For good."

He reaches into his jacket, drawing out a cigarette and lighting it up without a care in the world. As I turn to walk away, one of his goons snatches my wrist and yanks me backward, twisting it until I'm face-to-face with Rene.

"Anyone ever tell you you're prettier when your mouth is shut? Because I'm a lot less gentle than Mr. Duncan."

Claws dig into my arm as he casually blows the smoke right in my face.

I try my hardest to look unfazed.

"He's been here, hasn't he? Sniffing around like a hungry dog, I bet. Careful before you answer, I can smell him all over you."

My blood runs cold as laughter ripples around the table. I feel like a kid being picked on on the playground. My fists clench and I fight the urge to grab the nearest beer bottle, break it on the asshole with his hands on me, and drive it through his heart.

"Go fuck yourself, you insecure, *hideous* fucking worm," I spit.

In an instant, Rene is on his feet, a hand already holding me tight by the neck. He pulls me across the table and gets right in my face with an ugly sneer. There's decay on his breath, sickly sweet and hollow. I'm reminded of a rotting corpse and resist the urge to gag. I don't want to give him an inch.

"I own this fucking city and I could crush you and your friends in a heartbeat." He sinks a claw into my neck, slicing into my skin. My chin trembles and tears pool in my eyes, but I refuse to show him any fucking fear, even as blood runs down my skin. He sniffs at the air and leans in closer and closer until his forehead is pressed against mine. "The only thing you're worthy of is bleeding for me, you pathetic little cunt."

The mocking laughter at the table nearly overwhelms me, and my throat aches, holding back all the words lodged just behind my tongue.

"Now, do your job, and get me my fucking drink."

He releases me, but I'm frozen in fear, staring at the piece of human jaw bone that hangs from a chain around his neck. In the year we've been doing this, it's the first time I've been truly terrified like this. In my own bar.

One of his men snaps his fingers in front of my face, a sneer lingering on his lips.

"Did you hear him, bitch?"

I draw in a breath, and with trembling arms I push myself off of the table. My wrist aches, and I glance down to see a bright red handprint adorning it like a bracelet.

"One drink, and then you leave," I reply, keeping my voice as steady as I can.

He chuckles.

"Of course. You're the boss, after all."

I turn on the ball of my foot, storming through the crowd. When I reach the bar, Kirby's eyes are bouncing between Rene and I. Everyone looks as terrified as I feel, and I sniff tears away.

"Are you okay?"

"Five shots of O negative," I snap. "Get Bobby to bring it to his table. I don't want you going anywhere near him. Once they're finished, I want them fucking gone. I don't care if they have to be tossed out of here."

My voice is still shaking, along with the rest of me. But I won't break. I can't.

We never say it out loud, but we all know why I can't just kill Rene right now, and why Ares is standing by the door looking petrified. Deschamps is the most dangerous and powerful vampire in this city, and saying no to him is a death sentence, even here with all our rules.

We might have made deals with him, but he's more than willing to break them to get what he wants. He doesn't respect the humans in this city, at least not enough to give us a real say in how things are run. Deschamps has all the money and power. Why should he ever let us call the shots?

Kirby pours drinks, and Bobby is there in an instant, carrying the tray to Rene's table. I slip behind the bar, feeling a little more secure as I stand between Kirby and Ruby, both of them reaching down to squeeze each of my hands.

"What did he say to you?" Ruby asks.

"Something about bleeding for him." I let out a ragged sigh. "Not the most original insult I've heard, but..."

"He's terrifying," Kirby rasps, her eyes fixed on Rene as he takes small sips out of his shot glass. "He was gonna kill me the other night. I could feel it."

Ruby hangs her head, the guilt weighing her down.

"I'm sorry, Kirby. We shouldn't have let him in."

"He would have found a way." Kirby leans over the counter and smiles at Ruby. "Besides, you're not allowed to apologize. You saved my life."

She holds her head up high. I can still see the bite mark on her neck that's been covered by makeup.

"I'm not gonna give that fucker the satisfaction of scaring me now."

I squeeze her hand harder. Despite the bravado, she's trembling.

"We just have to be cordial," Ruby murmurs. "Give him what he wants, and he'll leave."

Rene winks at us from across the bar as he lifts what's left in his shot glass and tosses it back. Bobby stands a short distance from their table, one hand on his gun. It feels like someone lit a stick of dynamite and we're all just waiting for it to go off.

Bobby takes a step forward and Rene laughs, rolling his eyes as though *he's* the victim. He gathers his group with a wave of his hand. As they get to their feet and head to the exit, Deschamps catches my eye one last time, giving me an exaggerated bow before he disappears out the door.

Be Cordial? Give him what he wants? I'd rather watch him choke as I jam my gun between his teeth.

It looks like Dominic and I might have something in common after all.

DOMINIC

DUNCAN TOWERS

THEO'S STANDING IN FRONT of the entrance, smoking furiously as he paces back and forth.

"Where is he?" I demand as I slam the car door.

"Locked upstairs." He tosses the butt on the ground, crushing it beneath his shoe. "I shut the elevator down — Mateo, you keep watch."

"Yes, sir."

As I was making my way out of Nox, Mateo burst in to tell me that someone had broken into my penthouse. I didn't want to be dealing with this shit tonight, but Rene refuses to give me a goddamn break. The whole thing has almost killed my high. Someone's gonna pay for that.

I storm through the front door, Theo already at my heels as Mateo leans up against my car, unsure of what to do with himself.

"And the formula?"

"Locked away," Theo snorts. "Remember, genius?"

"Right," I sigh as we head inside toward the elevator.

"You got laid," Theo remarks, looking me up and down.

The elevator dings and the doors slide open.

"You didn't."

I step inside and lean against the wall while Theo taps his foot impatiently.

"Yeah, because I'm out here trying to find someone to make that fucking bullshit for you."

"That *bullshit* is going to make us rich."

Even through the steel doors and walls, I can smell Rene's fucking goon in my sanctuary. The elevator dings again and the doors click as they slide open.

"How'd he get in?"

I step into the apartment, sniffing at the air. Cheap cologne, and under that, the smell of blood and sweat.

I freeze, a tingling sensation running over me. He sent a human.

"Front door was wide fuckin' open." Theo glances around. "You forgot to lock it again."

For the humans Rene's employed, this kind of thing is usually a test of loyalty. A cruel smile spreads across my face and I glance over at Theo, who's already licking his lips. It's too bad this loyal bastard's only making it back to his boss in pieces.

"You wanna hunt?" I whisper.

Theo nods.

It's rare that we get to do this. Humans are scattered like leaves in the wind, so we get our meals in places like Nox, or buy direct from the Blood Bank. But I have to admit, it's embarrassing having a business meeting while you're basically drinking out of a giant Capri Sun.

And you still can't get the goddamn straw in.

I take the lead, Theo following behind me, a pattern we've known for most of our lives. The intruder's been trapped in the bedroom, and there's no second way out. The windows are sealed and painted over; the room replicates a coffin without having to sleep in one. I keep it cool and dark with only one light on the nightstand for ambience.

Whoever is in there is trying to control their breathing, but the smell of sweat-stained polyester gives them away completely. I'm shivering in anticipation, my mouth watering. It's not just about the blood, it's about the desire to rip and tear into flesh. I want to pull this person apart, sink my claws into their chest and bite into their still-beating heart.

If only I could share this feeling with Sofie.

I silently make my way into the room and around one side of the bed as Theo shuts the door, his bright yellow eyes shining ominously in the dark. They're in here, but not simply waiting for the slaughter out in the open. I motion for him to look under the bed while I leap silently into the air and land on the mattress, letting it sink beneath my weight. A soft gasp slips out beneath me, barely perceptible under the squeaking springs, but Theo is already on all fours, crawling like an animal as he bares his fangs. I love to watch him hunt, it's like watching an artist work.

"I can smell you," he rumbles, his voice razor sharp, as I crouch down to get a closer view. "You should know by now that breaking into a vampire's home is *very* unwise."

All I hear is a heart beat like a jackhammer. Theo looks up at me and grins before reaching under the bed.

"Got you."

Everything goes wrong as something hits Theo's throat, and he lets out a garbled growl. I'm right there to snatch the intruder's wrist and wrench it upward, snapping his arm like a twig against the bed frame. A pained cry echoes through the room as a small dagger clatters onto the floor, covered in blood. Theo kicks it away before he staggers backward, holding his throat and gagging as he slams against the wall. Blood pours through his fingers as I drag the intruder out of the darkness and into the living room.

He's young, maybe around 20 years old, pale, with a soft face and a bulbous little nose topped off with dark eyes and a head of dishwater blond hair. His breathing is heavy, spiked with little wheezes and groans as he drips with sweat. His broken right arm hangs limply at his side.

"Theo, you good?!"

"The fuck do you think?!" Theo stumbles out of the bedroom, blood dripping on the floor. "He's one of Rene's dogs. Got me right in the neck."

"Yeah." I hold the intruder against the wall and sneer at him. "I could smell cheap clothes and bullshit the second I stepped through the front door."

I grasp his broken arm, pulling until I feel the bone fully disconnect. The shriek he lets out sends an excited shiver down my spine. I know that arm is only being held in place by the sleeve of his suit and a bit of skin. One more tear and it'll come right off.

I grab him by the throat, lifting him over my head and hurling him across the room. His body makes a dull thunk upon impact, but to my delight, he doesn't immediately pass out from the pain. This human is incredibly durable. Maybe that's why Rene kept him around.

It's only a moment before he scrambles to his feet, trying to reach the elevator.

"That's a good try!" I call in a sing-song voice. "You made your way in, but there's no getting out!"

He ignores me, throwing himself at the sealed elevator door and furiously pounding the button with his good hand. Theo stumbles out behind me, and I can see the wound on his neck is still gaping, completely unhealed. Shit, silver dagger.

He won't die, but he's in a lot of pain.

"There's blood in the fridge," I tell him.

"I think I'll take it straight from the source," he gurgles as the intruder presses his back against the wall, trembling as sweat pours down his face.

A dark stain forms at the front of his pants and I chuckle, watching his eyes flick toward the window.

"Don't–"

It's too late. He's sprinting for it through grunts of effort and pain. His limp arm flails pathetically in his sleeve as I sigh and check my watch. We have two hours until the sun comes up. That's more than enough time.

I glance up when I hear the thud. His body is slumped limp on the floor below the window. Idiot tried to throw himself through double-thick glass. Theo is already beside him, picking him up by the hair and dragging him to the middle of the room.

"Grab a chair," he barks at me.

I raise a brow at the sharpness of his tone, but say nothing as I drag one in from the dining room. Theo props our guest up in it while I take some rope out of the closet, along with a set of knives and scalpels. I toss the rope to Theo and let him get to work while I lay the blades out on the coffee table, dragging my fingertips along the handles.

"Hello, my babies. I've missed you."

While Theo secures the knots, I make sure each knife is perfectly sharp, testing it by pricking my finger. We could do this with our teeth and claws, but there's something so deliciously cruel about using a blade.

"We've gotta make him talk."

"I know." I pick up a large serrated knife and flip it between my fingers. The intruder's head bobs, and he groans. "And we will. I just want to listen to him scream first."

I press the blade into the man's neck and grab his head, holding it in place as I begin to slice away at Rene's brand. I'll keep it in a jar along with anything else I decide to remove. My own little trophy shelf.

The pain shocks the intruder's eyes open, and he squeals like a stuck pig, sweat making his skin slick as I continue to cut.

"You keep moving and I'm going to slit your throat." I grip his hair and force his head back, holding it in place. "It won't be as fun if it's an accident."

"Go fuck yourself," he spits.

His voice quickly morphs into an agonized wail as I tear the rest of the brand off, letting the bloodied piece of skin fall to the floor. Just to add insult to injury, I sink my teeth into the wound, glee flooding my chest as he lets out another scream.

The man's head slumps as I dislodge my fangs, his breathing shallow and punctuated by little more than a slight wheeze. Theo reaches down and grips his chin, wrenching his head up to face us. More pained sobs ooze from the man's lips like honey, along with the trickle of blood that drips from his wound. This whole scene is delicious.

"Why did Rene send you?" Theo demands.

The intruder's glassy eyes find Theo's and he somehow manages a smile, shaking his head.

"The longer you hold out on us, the worse this is going to be," I mutter as I pick up a bigger knife and grab his broken arm, cutting through the fabric of his suit.

My blade digs into his flesh again, this time much more pointedly piercing the joint of his elbow. It's easy, like cutting into butter. I can hear the blade squelch as the flesh gives way, but I hold steady, slicing through muscle and tendon until his arm drops to the ground. This time he barely makes a goddamn sound, only watches in shock as I place the severed arm on his lap.

This is going to be a bitch to clean up.

"I know you're here for the formula."

The man looks up at me, somehow still defiant as he drips sweat and blood.

And then the shrill ring of the phone cuts through our perfect little moment. I can see our guest grin out of the corner of my eye.

"Now, what do we think that could be about?"

DOMINIC

DUNCAN TOWERS

I FLIP THE BLADE in my hand and jam it into the intruder's gut. His agonized cry is like music as I lean over, patting him on the head.

"Hold that for me, will ya?"

Theo hands me the phone, his yellow eyes betraying some frayed nerves. I lift the receiver to my ear and exhale.

"Hello, Dominic."

My muscles coil.

"Rene."

The human laughs hysterically in the background, interrupted only by little groans as he struggles with his many wounds.

"It's been a while since we had a proper discussion. Like gentlemen."

I scoff. Rene was always dragging Theo and I in for meetings like he was the fucking vampiric Godfather. He'd sit behind an enormous desk in an ostentatious office and tell us every single step of a plan, down to the last letter. He treated us like fucking children. It's natural to get sick of that bullshit after a while.

"What's the matter, don't have the guts to meet me in person? You sent one of your little bitches to do your dirty work for you? Hey, you want me to make him sing for you? He's a real fucking talent, listen."

I yank the knife from the human's gut and drive it straight down into his thigh. He lets out a screech that slices through the air like the string section of a symphony. I know it won't mean anything to Rene. It's low-class showboating, but I don't care. I need to take this rage out on *something*.

"Do it again," Rene chuckles. *"Actually, can you put him on the line? I want front row seats to your little show."*

I slash the human across the face with my claws. Deep cavernous cuts form and his wail digs into my bones like teeth while Rene cackles on the other end of the line.

"You know, even as predictable as you are, you're becoming quite the thorn in my side. You've spent so much time trying to get to me that you can't even see the mistakes you're making. Every once in a while, the fallout of one of your little idiotic adventures actually causes me a bit of grief. Not sure if you deserve credit for just being a fuckup, but at least it keeps you in my thoughts."

Rene is over 600 years old, and he's always gotten off on treating me as his subordinate. Like a child. Violent hatred gathers at the base of my throat, acidic and painful.

"Well, you know how it goes... I antagonize you, you sit in your fucking villa and do nothing. Still loving the life of a coward?"

"Not this time, kid. You burn down my lab, you kill my men−"

I scoff.

"Your *man* just broke into my penthouse. Fair's fair, Deschamps."

"I thought it was a fortress, Dominic," Rene chuckles. *"Shouldn't it have been a little harder for a single human to make his way inside? Or is something making you sloppy?"*

No. There's no way he knows about her, and I'm not about to give him any new info for free.

"Look, unlike you, I'm a busy man. What do you want?"

"I want my formula back in my hands, I want payment for that warehouse, and if there's a bit of extra time, I'd be happy to have your head on a fucking pike."

Empty threats. Rene is full of them, and I'm already tired of playing this little game.

"Oh, is that all? You should have just asked nicely, old man. Maybe I would have given you back your little project. Now though? I think I'm gonna get your dog to tell me everything I need to know."

The line is silent for a moment, but his voice is calm when he speaks up again, cold enough to chill my blood.

"Dominic, I've been onto you since the night you broke into that lab. I just wanted to see what you would do, and you disappointed me. You're pathetic. Inexperienced. Childish. You have no idea what it means to rule."

"Fuck you!"

I can hear him chuckle across the line before letting out a contented sigh.

"You'd best keep a little more calm and think about exactly what you're going to do, especially now that you've got something to lose."

I bristle, goosebumps cascading down my spine like ice water.

"She really is quite a beauty. The only thing I can say against her is the smell. You're all over her. I can't get within a few feet before I want to retch."

If he touches her, I'll slice him open and choke him out with his own intestines.

"Sofie, was it? Doesn't take much to get people to talk, you know. For a bunch of humans who seem so ready to band together and protect each other, they are all too willing to give out valuable information. Half the time, they don't even know what they're saying, or who they're speaking to."

"Whatever you think you have, it's nothing."

Every word feels like I'm swallowing cotton.

"Are you sure? You're really such a simple creature. Did you already forget what happened with Selene?"

"How dare you say her name," I growl.

"Well, she was screaming mine by the end."

My rage swirls into an inferno, consuming all logic.

"I'm going to rip you apart, piece by fucking piece."

*"No, what **you're** going to do is give me that formula. If I have it by the end of the week, maybe I'll let you keep pissing away your life in that tiny tower of yours. Maybe I'll even let you keep your new little whore."*

"Why is it so important to you?"

Rene chuckles.

"You'd love to know that, wouldn't you?"

"What are you gonna do, sell it? Ship it out to other cities?"

The louder he laughs, the angrier I get.

"Do you really want to make it, Dominic? I'll tell you what it is."

Lies, but my silence is the only answer he needs.

"It's power and money in a little vial. Whoever controls it controls the city. Maybe more."

"Why are you telling me this?" I ask.

"Because you don't have a plan. You never have and you never will. Meanwhile, I've been working on this since we found out what our blood could do for the humans. Do you know how exhausting it is to make deals with them? They demand respect, but why should we respect a species that only destroys itself over and over?"

"So that's it, it's just a drug after all."

"It's far more than that, child, but your tiny brain could never grasp its complexity."

I puff my chest out as though he were standing right in front of me.

"You want a war? I'll bring it right to your fucking doorstep."

"Did you forget, Dominic? You already have. You should have been content with the territory that I generously let you scrape together, but you've always been a covetous little wretch. I'm going to enjoy taking your head. I'll parade it around Santa Cruz, right beside your little girlfriend's."

"Don't you touch her." My teeth clench so hard they threaten to grind into dust. "Don't you *dare–*"

"Better get to her quick, Dominic!" Rene sings, just as the line goes dead.

He's bluffing. He has to be.

Rene's little minion laughs again, and something inside of me snaps. I swing the phone, hitting him in the side of the head and creating a crater in his skull. The pungent scent of blood and viscera fills my nostrils as Theo leans down, checking his pulse.

"Still alive. Durable fuckers, aren't they?" His tone is melodic and playful.

I lean forward, jaw clenched tight, and remove the knife from the man's thigh. He lets out a strangled grunt as his body lurches in place.

"You're gonna be a good little lapdog and scream nice and loud for me." I lean in close and lick the side of his face. "That call put me in a bad fuckin' mood, and this is the shit that really gets me off."

When I pull back, a wad of spit lands on my cheek. Humans are so adorably stubborn.

"You have *no* idea what Rene has planned for you... for all of us."

"You're all so goddamn gullible. Let me guess, he's going to make you a vampire, right? He'll give you a whole new life, full of wonders you never dreamed of," I gesture with the blood-soaked blade and stare out at the night sky with a smile. "Power, money, blood... he'll promise it all, but it's a pipe dream. You would have just ended up trapped under his thumb."

Theo stares at the man with a stony expression. We've both played this game before. There's no room for real freedom with Rene.

"But hey, at least now you can avoid all of that."

"You're gonna die, Duncan."

"Christ, I wish you'd shut up," I snarl as I pry his mouth open with one hand.

He chokes and sputters, and I grip his tongue, sinking a claw into it to keep it from moving as I slice through the thick muscle with the knife. He lets out a strangled wail and tries to wriggle away, but it's futile. The ropes are too tight, and even if he got free, he's in far too much pain to run.

Theo chuckles beside me, and the grind of his lighter catches my attention.

"Been a while since we did this, huh?" He blows a smoke ring.

"Too long, pal."

My blade slices through the last bit of muscle, and the tongue comes loose. I pull back and lift it up to the moonlight.

"This'll look great on my mantle."

Theo has already latched on to the side of his neck, drinking greedily as the tip of his cigarette burns to ash. I lick the blood from my fingertips and drop to my knees, both of us fully giving in to the thirst and draining what's left of my little intruder until he's dry.

Theo rips his mouth away and stares up at the ceiling as his chest heaves, mouth smeared with red. His eyes roll back like he's just seen God.

"You good?" I ask, gesturing at the half-knit wound in his neck.

He nods, coming down from the high of a fresh kill.

"Should be almost healed by morning."

I lean over to inspect the wound, making sure he'll survive the night.

Vampires are an inherently lonely species. We age much slower than humans, which means that we see a lot of the world change. I often feel like I'm sitting in a moving train watching the landscape whir past me. Months turn into years, which turn into centuries. I've lost my parents, my brothers and sisters, friends, and a wife. It always feels like the universe is taking from me to square some kind of debt, but Theo's the one constant I've been able to hold on to.

"You stay here tonight. I'll give you a change of clothes."

"Thanks, Dom."

I grin at him.

"Brothers, right?"

He smiles, his eyes bright and beautiful.

"Brothers."

Back when we broke away, I promised Theo the same thing that Rene promised me: Power. Except this time, I'll deliver. He deserves that much.

The formula is the key.

"Hey, you wanna blow off some steam tomorrow night?" He asks. "You know, like the good old days?"

Now that's something I wasn't expecting.

"What are you thinking?"

"The feeding rooms at Nox are open, and you've gotta come up with a plan for your cute little bartender, right?"

Rene's threat hits me again. He's right. I have to keep her safe.

"We should go. Now."

I go to stand but Theo stops me, a hand on my shoulder.

"Sun rises in half an hour. If we can't get there in time, then neither can he."

"Unless they're already there. Theo, they–"

"Dom, Nox is closed, remember? Has been for at least an hour now."

I jiggle my leg, anxiety flooding me in waves.

"You think he's lying about her? About what he's planning to do?"

"I don't know," Theo sighs, "but for once in your life, you need to sit down and think before you do something stupid."

I groan as he stands and struts toward a mirror to take a look at the damage on his neck.

"Jesus, I'm gonna need to wear a fuckin' turtleneck. Look at me! I look like Ichabod Crane!"

I can't help but grin.

"At least you've still got your head."

DOMINIC

DUNCAN TOWERS

"You got a plan? You've been awfully quiet since we got up."

Theo's been on my back even more than usual lately, and the ride over to Nox has been no exception. I know he's just looking out for me, but it's been getting on my nerves.

"Best plan of all time: I'm gonna ask her to dinner."

He scoffs.

"You're kidding."

"The way she was looking at me last night, there's no chance she says no. Then, when she's on my turf, she's playing by my rules."

He looks at me like I have two heads.

"How arrogant are you, honestly? This is the dumbest plan you've ever come up with!"

"Blow me, you shitbag," I mutter.

"It's too passive! How the hell are you going to make her trust you? Your dick isn't a magic wand, Gandalf."

"Gandalf didn't have a wand, he had a staff, you idiot. Did you even read the book?"

"Prick," he mutters.

"That's a no, then. And you didn't hear the rest of the plan, you're always jumping to conclusions."

"Oh, so *ask her out to dinner and hope she really, really likes me* wasn't the whole thing? Good to know."

"I'm going to find out why Rene knows so much about her, and *what* he knows. If she's useful to him, she's useful to us. I called Mateo while you were asleep to bring over some tranquilizers–"

"Oh, it just keeps getting better," Theo grumbles as he focuses on the road and grips the steering wheel a little harder. "What's next? Hold her hostage?"

"Hey, that's exactly it," I reply. "Good anticipation."

"Okay, great, thank you for explaining the extra steps. It really is your finest work. True genius."

Theo parks near the curb and kills the engine, checking himself in the mirror.

"Hey, does this outfit look stupid?" He asks.

I give him a quick glance up and down.

"Well, it's a really nice scarf," I grin. "That said, I think adding it on top of the turtleneck, *with* the leather jacket might be your problem."

He groans, slamming his head back against the seat.

"Fuck this. You go in, I'm going home."

I light a cigarette and turn to him, taking the scarf off and shoving it in the glove compartment.

"The turtleneck and jacket are fine. I don't know why you added a scarf."

"It's an ascot, you uncultured prick," Theo mutters.

"Well, you look like Mr. Darcy if he joined a motorcycle gang."

"Shut up. You know I'm not good at this stuff."

While most vampires are extravagant, Theo's never really gravitated toward that side of things. He has ten of the same suit that he rotates, and never really ventures out of his comfort zone. His fashion sense only evolves when it has to, whereas I've collected clothes from every decade I've lived in.

"Here," I mutter, fixing the collar of his jacket. "Much better. Let's go."

We step onto the street and head straight for the front door, only stopping when another lumbering bouncer covered in tattoos puts his hand on my chest. His biceps are almost as big as my head. Anyone else might be a bit intimidated, but I ripped a man to shreds last night and his tongue is sitting on my shelf, so I'm not too impressed.

"Easy there, big fella," I chuckle, putting my hand on his forearm, claws extended. "Don't wanna spike that blood pressure, do ya?"

"You wait in line."

Ridiculous.

"I run this fucking city. I don't wait in lines."

The bouncer looks me up and down for a *long* time, struggling with the complex mental process of remembering a single face, before he finally pushes the door open.

"No fucking around, and *no* antagonizing the staff. Is that clear?"

I smile at him, wondering why I'm getting the third degree suddenly. I give his arm a firm squeeze.

"You have my word."

He nods, staring me down even through his mirrored sunglasses.

"Welcome back to Nox, Mr. Duncan."

"Now that's the kind of hospitality I expect," I reply.

The music is already pounding as we step inside. Vampires linger near the bar and lounge in booths, while others are being let in slowly behind us. There's a nervous excitement in the air. Feeding night.

I promised I'd be back, and I need her alone.

Out of the corner of my eye, I can see someone striding up to me in a tight black dress and thigh-high boots. Sofie's friend. Her eyes are already bouncing between me and Theo, sizing the two of us up. She sticks out her hand as she finishes her approach.

"Mr. Duncan, my name's Ruby Connors. I assume you're here for feeding night?"

"You assume correctly."

She has a great fucking figure. Full hips, gorgeous breasts that almost spill out of the top of her dress, and perfectly painted red lips. Theo is having trouble keeping it together, his eyes alight with lust. She points at the roped-off section near the back and looks over her shoulder.

"Well, if I'm not mistaken it's your first time, so let me explain. You pay up front to that *delightful* man at the door. Cash only. You find the room with your girl, you knock, and you wait for her to let you in. Any bullshit, up to and including trying to kill our staff, their heart rate monitors alert security and you're thrown out on your ass, or executed. Dealer's choice." She crosses her arms over her chest, that pleasant smile never leaving her lips. "Sound fair?"

"I suppose it depends on who the dealer is," I reply.

She holds up a gun.

"Little Miss 9mm."

I crane my neck, scanning the rooms behind her.

"Where's Sofie?"

"You haven't answered my question. Are we clear?"

"Yeah, yeah, Little Miss 9mm, I get it," I sigh. "She's back there?"

"Look, Dominic, you might run this city, but *we* run this fucking club. I don't want to repeat what happened with your little rival the other night."

"We'll be on our best behavior," Theo assures her.

"That's what I like to hear!" She gives me a quick condescending pat on the arm. "Enjoy your evening, gentlemen."

Theo and I head toward the door, another bouncer puffing out his chest when he sees us. It's honestly fucking hilarious. I love it when they think they're tough stuff.

"It's $1,000 an hour," the bouncer grunts as we reach him.

"Christ," Theo sighs. "Highway robbery."

"If you've got an issue with our prices, you're free to fish rats out of the sewer grate out back. That comes free of charge."

Theo scowls at him while I dig out a stack of hundred-dollar bills, counting them quickly.

"I want two hours with Sofie. The rest is for my friend to feed on whoever he chooses."

Theo quickly pulls out another wad of cash of his own.

"Tack on a bit of extra time for me, too. Fuckin' starving."

"Now that wasn't so hard, was it, boys?"

He counts the money out, holding a few hundred-dollar bills up to the light. I snort. He doesn't even know what the fuck he's looking for, he just wants to make us sweat. Finally, he tucks the cash into a small box before opening the door for us.

"Sofie's in the room at the end of the hall," he informs me before turning to Theo. "You can pick whoever you want. Their names and photos are outside of the rooms."

The hallway is glowing with blue and purple lights with mirrored walls. I smooth out my black suit with both hands before pushing my hair back, making sure that silver streak is prominent.

Theo's still scoping out the pictures on the doors when I find Sofie's room, and I decide to leave him to his work. Somehow I feel nervous, but not in that fluttery way that humans do. It's more of an anticipation, like right before the hunt. My body is still wired from last night. Killing that motherfucker really brought something bestial out of me.

My jaw tingles, already longing to feel Sofie's blood running down my throat. I stop in front of the door and grasp the handle. It burns just a little. Silver. Smart.

I twist the handle and step into the room, ignoring both the instructions and the searing pain soaring through my arm.

There she is, perched on the couch, copper hair pulled into a high ponytail that cascades down her shoulder. Her tight blue dress resembles a deep and mysterious ocean shimmering beneath the dim lights. She looks statuesque, a sharp jaw, blush sculpting out her cheekbones, and that beautiful dusting of freckles across her little button nose. But it's those eyes, burning and piercing, that really draw me in.

I drag my tongue across my lip and she tilts her head, a glass of whiskey balanced on her bare thigh as her high heel dangles from the tip of her toe.

"I didn't think you'd show up," she whispers.

"I paid for extra time. No interruptions."

She hums. The way she twists her glass on her thigh makes me want to drop to my knees right in front of her. I want to spread those legs and bury my face between them to see what she tastes like.

"You know how these rooms work?"

"Your friend explained it all loud and clear."

When I take a step toward her, she straightens up, putting her foot down and sliding it back into her heel.

"So you know the rules, and you still didn't knock? You must be extremely confident tonight, Mr. Duncan." She glances at the small bar that's tucked toward the side of the room. "You want a drink?"

I cross the room and take a seat beside her, draping my arm across the back of the couch. My fingers brush lightly against her neck, watching goosebumps appear like magic. She looks like she's never done this before, big doe eyes darting around as she draws in a deep breath.

"I'll take a bourbon for now," I hum, studying the way her chest rises and falls. I can smell her blood and hear her heart thrumming against her ribs like a drum.

She pushes herself up off of the couch and struts toward the bar, hips swaying with each step. She's got a great ass; gorgeous legs with firm muscles I want to sink my teeth into.

There's less confidence in her bartending skills tonight. Her hand trembles a little as she pours the drink. Is it the fact that we're alone that's making her nervous? This is her territory. She should be comfortable here – own it, even.

She takes a tentative step toward me, thrusting out the glass a little too roughly. When our eyes meet a rush pulses through me like an electrical current.

"You can relax, you know."

"Is this the part where you tell me you don't bite?" She teases.

"I'd never lie to you, Sofie." I take the glass as she sits back down. "So, is this a new thing for you? How often do you do this?"

"Only a select few weekends," she replies. "Ruby and I mostly just rotate in to give people a break." She plays with the rim of her glass, looking at me sideways. "Is that really how you want to spend your time, playing 20 questions?"

"I just want to know why you look so afraid."

Sofie snorts as she takes a quick swig of her drink. It's the first sign of attitude I've seen from her all night. I like it.

"Try not to drink too much of that," I tell her with a smile.

Alcohol is a blood thinner, and I doubt I'm going to be showing much restraint tonight.

She turns, staring me right in the eyes and drains the rest of her glass in one go. Her insubordination gives me a rush of adrenaline, and I toss back my drink in an instant and pull her closer to me. She squeaks a little, and I dip my head to nuzzle in the crook of her neck. The smell of the blood in her veins and the alcohol on her breath force my lips to part.

I'm starving, craving her.

"You never answered my question," I purr, reaching for the glass in her hand and tossing it to the floor. "What are you afraid of?"

She gasps as I drag the tip of my nose along her pulse point, feeling it thrum so close to my bared fangs.

"I'm not going to hurt you. No one will while I'm around."

She's shivering beneath my touch, sparks shooting off of her skin. I wonder how many vampires she's let kiss her before they drink from her, how many of them she's fucked. I want to be better than them; I have to be the only thing she thinks about when she goes home in the morning.

I want her to lie in bed struggling to sleep while she thinks about me and only me.

"Nothing scares me, Dominic, least of all you." She parts her thighs, flashing me a confident smile. "Besides, I don't think you could hurt me if you tried."

I love a woman who knows what she wants. I slip my hand between her legs, relishing the heat radiating from her skin.

"Well, it's your territory, so you make the rules. Is that something you want? Would you like me to hurt you?"

"I don't know," she whispers. "It all depends on you."

My eyes dance around her features, her pretty plump red lips parting as she wets them with her tongue. I want them colliding with mine. I want them around my cock.

"I want to drink from you," I whisper as she leans into my touch. "It'll only hurt if you want it to, but–"

Her mouth flickers into a smile. My cock throbs and aches, and all I can think about is feeding, fucking, or both.

"I can take it," she purrs.

I grin.

"Of course you can."

I lean toward her slightly parted lips, ghosting them with my own for a brief moment before I dip my head and dive straight for her throbbing vein. The moan escapes her lips before I've even touched her, and that sound is all the encouragement I need to drive my fangs deep into her tender flesh.

It's all shades of copper at first, but soon I taste the real notes, like wine or whiskey. She's a little on the sweeter side, like a sour candy or a popsicle. I tasted some of her in the supply closet, but not enough to really appreciate the complexity.

The back of my jaw tingles and I can feel saliva rushing forward as I suck a little harder every couple seconds, all while being careful not to take things too far. The goal of a bite like this is not to kill within seconds, it's to drink continuously until we're both satiated.

My head swims with visions of her deepest self. I can taste everything: the sunlight she sleeps in to protect herself, her fears and anxieties, and her hope that someday, she'll get out of this.

Her hope that things can change.

I reach between her legs and tease her through her panties, finding her already quite wet. She rocks her hips in quiet desperation as sultry moans fill the room. I love this tension, stretching like a rubber band just waiting to snap. I drink deeply, finding her clit and stroking it slowly, working it until it pulses against my finger.

The moan that escapes her throat makes me crave more. I want her blood running down her tits, and I want to lick it off while she rides me like a fucking animal.

She's going to come on my cock. I want to be buried so deep inside of her that she never forgets me.

I remove my fingers, intent on reaching for my belt, when she grips my wrist tightly. Her skin is so warm, decadent. I dislodge my fangs, looking up at her. She turns to face me with a smile like warm sunlight.

"I never said stop."

SOFIE

Nox Nightclub

EVERYTHING ABOUT DOMINIC EXUDES pleasure and power. That's something I might have rolled my eyes at a week ago, but so much about him compels me. His touch is gentle, even the way his fangs sink into me is delicate. The way he told me he wouldn't hurt me threw me for a loop.

I gasp when he withdraws his fingers and my hand snatches his wrist on its own, trying to force his fingers back toward my pussy to finish the job. When he dislodges his fangs and lifts his head, his eyes are that bright golden color, the color of the sunlight he can never see.

The way he stares at me, like he wants to devour me whole... it's an adrenaline rush. I've never felt this way in the feeding room, save for once. It was my first day, and at the time I chalked it up to nerves, but the woman who fed from me was exquisite. Her bite was nothing but pure pleasure, just like Dominic's, and the sex was even better.

"I never said stop."

Dominic licks the blood from his lips.

"I was just warming you up."

The dim light makes every feature on his face look as sharp as his fangs. I listen to the low, rumbling sound of his voice as his hand slides up my thigh again. The eyes of an ancient predator dig into my own like knives. I can feel blood leaking from the little wounds in my neck. He dips his head, running his tongue over the tiny little spots, soothing the pain.

"Tell me what you want," he whispers. "I'll give you anything."

What does that mean?

"Fuck me."

The words just jump out, completely unbidden, but it's what I want right now; to satiate this raw hunger that tears at me from the inside out.

Suddenly, I'm being lifted into his lap, forced to straddle him as he continues to stare straight into my soul. My hands reach for his belt buckle, but I stop just short of undoing it, glancing back up at him. A sharp claw traces a line down the side of my neck, just barely breaking the skin. I hiss softly and Dominic smiles, eyes dancing with a playful cruelty.

"I didn't expect this to be so–"

"You knew exactly what to expect the second I walked through that door. Even now it's written all over your face, little dove."

The nickname drips from his mouth, sticky and wet with what's left of the blood he took from me. I lean forward to capture it against my lips, tasting only a fraction of what I imagine he experiences every time.

I don't have a lot of regulars, that's Kirby and Ruby's thing. They like to forge relationships with vampires, get some little perks to keep money and supplies coming in. I'm in more of a strategic management role.

Dominic breaks the kiss and slides his fingers beneath my chin, thumb resting just under my bottom lip. Slowly, he tips my head upward.

Maybe some more on-the-job experience isn't so bad.

"We help each other out. You take what you want, I take what I want." He smiles as I struggle to maintain my focus. "Are you listening?"

I nod, and he looks down at my nervous hands resting on his belt.

"Then be a good girl and take care of my cock."

My heart is thumping wildly, a chaotic beat against my ribs. It's those eyes, still glowing golden, and underlined by the little stain of crimson on his mouth. He might just be the most beautiful man I've ever laid eyes on.

I unbuckle his belt and slowly unzip his pants, reaching in to wrap my fingers around his cock. He's thick, his skin still cool to the touch, and it's only moments after I make contact that his head rolls back, exposing the dark tattoos on his neck.

His Adam's apple bobs as I lick my palm and stroke him slowly, watching the muscles in his neck tense and pulse each time my thumb glides over the tip.

"That's it," he groans. "Just like that."

I keep up the pace, my own thighs soaked with sweat from the anticipation of what's coming. This entire experience hasn't gone at all like I expected. I even liked when he fed on me, the burning sensation quickly warping into pleasure. A lot of vampires are too eager, and it's just about dealing with the pain, but Dominic's made the entire experience so fucking sensual.

I want this every day.

He lifts his head and his hands cup my face before he pulls me in for a deep and sensual kiss. My pussy aches, a low and desperate pulse nearly sending me over the edge.

"Need you," I whimper against his mouth.

I pull my panties to the side so that I can sink down onto him. He growls, his tongue diving further into my mouth as he fills me up. It fucking stings, and I have to tear myself away to cry out at the ceiling as his cock nearly rips me apart.

Dominic sinks his fangs back into that same spot, and a wave of pleasure forces my hips to buck on top of him as I take him deeper and deeper until he finally bottoms out. I can feel him draining the life force right out of me, but I'm too caught up in the moment; his hands on me, his teeth in my neck, and the way his cock hits that spot deep inside of me all combines to turn me into a quivering mess. I rock my hips faster. I need more.

I've heard vampires are so invested because we taste better when we're brought right to the brink of climax, but I don't know how true that is.

Maybe I'll ask once this is all over.

Dominic's fangs dislodge, and a moment later his lips are locked with mine all over again. Our bodies move in tandem and one of his hands wraps around my waist, sliding down to my ass and giving it a rough squeeze. He breaks the kiss to nip at my ear with a bared fang, and I taste my own blood on my lips. Any other day I might be disgusted, but I'm too drunk on the power he has over me to care.

"I knew you were gonna be an animal the second I laid eyes on you."

"You don't fucking know me," I hiss through clenched teeth.

He licks at the blood on my neck and sucks at the wound once more. The softness of his lips, the knowledge that his fangs could rip me apart at any moment, and the sting of his stubble are the perfect combination. Heat spreads down my lower back, making my toes tingle. I'm trying to control myself as much as I can, but I can feel my climax building to the point of no return.

"You think I don't know you? Can any guy make you come just like I did last night? You were so fucking desperate for it, and I gave you *exactly* what you needed."

Dominic snarls as he reaches up my back and unzips my dress, his fingers making quick work of the straps to free my breasts. He dips his head to swirl his tongue around each nipple, biting down gently. He lingers right on the verge of brutality and gentleness, and I let out a cry, my hips crashing against him like harsh waves against a shore. In all this bleakness, the only joy I can find is in a fucking orgasm. For a few moments, I'm not a miserable bitch who's always looking over her shoulder, or worse, just waiting to die.

Dominic's mouth curls into a malicious grin, his eyes glowing like the flames on a candle. I want to resist him, just because I can. Because he's paying for two hours, and it hasn't even been 40 minutes. My hands find his shoulders, and my hips slow right down, making big circles as his cock glides against my G-spot.

But I'm not in control for long. His fingers wrap around my throat and he pulls back, forcing me to stare straight into his eyes.

"I think I can make you scream my name."

I like power play. I can't deny that I'm still a little afraid of this man, of the fact that he could end my life as easily as he could whisper, but I believe his promise. He won't do anything to *really* hurt me. Not unless I ask.

Dominic bites into the top of my breast and feeds again. My head is thrown back in the chaos of it all, my body betraying me completely with his assistance. He releases my throat and squeezes my ass, bouncing me up and down on his cock.

"Oh my God!"

My head is swimming, and I can't stop the pathetic moans and whimpers that are escaping from my lips like confession as he drinks from me. He's leaving marks, *his* marks. I'm going to be covered in bruises and puncture wounds, but the only thing I'm focused on is getting what I want.

My eyes roll back and I moan louder. His name, God's name, the Devil's, anything to fucking get me there. I'm aching for it.

And then it all comes to a grinding halt. He's pulling his fangs out of me and lifting me off of him. He's tossing me onto the seat next to him like I'm a doll. I stare up at him in confusion. There's blood all over his mouth as he gets to his feet.

He sheds his jacket and unbuttons his shirt, exposing a heavily tattooed torso. My chest heaves, and I feel like I've just been ripped out of a dream.

"The fuck are you doing?" I pant, steadying my breathing.

"Don't worry," he rumbles, licking my blood from his lips. "I'll give you what you need. But first, I want to do something I've been thinking about since I laid eyes on you."

Slowly, he sinks to his knees and crawls toward me, a devilish smile eclipsing his features. I feel like I'm being hunted, and I love every second of it.

"By my count, you're mine for *at least* another hour, and I'm getting my fucking money's worth."

He leans forward, spreading my legs as he glides his mouth up and down my thigh, smearing more blood on my skin. All I can do is watch him as he licks it away, his mouth moving higher and higher up my thigh, those eyes still digging into me.

"I'm gonna come back here over and over again. I've got all the money I need, and I wanna spend it on you."

He sinks his fangs into my thigh, and I cry out as the rush of pain and euphoria nearly makes me come. My fingers lightly circle my clit, and I let out ragged grunts while he drinks from me. I flick it slowly, my pussy quivering and aching to be filled up. Suddenly, like he's reading my mind, Dominic grasps my wrist and moves it out of the way, sliding his fingers inside of me. My head falls backward, eyelids fluttering, and I no longer have control. His fingers curl, stroking my G-spot as I tease myself, pinching my nipples while he continues to feed. The buildup just makes it that much better.

"Check your heart rate," he orders as he tears his mouth away from my skin.

I blink through the euphoria, trying to clear my head.

"What?"

Dominic gestures to the watch on my wrist and I glance at the monitor, frowning slightly when I see that the number has dipped a little more than usual.

"It's a little low, but I'm okay."

He shakes his head, bringing himself slowly to a halt.

"I don't need you passing out on me."

He slices his palm open and presses it to the wound on my thigh to stop the bleeding and heal the puncture wounds. It's a small act of kindness, but coming from a vampire, it may as well be a miracle.

"Now," he whispers, ripping my panties with one hand and tossing them aside. "These are in my fucking way. *Again.*"

I gasp as he spits my own blood onto my cunt. It's unsanitary, it's disgusting. It's fucking *hot*.

Dominic drags his tongue along my clit as our eyes lock, and I let out a ravenous moan.

"You're a filthy little thing, aren't you?"

It's more of an observation than a question, and he's right. I feel like a caged animal finally being released.

"Say it," he demands. "Say it or you don't get to come."

He brings me right to the edge and then pulls me back just as he can feel me tumble over. I keep bucking against his face, desperate for more pressure, but he slows right back down, his fingers, his mouth, everything. My breath is ragged as he pulls away, my blood still staining his lips.

"Please," I beg.

He smirks, leaning back to stroke his cock. He wants me to see it. Precum leaks from the tip, making the entire thing glisten. My body shifts with discomfort, the ache becoming more and more intense by the second as he stares me down.

"Please what?"

"I'm a filthy little thing, Dominic!" I'll tell him anything he wants. "*Please*, just fuck me!"

He chuckles.

"So you *can* do as you're told."

His voice is pure gravel, husky and deep as he stands up, looming over me, lips hovering above my own. My heart is pounding, and there's not a single coherent thought running through my brain. The only thing I'm focused on is him.

He takes a step back and strips off his unbuttoned shirt, tossing it to the ground. He's muscular, with a strong broad chest, chiseled abs, and toned arms. I can see the indents in his hips that peek out of the tops of his pants, forming a deep v that points right to his cock.

His skin is pale and covered in dozens of black and gray tattoos that stretch all along his chest, arms, and stomach. Some look like they were done with a knife and ink while others are deeply shaded, with more detail and intricacy. Runes, crows, the Virgin Mary with bleeding eyes, upside down crosses, many with words written in a language I can't read.

"Turn around," he orders. "Put your hands on the back of the couch."

I do as I'm told and feel his icy hands run up the backs of my thighs. He gives my ass a rough slap, the sharp sting forcing me to cry out. Dominic soothes the spot with his hand, and I can feel the rings on his fingers as the welt on my ass grows warmer.

"You like that," he rumbles.

It's not a question, he's telling me exactly how I feel. I'm starving for pleasure at this point, and anything he gives me, I would take. I've never been this high on someone before.

"Yes."

"Sir," he demands. "Be a good little slut and call me sir."

My cheeks warm, and I nod.

"Yes, sir."

His tongue is on my clit again, large hands spreading me wide as he devours me from behind. I relish the coolness of his mouth and a delightful pressure from this new angle. My back arches and just before I can get into it, he denies me again. I glance over my shoulder to sneer at him.

"You know, that's really starting to piss me off."

Dominic swings his arm back, his hand connecting with my ass as a loud *crack* that echoes through the room. I yelp, my clit pulsing and my thighs drenched with my slick and blood. He leans in, his cock brushing against my aching pussy.

"I paid for you. That means you're mine tonight."

I cry out at another strike that feels like it might shatter my entire body.

"Tell me," he demands. My mouth opens, but the words are lodged in the back of my throat. He hits me again, even harder this time. "*Tell me.*"

"Yes, sir," I grind out through clenched teeth. "I'm yours, sir."

He's driving me insane, and he knows it. Every part of me is trembling like a leaf.

"You know what I like about humans?" He asks.

"No," I squeak out.

"You're so fucking desperate, it's pathetic." He leans over, gently biting on my ear.

God, why do I want him to keep talking to me like this?

"I can smell it on you," he continues. "You're gonna be a good girl and take every inch of me, and when I tease you, when I let you suffer and writhe, you'll thank me for it."

The dominant edge to his voice makes me want him even more.

"Yes, sir! Thank you, sir!"

"That's my girl."

He pushes his cock inside of me with a grunt, filling me up. This time, the pace is brutal and vicious as he fucks me. It's all about him and his pleasure. His hand slides around my throat and I can feel him squeeze, pressing down on my windpipe and cutting off blood flow and air. It's just enough that I can still breathe, but I'm starting to get dizzy as his hips continue to crash into mine.

"Fuck, you're so wet," he groans. "You wanna come for me?"

"Yes," I manage to choke out. "Please, sir!"

"You're close. I can feel it."

He squeezes my throat a little tighter and my thighs tremble. Dominic snarls, driving himself inside of me over and over.

"Make a big fuckin' mess all over my cock."

I'm barely holding on to the back of the couch with one hand while my other is furiously rubbing my swollen clit. Dominic sinks his teeth into my shoulder one final time. The pressure of his hand around my throat and his bite sends a jolt of pure euphoria coursing through me and I come so hard that my vision grays out.

"Oh, God!"

He's brutal and relentless, pushing my face back into the couch and holding it there as he pounds into me. Slapping sounds fill the room and I can hear him grunting and growling as he fucks me even harder.

I manage to catch a glimpse of him out of the corner of my eye, his head thrown back and his eyelids fluttering. His body is gorgeous, muscles rippling beneath his skin. That perfect jawline, those abs... *fuck*. I'm already getting close again. I keep rubbing my clit, feeling my own blood trickle down my arm as he presses me even harder into the cushions.

A second climax hits me, softer this time as it rolls over my entire body. I couldn't even read the monitor on my wrist if I wanted to, but I don't give a shit. He crashes into me one more time before letting out a sinful moan as he comes. I collapse, my forehead pressed against the couch, desperate for air but reveling in the afterglow. The alley, the broom closet... nothing has even come close to this.

Dominic leans forward, pressing all of his weight into me, laying a soft little kiss on my shoulder. I can feel the heat of his breath, and the tiniest sting of his claw as he traces playfully along the back of my neck.

"It was finally nice to meet the real you, Sofie."

DOMINIC

Nox Feeding Room

Sofie's slumped against the couch, a big drunken smile on her face and her eyes drooping from pleasure and blood loss. I'm obsessed with the way her skin has paled and her freckles have become more prominent. I want to kiss each one of them, count them like stars, but I hold myself back. It's all too desperate, and there's nothing I hate more than seeming soft. I grasp her wrist, and check her heart rate monitor.

All I know is that I can't leave this woman alone.

"Where's your first aid kit?" I ask, tucking my cock back into my pants and beginning to search.

"I'll get it," she mumbles.

She has a red mark around her neck from my hand that'll turn into a bruise before long. Delight fills me up as I realize that she'll be wearing me on her body.

"Stay there."

She tries to get up and I hold my hand out, motioning for her to sit.

"I said stay," I bark. "Where is it?"

She stares at me with suspicion.

"Behind the bar," she finally rasps. "Bottom shelf."

I round the bar and crouch down, spotting a bright red bag with a white cross on it. Inside are sutures, alcohol, and bandages. Pretty much everything I need.

"I can do this stuff myself," she mumbles as I stroll back toward her and take my seat.

"Well, you let me feed on you, so I can clean up the mess I made."

"Let you?" She laughs, her eyes sparkling. "You paid for it."

I grab what I need and pour some alcohol onto a cotton ball, pushing her ponytail back. Carefully, I clean the remnants of blood that I wasn't able to lick off.

"If I'm going to be coming back here, I want you well taken care of."

"You want to be a regular?" She asks, an unintended yet hopeful lilt in her voice.

"Well, yeah. I had a good time. Did you not?"

"No, I did."

I continue to clean her up, sliding off of the couch and onto my knees in front of her, spreading her legs to clean up her thighs with another cotton ball. She hisses softly as I run it over the deep bruises I made with my teeth.

The puncture wounds have closed over already. I can't help but leave kisses in my wake as I fix her up. Her skin is so warm, I want her pressed against me while I sleep.

Once we're finished, she fixes her dress while I grab a pack of cigarettes that were nestled in my jacket. I toss it to her and she pops one in her mouth before I flop down next to her, lighting hers first before my own.

"You know I still don't trust you, right?" She announces, staring at me like I should be surprised. "This was business, it didn't change anything."

I lean forward, moving my hand up to cup her cheek. She flinches a little at first, but then slowly relaxes into my touch. I enjoy watching her warm up to me.

"For someone who seems like such a smart girl, you sure are ready to get in bed with a vampire you don't trust. Just something to think about."

A cocky smirk crawls across her face. There's something dark and mischievous about her that keeps my interest piqued; every time I fuck her, she shows me another piece of who she really is.

"Yes, Dominic." She leans forward and runs a fingernail down my bare chest, almost digging it into my skin. I groan and my cock twitches. "I'm a *very* smart girl. They don't just hand out PhDs in experimental medicine for nothing."

"Experimental medicine?" I ask excitedly, dropping my mask for just a moment.

"Uh-huh. I studied hematology."

"What's that?"

"Blood, Mr. Duncan. I thought you'd know, considering how much you love it."

"Blood," I repeat, nodding as I stare into the distance. Theo can stop his search because life just handed me a big glass of lemonade.

"But I'm not just smart with blood," she whispers. "I know exactly who to trust and who to toss out on their ass."

"Like Rene?"

I immediately regret the question.

She bristles at his name, and her fear ripples through the room, changing the mood completely. I lean forward, knowing she's hiding something from me. Her eyes are suddenly fixed on the ground, and my desire to rip Deschamps' throat out returns with a vengeance.

"Did he do something?"

She examines her chipped nail polish, shaking her head as I watch the hairs on her arm stand up on end.

"I don't want to talk about it."

I'd never blame a human for being terrified of him. Rene gets off on doing the most heinous shit without a care in the world, and this is coming from someone who has a man's tongue sitting in a jar at home.

I drain my drink and get up to make another, sensing her discomfort. We need a change of pace. Rene is a fucking boner killer.

"So what exactly did you do? With blood, I mean."

She holds out her now empty glass, clinking the ice cubes together.

"How 'bout I tell you after you top me up?"

I crush my cigarette out on the bar, pour us more whiskey, and sit down next to her, running my fingers playfully through her hair.

"Not sure if this is really in your wheelhouse, but I worked at the blood bank, way before all this shit went down. Tested samples when people donated, looked for blood-borne pathogens, stuff like that."

"So you pretty much know everything there is to know about blood, huh?"
She tenses up a little.

"I wouldn't go that far."

"What about vampire blood?"

"I'm familiar with it. At least enough to know the inoculations won't turn us into vamps, no matter how far that rumor spreads."

I chuckle.

"Not sure it'd be the best evil plan for us to try. If everyone was a vampire, the food sources get pretty fucking thin."

"That's what I've been saying!" She laughs, her warmth flooding back into her features.

It's a glimpse of who she really is, but only for a second. Sadness quickly pushes out the brightness in her eyes, and I sense trepidation all over again. She only allows herself these small moments of vulnerability, and so it's impossible for her to trust me. We're not on equal footing.

"Why did you ask me about what I did?"

If she's worked with blood before, she might be able to synthesize this formula, but I can't just open with that. I keep calm and flash her the most charming grin I can muster and she melts, her gaze softening immediately. It's easy because she wants it to be real.

"I'd like to get to know you."

"To know me?" She laughs. "What for?"

"Have dinner with me tomorrow night."

There's a long pause before she bursts into giggles, pressing her hand to my forehead.

"Are you sick? Can vampires get sick?"

I feel heat in my belly. Embarrassment. But I grit my teeth and swallow it.

"Have dinner with me," I repeat. "Tomorrow night."

"Dominic, I have a job. I don't really get a lot of time off, especially with zero notice."

The fact that Rene still hasn't come at me with everything he has is a miracle, and I'd be a moron to not take advantage. I know the storm that's coming, the danger he poses to the both of us, but she doesn't. He sniffs out and exploits weaknesses, but this time he's slipped up and told me too much. If I can convince her, if I can keep her safe, I can take him apart piece by piece with no fear of repercussions.

She can make me that formula, and I can crush Rene like a fucking cockroach.

"You're the boss, aren't you? Just take the night off."

She scoffs. Her attitude makes me want to bend her back over that couch and *make her* obey me. But for her, I'm willing to try a different tactic.

"I'll pay you."

"You can't get everything you want with money."

"That hasn't been my experience."

"If you want to fuck me again, we can do it here."

"It's more than that."

"More?" She asks with a raised brow.

"I'd like to get to know you better. Talk to you. This place is a little... loud, don't you think?"

"Dominic, I can't–"

"Two hundred thousand dollars."

I'm desperate, and I hate being desperate, but I fucking *need* her. More time, more of her scent, her mouth, everything. I can keep her safe at my penthouse.

"I'll give you two hundred thousand dollars to have dinner with me tomorrow night. You can do whatever you want with it. I'll take you to Nox the next night for your shift, drop you off and leave you alone if you like. I *promise*, Sofie."

Crimson blooms along her cheeks and travels down her chest as she exhales, staring me down for a moment before draining the rest of her drink.

"Wow, you *are* tenacious."

I grin and reach out, hooking one finger beneath her chin to lift it.

"Say yes."

"I'll talk to–"

"Say *yes*. One night. Don't make me beg."

There's a storm raging behind her eyes as she studies my face. She doesn't fully trust me, not yet.

She's smart.

"Begging, huh? I'd like to see that. You look real good on your knees."

She's got me right where she wants me, and she knows it.

"You think this is funny?"

"I think if you want to *have me* for dinner, you need to work for it."

She brushes my cheek with her fingertips. My eyes flutter at the warmth of her skin. I've rarely craved the sunlight before, but lately dreams of a silent sunrise, hand in hand, have been haunting me. Of course, that fantasy quickly gives way to the reality of a quick and ashy end, but it's nice to indulge in romanticism from time to time.

"You get on your knees and beg for me, and we might just have ourselves a deal. I'll want that money, too, of course."

The newfound confidence radiates off her, and I can't help but smirk.

"Of course you will."

"Symbiotic relationship, right?" She asks with her own wide grin.

"Oh, is that what this is?"

"Just what I thought. You don't want to give up even a sliver of power, do you?"

"That's not true."

"Then prove it to me." She flicks her head. "Drop to your knees and beg."

With clenched muscles, I shift my body and slide down onto the floor, moving in front of her so that I'm resting between her thighs. I can hear her breath hitch in her chest as I kiss my way up each leg, showing her a sweetness that feels almost like a stranger to me.

Her fingers run through my hair, pushing it back as my lips ghost along her skin.

"No cheating, Dominic. You know the rules: I need to hear you beg," she whispers. "Just once."

The tension between us is suffocating, and her muscles tremble with each kiss.

"Please," I rasp.

She smiles.

"Louder."

My chest heaves, along with hers. Sparks rush down my spine and I ache to grab her by the throat, pin her down and show her what a fucking animal I am. The blood in her veins sounds like the ocean being kicked up in a hurricane.

My lips move higher as she spreads her legs.

"I need you," I whisper.

"Need me?" She tugs at my hair and I think about the last time a woman had me in this position. Funny enough, she tried to kill me.

"You *need* me?"

My throat feels like it's made of sandpaper. This is humiliating, but I kind of like it.

"Need to see you, need to touch you, need to know you."

"Why?"

"I don't know." I breathe deeply. This has turned into a hell of a lot more than begging. "Please, Sofie."

"That's all you had to say." The smile on her face is my answer as she tips my head back. "I just wanted to see the big, bad Dominic Duncan on his knees for a human, and a woman no less."

I can't contain myself anymore. I pull her down on top of me and we tumble to the floor, clawing at each other as our lips crash together.

"It turns you on, doesn't it?" I ask as she places her hands on my chest. "Me, on my fucking knees. Begging for what you know goddamn well I could just *take*."

"Yes," she moans.

I'm greeted with little pops of electricity when I touch her. She gasps, grinding herself against my cock. Can she feel the connection between us like I can? Or is this just lust and hormones swirling together to create more chaos? At this point, it doesn't really matter to me.

My hand finds its way around her throat, and her moans get louder. She's still fucking soaked. I can feel it through my pants. This is going to be faster and more desperate than before. Tomorrow night, I'll get her all to myself. No time limits, no interruptions, no sharing her with anyone else.

I squeeze her neck harder, cutting off a little bit of airflow. Her face turns pink, and she moans, eyelids fluttering and her tongue slipping out to flick across her bottom lip. I love the sensation of her pulse beneath my palm as my claws sink into her skin.

"You're mine," I whisper. "I'm going to come here every fucking night. I'm going to fuck you, and I'm going to take what's mine. I don't care if it's a feeding night or not. You. Belong. To *me*."

"Big talk from a man who's pinned underneath me," she purrs. "I think you like a woman who takes control."

I loosen my grip around her throat and she shimmies her way down my body and unzips my pants. I lift my head in time to watch her take my cock out and swirl her tongue around the tip. Her mouth is incredible. She's so goddamn gentle, even in the way her dull teeth scrape across my skin and she threatens to bite down. I don't believe her for a second.

My eyelids flutter, and my back arches as she takes me all the way down her throat. I bury my hand in her hair, forcing her head down until her nose is pressed against my pelvis. She gags and coughs, but I don't let her come up for air. Not yet.

She's right, I like a woman who takes control, but I don't relinquish power easily. I want to see her fight for it.

"All the way, little dove," I groan. "I knew you'd look pretty with my cock in your mouth."

I wrap my hand tight around her ponytail and keep her head down until she's gagging on me, saliva dripping from her lips.

"You can take it," I whisper. "You like being treated like a toy, don't you?"

The benefit of our senses means it's easy to read our partners. It means we can go all the way to the edge, just a sliver away from too far, and still bring them back. I pull her off of me and she gasps like she's just emerged from water. Those big doe eyes nearly bulge out of her head, and a line of spittle connects her mouth to my cock. I want to rip her to pieces and take care of her every need at the same time.

If she says yes to dinner, I'll be able to do all of that and more. I've already set a plan in motion, and the pieces *will* fall into place.

I beckon her over with a finger.

"Ride me."

She crawls back up my body and straddles my hips again, sinking down onto my cock. Her fingernails dig into my skin, leaving tiny half-moons behind like she's trying to punish me, and it turns me on more than I care to admit. I haven't been with many humans who are brave enough to tear into a vampire.

She's close, clenching around me. I can feel her aching to come, only caring about her and her own pleasure. I roll her nipples between my thumb and forefinger and she cries out, her back bowing as she looks up at the ceiling.

"Oh, God!"

Lightning crawls through my veins as I cup her breasts, resisting the urge to pierce her tender flesh with my claw.

Control the beast, Dominic.

"There's no God here," I breathe. "It's just me."

That throaty laugh makes my cock twitch inside of her.

"You've got a real fucking ego, Dominic."

"You're the one who's about to come *all* over my cock." I pause and grip her hips, forcing her to fuck me harder. "Again."

Her pussy flutters and pulses, her swollen clit rubbing against me. I reach down with one hand and circle it with the pad of my thumb as my claws retract. I want to be gentle, even if she doesn't; she has to have a reason to give me her trust.

I'm going to need it.

A smile tugs at the corners of her mouth and I can't help but notice how blissed out she looks, her cheeks a bright shade of rose petal pink as she gets closer and closer.

"Please," she rasps. "Fuck, Dominic."

"Now who's begging?" I rumble. "Tell me what you want."

"Make me come!" She gasps. "Fuck, please, make me come and I'll do whatever you want!"

"Anything?"

She collapses on top of me, the only thing moving are her hips. A sob ripples from deep in her body, her mouth colliding with mine in a feverish and animalistic kiss that leaves both of us breathless. I don't even care if I come again. I just want to hear her moan.

"Keep making those pretty sounds for me, Sofie."

She moves her hips faster, my cock pounding into her as we fall back into our chaotic and furious rhythm, trading grunts and groans back and forth. I snarl in her ear, the knot in my stomach growing tight again. She's so fucking wet. I need her, need to be buried in her, need to have her by my side all the time.

Sofie lets out another loud moan that sends me over the edge. I can't stand it anymore, rolling the two of us over in the blink of an eye as I pin her arms above her head. Her lips are parted, stained with fresh new blood. I must have nicked her with my teeth during a kiss. My bloodlust is so insatiable that I'm unable to resist and bite into the top of her breast. The second the warm, coppery liquid touches my tongue, I come so hard my vision whites out. Sofie screams, clenching around me.

"Dominic!" She keens. "Fuck!"

I dislodge my fangs and smear the blood all over her bare tits with my tongue, dragging it up her neck and marking her as mine. Her body relaxes, melting into me as her legs wrap around my waist. She's breathing hard, wheezing a little as I pull back, the bottom half of her face stained crimson.

Everything feels right. It just fits.

And all I can think is she'd make a beautiful vampire.

SOFIE

DUNCAN TOWERS

"DINNER? WITH *HIM*?" RUBY exclaims as I fix my hair in our bathroom mirror. "I can't fucking believe you."

She freaked out when I told her what Dominic proposed, and she freaked out *again* when I told her I agreed to it.

"Honestly? Neither can I."

There are tubes of lipstick and eyeliner scattered all over the counter, scattered in with everything else I've dug out of my makeup case. I'm already doubting my outfit choice. What does someone wear to dinner with a crime boss, or a vampire for that matter?

In the end, I opt for a simple, low-cut black dress that hits my mid-thigh. Something Dominic would like, I hope. My hair is wild and wavy. No sense in styling it if he's just going to wreck it all later.

"Look, it's obvious why he invited you, but why the hell did you say yes?"

"Because he's paying me 200 grand, Ruby. That's enough to improve security and make things safer. Just imagine what we could do to this place with that kind of money! Who the fuck could say no to that?"

With my ring finger, I smudge the brown liner beneath my eyes a little more, trying to make them look less like Charlie's. Sometimes it's hard to look in the mirror without seeing him. We had the same eyes. It was the only way I could tell for sure that he was mine. Otherwise, he looked just like his dad.

Sometimes, I feel like the things that make me who I am are just puzzle pieces of the people I've lost. My mother's dimples, my dad's nose and broad shoulders.

"Sure, it's a crazy amount of money, but the emphasis is on the crazy! How do you know he's going to hold up his end of the bargain?" Ruby's voice gets higher in pitch. "Do you know what he's done to people? To other vampires? Kirby says he bit a guy's tongue off. *Off*, Sofie! Pulled it out by the fucking root and sucked on it like a fruit roll-up!"

"I think Kirby has an overactive imagination."

"You know he's a vampire, right? Or did you miss those big signals, too?"

She's not wrong. It seems absolutely insane to be putting my trust in one of them, especially outside of the protection of Nox, but Rene showed me even that has its limits. And Dominic... he's not the same. If he wanted to hurt me, he could have. Maybe not in the club, but in the alley? He could have drained me dry and left me for dead. He's not in this for a quick drink, he wants more.

Our apartment buzzer interrupts my half-formed retort. The thing sounds more like an air raid siren and Ruby jumps, clutching her chest.

"Jesus Christ!"

Nobody comes here anymore, so whenever the thing rings, it scares the shit out of us.

We're hyper vigilant. Every creak at night sounds like a vampire trying to get in. We put bars on the windows and four locks on the doors. There are weapons under our beds and we're always prepared for the worst.

But this time, I know who's standing out front waiting for me. My heart races and I snatch my bag off of the counter, double checking I packed my gun just in case things get out of control. I even have a small silver dagger strapped to my thigh, half for some extra protection, and half because I'm pretty sure Dominic is into that shit.

Ruby jumps off of the counter and stops me in my tracks, fixing one of my flyaways. Her brows are scrunched together and she's chewing on her thumb nail. Our eyes meet in the mirror and I smile.

"It'll be okay."

"Make sure you come back, okay?"

"I will," I reply, turning around to kiss her on the cheek. "I'll be at the club tomorrow night. He promised."

Ruby sticks out her pinkie finger, and we link them, giving three little shakes. It's our little pact when things get serious.

"Can't break the promise now, no matter how good that vampire dick is."

Another buzz and I glower as I head toward the door.

"Jesus fucking Christ, I'm gonna kill that guy."

I look at Ruby one last time, giving her a small wave.

The second the door shuts behind me, my heart is in my throat. Dominic was playing on my turf before. I have no idea what he's like on his own and in his own territory.

When I reach the lobby of the apartment, I spot a man in a black suit with slicked back blonde hair waiting for me just outside the foyer. He'd look like a surfer if he weren't so pale. Maybe he should borrow some of Hunter's self tanner.

He's shorter than Dominic, with muscles that threaten to bust right through his suit. His face is twisted up, like he can't choose between scowling and wincing as his foot clicks impatiently against the tile. I can hear the *tap tap tap* through the glass doors as he checks his watch, huffing every few seconds.

"Hi!" I call out, pushing the front doors open. "I'm so sorry, I was–"

"Mr. Duncan doesn't like to be kept waiting," he snaps, jaw ticking with irritation.

I frown, exhaling softly as I adjust my purse.

"Okay, dickweed, chill the fuck out," I mutter under my breath as I follow him over to an unmarked black car.

The warm air wraps around me like a blanket, along with the smell of trash that's become a permanent fixture in Santa Cruz. If you want fresher air, you have to go to the mountains and brave the less civil vamps and some of the most fucked up humans you've ever seen.

The man opens the passenger door for me and I slip inside, buckling my seatbelt as he strolls around to the driver's side and climbs in. I watch him adjust the rearview mirror and glance behind him to make sure we're alone. I'm not sure if that makes me more or less nervous.

"Dominic pays you well to do this, I take it?"

"I'm here to drive, not to talk," he growls, thrusting the key into the engine and turning it over.

"Seems like you and I have a lot in common," I remark.

For the first time, I feel like I've met my match. Hates his job, hates people, and he's got a grumpy disposition. Sometimes it sucks to look in the mirror.

My chauffeur stares straight ahead, but a small smile tugs at the corners of his lips. I want to ask him what his name is, but when I look over again, his expression has already soured.

The ride is quick and quiet, the same direction as I drive to the blood bank. There's almost nobody on the street, save for small packs of stupid young vampires looking to hunt any human who dares to venture outside. I draw in a deep breath as we pass them, the driver slowing down to take a turn. One of them makes eye contact with me: a redhead with piercing yellow eyes. He smiles, baring his fangs. The driver scoffs.

"Don't let him intimidate you."

"You know him?"

"Yeah. His name is Jared." He smirks. "What kind of fuckin' vampire is named Jared? You know what I mean?"

I try to hold back a chuckle as he turns a corner.

"What's your name?" I ask.

He shakes his head, and I sigh.

"Okay, fine, Mister Mysterious. What if he follows us?"

"If he touches Dominic's property, he'll be dead before he hits the ground," the driver replies.

My brows snap toward my hairline. If that's what this is, he might as well just turn this fucking car around. I'm not going to be some suckhead's property.

"Is that what he thinks I am?"

"I'm just the driver, doll," he replies with a shake of his head. He parks the car in front of the towering high-rise and grabs his gun off of the dashboard, cocking it. "Here we are. I'll walk you inside."

When I step out, I feel like a walking lunch. Totally exposed. Dread pools in my stomach, crawling its way through my body as we rush into the building, through the black tinted glass doors.

I'd only ever seen Duncan Towers from a distance, and never had a reason to step inside, but it's strangely both less and more than I expected. The building smells clean and fresh. Modern, with black and gold marble floors, and a few matching wingback chairs in the lobby that look like they were bought strictly for decoration. I wouldn't be surprised if no one's ever sat in them, or anywhere in the lobby for that matter, as the echo of our footsteps ring out through the hollow surroundings.

I spot a stained glass window in the back that looks like it was lifted from a church. A few small sconces line the walls, making the room glow a warm golden color. I let out a whistle, and as if on cue, the elevator dings and Dominic steps out.

He's wearing a dark red suit with a slightly unbuttoned black dress shirt. His tattoos are on full display, along with his well-sculpted chest. There's dark stubble peppered across his jaw and his eyes are the most intense shade of electric blue, somehow brighter than I remember them being back at the club. The second he sees me, a warm smile lights up his face. My mouth is immediately dry, desperate for a cool drink.

He turns to the driver.

"That'll be all for tonight, Mateo. You can go... frolic."

The newly named Mateo flashes him a sly smile and winks, his grumpy disposition melting away with the all-clear from his boss. He flashes us both finger guns, spins on the balls of his feet, and struts out the door whistling.

"I hope he didn't give you a hard time," Dominic murmurs. "I would have sent a human driver, but my last one had an... unfortunate incident with one of Rene's men."

"Mateo was a perfect gentleman."

"Glad to hear it. He's still young. I told him he had to behave himself."

Dominic stretches out his hand. He's like a fucking magnet, and I can't stop myself from closing the gap between us and sliding my palm against his. He brings my knuckles up to his lips, kissing them before he pulls me close, his lips ghosting my neck.

"Thank you for coming."

I try to think of something impressive to say, something to let him know I'm still a force to be reckoned with. Unfortunately, nothing comes to mind, and I wing it.

"Thanks for being hot and rich."

He laughs and pulls back, tilting his head as he grasps both sides of my face.

"Can I kiss you?"

"Oh, you're asking for permission this time?"

He sighs, shrugging his shoulders and running his thumb back across my knuckles. I feel like a mouse that's been caught by a lion.

"Well, I promised myself I would be a gentleman." His tongue runs across his lips before lingering on one of his fangs. "At least for a while."

I nod quickly, letting his mouth melt into mine. It's soft and delicate, so much different from before, although I recall it may have started this way once or twice. Dominic kisses my top lip first before pushing his tongue inside of my mouth and tangling it with mine.

His hand slips around the back of my neck and I'm breathless; completely at his mercy as I'm pressed against him. I bite down on his lower lip and tug, giggling as I listen to him moan. Dominic breaks away, reaching up to wipe away some of my smeared lipstick.

"Let's go upstairs."

We step into the steel elevator, and he presses the button for the top floor.

"Are there other vampires who live in this building?"

"It's just me."

"You live all alone in a high rise? Seems kind of wasteful and cliché for a vampire, doesn't it?"

He glances at me with a grin as he twists one of the skull rings on his fingers. It's silver with two black stones set in its eyes.

"Smart, aren't we? Actually, I originally wanted it to be an apartment building for us – vampires, that is – but The Bank had other plans."

"Gee, I wonder why," I remark wryly as the elevator climbs higher. "A bunch of vampires a block from a building full of blood seems like a disaster waiting to happen."

"I guess that's the human way of looking at it. Either way, I mostly use this place for storage now."

"What kind of storage?"

"Cash, guns, drugs, whatever we need." He pauses. "But I assure you, you're safe here. I have state-of-the-art security. Bullet *and* vampire-proof glass, alarm systems, the works."

"I think I can trust you," I whisper.

He raises a brow.

"Really?"

"At least as far as I can throw you," I tease.

"Fair enough."

"But, wait a second, what the fuck is vampire-proof glass supposed to–"

The elevator dings and the doors open, and my jaw drops when I see his penthouse. It's massive, thick black blinds pulled up to let the moonlight cut through the room and bathe everything in an ethereal silver glow. The place is sparsely but purposely decorated with a record player, a small side table next to a sofa, and some bookshelves stacked with volumes old and new. I guess Dominic doesn't really see the need for a television set, but really there's much on cable anymore. I mostly use our TV to watch old videotapes.

Across the room, I spot a tall shelf filled with vinyl. Other than what we listen to at work, Ruby and I don't have many albums. I can't help but wonder what vampires listen to.

The entire place is open concept with the same black and gold marble floors, charcoal walls, and even the sconces from the lobby providing a low ambient light. At the end of the room I turn and spot a dining room table – black, of course – with a bottle of wine, two crystal goblets set out. In the center is a bouquet of dark red roses sitting in a black vase.

"Wow," I whisper.

Dominic turns to me and smiles, his eyes twinkling as he waits for me to say something backhanded, but I have to disappoint him.

"This is beautiful."

He blinks, a little surprised, before gesturing toward the dining room table.

"You want a drink?"

"Please."

Dominic picks up a bottle of wine that looks older than Ruby and I combined, popping the cork out with his claw. I watch him sniff at it for a moment, savoring the aroma before he pours us each a glass.

"I haven't started cooking the meat yet. I realized I still needed to ask you how you like your steak."

"I haven't even seen a steak in five years, let alone eaten one."

I take a sip of wine and groan. It's delicious, oaky, and heavy on my tongue. I catch small hints of berries and an almost jam-like quality. Back before everything went to shit, Sam used to have a pretty extensive wine collection. It was mostly an excuse for me to get drunk, but I learned a few things from him.

"Well, I thought after what you provided me last night, you deserve a proper meal of your own."

"You must have had someone drive pretty goddamn far to get that food. As far as I know, no one in the city's got anything anywhere near a steak dinner." I pause and smile. "And I like it medium rare. Thanks for asking."

He lifts his wine glass to his lips.

"Perfect."

Dominic places the glass carefully on the counter, shrugging off his jacket and draping it over the back of his chair. He rolls up his shirt sleeves to expose his heavily tattooed arms, pulling out different utensils from the cabinets.

I follow him around the kitchen like a pathetic little puppy dog until I finally force myself to sit down at a bar stool while he rummages around in the fridge. I spot bags of blood, almost identical to the stock that we get from The Bank. I wonder if he has humans make runs for him, or if they actually let him inside the building, but I decide not to ask. It's really not what I'm most interested in tonight anyway.

For a little while I stay silent, simply watching him glide through the kitchen, but soon I feel the silence weighing down the room.

"I didn't know vampires cared about cooking."

He takes out a large knife, flipping it in his hand. He chops up some rosemary and slices off a knob of butter, tossing it into a hot pan. It crackles and sizzles from the heat, and the smell gets more intense.

"You know, we worked side by side with you before everything went to shit. Some of us even worked in kitchens. None of you ever really knew."

I smirk, lighting a cigarette.

"Oh yeah, licking blood off the floor?"

He laughs.

"Not my style."

"I'm just teasing."

"I know. You do that a lot."

I wet my lips.

"You seem to like it."

He places the knife on the counter, the tiniest inkling of a smirk on his face as he struts toward me. The moonlight's hitting him at the perfect angle, carving out his cheekbones as a few strands of dark hair fall into his eyes. I have to resist the urge to brush it away.

"Is that what you think, little dove?"

I inhale deeply and blow a smoke ring as his eyes land on the vein pulsing in my neck. My heart rate has stabilized since I stepped in here, but it's still running significantly faster than normal.

"I think if you wanna get laid tonight, you should make me one hell of a steak."

He reaches out to cup my cheek, and I shiver beneath his cool fingers. His touch is electric.

"You really make a guy work for it, huh?"

"That's what makes it all worth it in the end."

I can't help but smile to myself as he turns back around and chops up another onion. I haven't had a home cooked meal in years. It's mostly been canned food, boxes of mac & cheese, and MREs that Ruby had been stocking up for years. Our pantry is a doomsday prepper's dream, but prices for fresh produce are so high with so few farmers left, and even fewer outside of Rene's reach. I wonder again just how far Dominic had to go to get that steak, or who he sent to get it for him.

I feel completely out of place in this penthouse, like it's all a ghost of the life I had before that had all but disappeared. We used to live near the Board-walk in a beautiful beach house with a big backyard and a view. Now, Ruby and I sleep on shitty mattresses in her living room and use her bedroom as a pantry-slash-weapons storage container.

"So, I guess the question is, do vampires eat human food?"

"We can. I like the taste of it, but it's not a necessity. Humans taste better than the food they make."

"And what do I taste like?"

I want to know what makes me so addictive, why he keeps coming back.

Dominic turns and rolls his sleeves up a little higher, his forearms flexing. Heat pools between my thighs just watching him. If my mother were still alive, she might say he was husband material based on the cooking skills alone, but she would fucking hate the tattoos. When he looks back up at me, his expression is soft, almost sweet, full lips parted as he draws in a breath.

"A little like a popsicle melting in the sun, when it drips down your hand and you have to lick it up because you can't bear to waste a drop."

I chuckle and take another pull from my cigarette.

"A popsicle melting in the sun? Sounds pretty dangerous for you, don't you think?"

"We understand metaphors, Sofie," he pauses for a moment, looking out into the night. "Besides, we were all children once."

He seems almost sad, but not exactly. More nostalgic than anything.

"Well then, if you're an expert, what kind of popsicle would I be?"

"Cherry."

I snort. He didn't even miss a beat.

"What? Is that bad?"

"It's so cliché, Dominic! Have some creativity!"

"Ah, well, if I suppose you don't want the truth, will you settle for Strawberry?"

"Better," I reply. "But still kind of hokey."

"You really like to give an old man a hard time, don't you?"

He doesn't seem so dangerous now, save for the knife in his hand. And the fangs. And that if he wanted to, he could kill me just for saying the wrong thing. Or for less.

But for now, even just for a moment, everything is calm and soft.

Everything is nice.

SOFIE

DUNCAN TOWERS

DOMINIC TAKES HIS SEAT as I look down at the meal he's made for us. Perfectly cooked medium-rare steak, asparagus, and potatoes. It reminds me of Sam's meals. He used to make a big fuss about having dinner as a family. It was important to him, and it became important to me.

A lump forms in my throat. I've really missed this kind of thing.

Still, despite how sweet it all seems, I have to wonder what his angle is. Does he want a cut of the club? Is he planning on moving in completely? Does he want us to freeze out Rene? Unfortunately, I'm painfully aware that none of these questions are good ice-breakers and I'd hate to dampen the mood.

"So, um, how old are you?" I clear my throat and smile. "If you don't mind my asking."

He sits and motions for me to pick up my knife and fork. I oblige him.

"I don't mind," he chuckles. "I'm 170, give or take. What about you?"

"29."

"Hm, you look younger."

"It's probably the freckles and the button nose." I cut into my steak and take a bite. "That or everything looks young when you're over 100." He flashes a wry smile, and I feel a little more at ease. "Seriously though, even when I had my son, I looked younger than I actually was, at least until the sleepless nights started. *Then* I looked my age."

He frowns.

"You have a son?"

"Had."

I can see that he wants to ask another question, but stops himself.

"And a husband, but I'm on my own now. A lot of us are."

"We have something in common," he murmurs. "The loneliness, I mean."

It must ache for them to love people and lose them, or to spend decades alone. Neither option seems particularly great.

"I guess so, yeah."

I take another bite of the steak. Rosemary, fresh black pepper, onion, and butter light up my tongue.

"This is seriously amazing, Dominic," I mumble as I go in for more. It's really hard not to pick the plate up and just shovel everything into my mouth. "So good."

He beams at me.

"I'm glad you like it. My mother taught me to cook, she was very good."

"Is she, uh... you know..." I clear my throat and point at my teeth.

He laughs, shaking his head.

"A vampire? No, she died when I was quite young."

"How young?" I hold up a hand. "Sorry, that's–"

"No, it's alright. I was fourteen."

"God, I'm sorry. That must have been awful."

Dominic nods.

"It was, but it wasn't as awful as what I did to the man who took her from me."

My stomach drops and folds in on itself.

"Who..."

"My father," he whispers. "I was asleep while he was killing her – and not just killing her, he was doing... more. I don't know how I overpowered him. I just wanted it to fucking stop."

Tears mist his eyes and he takes a deep breath, reaching for his wine and draining it before pouring himself another glass.

"I'm sorry," he whispers, the humiliation evident in the tightness of his jaw. He's choking on grief. "Not exactly appropriate dinner conversation."

"No, it's... it's okay."

This is the first vulnerable thing he's really shared with me and I don't really know how to reciprocate. I'm not good at this stuff. I've spent so long bottling up my grief that it's just fucking hard to pull it back out and lay it on the table. It's like reopening a wound that I was praying would stay closed. I nestle into the natural discomfort of trying to figure out what to say, but he speaks up first.

"Tell me more about you. What was life like before all of this?"

Here it comes, the conversation I always dread having. I stare at him as he swirls his steak in a pool of butter and blood before popping it into his mouth. I'm not sure how much information to give him, and I'm not sure if I'm going to cry.

"What do you want to know?" I ask.

"Everything."

"That'll be a lot."

"I've got all the time in the world," he replies. "And we have all night."

Mild suspicion takes root in my stomach, but I take another sip of wine and bury it. What could he possibly do with something as useless as my past?

"Well, um... I got my PhD young, while I was raising my son."

"That must have been hard," Dominic replies.

I blink, not really expecting this kind of conversation from him. Really, I just kind of expected to be mauled and fucked against the wall the second I got into this penthouse.

"In a lot of ways, yeah. But my husband helped to step in and raise Charlie." I clear my throat. "I lost them both five years ago."

Dominic's eyes soften, the icy exterior around him melting, and his body slumps a little.

"I'm sorry."

I shake my head. My mother always said I was made of tough stuff, but I never really knew what that meant. Ignoring my feelings? Drinking and fucking them away? If that's the 'tough stuff' she was talking about, I think I might be fucked.

"Everyone's lost people. It's kind of what binds us all together in this shitshow."

One of the worst parts of grief is sharing it with someone and not knowing what they'll do with it. It feels like handing out the most delicate part of yourself and having to trust they'll treat it with care.

"Five years, so it was the virus?" He asks, resting his knife and fork at the side of his plate. His expression is soft, yet pained, concerned eyes shining in the candlelight beneath dark and furrowed brows.

I can tell that he thinks I'm going to blame him somehow, but the plague wasn't the fault of the vampires, no matter how much they fucked us afterwards.

"My son got infected first, and then my husband. I lost them within a few days of each other. Sometimes I wonder why I didn't get infected too," I whisper.

I feel guilty every single day, but I never say it out loud because everyone around me feels the same goddamn way. We all wonder why we survived. The virus has something like a 90% mortality rate. It could be transmitted via body fluids – blood, saliva, stuff like that. Most of the people who became infected were covered in open wounds, and there was no way to stop it from spreading. Even changing someone's bed linens was a risk. By the time we found out that vampire blood could be used as an inoculant, nearly everything was already gone.

"I remember when they started to quarantine the infected. They kept them behind big plastic sheets in the hospitals for days while they degenerated." As I'm reliving it all, a wave of grief swallows me and tears gather at the corners of my eyes. It's been five fucking years since I verbalized this. "It looked like a fucking war zone. If you came to see family, you had to wear a hazmat suit. But when Sam saw Charlie, he took his helmet off, and–"

I have to stop, covering my mouth with one hand to keep myself from bursting into tears.

"I wish I–" Dominic's voice drops to barely a whisper. "I'm sorry, Sofie."

"Well, it was great for you guys," I reply as I dab my eyes with a napkin.

He rubs his chest as if something inside of it hurts. Is it his guilt? Or mine? Is this the first real sit-down conversation he's had with a human? Am I finally seeing the real Dominic Duncan, or is this all an act?

"We *thought* it was going to be great," he replies. "I don't think we considered what exactly we were walking into. We have a delicate relationship, humans and vampires. A lion relies on its prey for food, right? If there's no food left, they have to move on. But what if something just..." He snaps his fingers. "If you take away every single source of food for that pride? They'd wander and wander and wander, looking for something to eat until they died."

"Or they ate each other," I pop a piece of steak into my mouth, chewing dramatically.

"It does happen," he sighs, picking up his utensils and slicing off another thin piece of steak.

"Does that work? Drinking from another vampire?"

"It's not as nutritionally dense as human blood, there are obviously far fewer of us, and of course, it's frowned upon, but yeah, it works."

Dominic studies me in between bites. I wonder what he's thinking. Actually, I'm pretty sure I know what he's thinking, because I'm thinking about it too. It's about time we both found a distraction.

"So, what, are you in the habit of inviting humans over for dinner?"

He laughs and shakes his head.

"No, you would be the first in a long, long time."

A rush of electricity shoots up my spine.

"Then why me?"

"Because I want to get to know you."

A buzzer goes off in the back of my brain. I've been doing my job long enough to tell when someone's lying to my face. Vampires are experts in manipulation and charm, but when you work with them long enough you start to see cracks in the mask. It helps that I've always been good at sniffing out bullshit.

I lean forward.

"Tell me the truth, Dominic."

"I am telling the truth," he laughs.

"Bullshit."

There's a tiny nervous glint in his eyes, behind all the niceties and the newfound warmth. After I've stared him down for long enough, he pushes his chair away from the table and stands. I do the same as he moves past me toward the living room.

"Stay there," he insists.

I ignore him completely, following him to the living room.

Dominic takes a key out of his pocket and slides it into a drawer next to the sofa. I stand a few feet away, craning my neck to see him pull out a piece of paper and turn it over in his hands. His brows knit together and he seems nervous suddenly as he reaches to rub the back of his neck.

"You said you studied blood and experimental medicine, right?"

"That's right."

He rubs his stubble with one hand, almost as though he's trying to force the words out of his mouth as he walks toward me, closing the gap between us.

"I, uh... I need..."

I chuckle, and he visibly bristles at the sound. I step backward, but don't break eye contact.

"It really kills you to ask me for something, doesn't it?" I tease. "Should I make you get on your knees again?"

He's not taking the bait. There's something swirling in his eyes that I can't grasp onto, like trying to catch smoke with my bare hands. Dominic's gaze extends past me, landing on something in the distance as he slowly hands me the folded up piece of paper. He's afraid.

"Theo and I have been looking for someone who can make this. I have supplies – uh, downstairs in a lab."

"Supplies for what?" I ask, flipping the paper open.

Scrawled on the page are several formulas and the basic chemical composition for some kind of compound that uses hemoglobin as a base. *But* the molecular composition required isn't human. It's vampire blood, or at least it's structured like vampire blood.

Synthetic, that's my specialty.

Or it would be, if I ever got my research off the ground.

Something like this would have taken years to get right, and would have required a level of sophisticated knowledge that's beyond me. I scan the rest of the page, unable to really piece it all together on the spot. It looks complex, almost like a puzzle. I used to love solving puzzles, but this would take time.

"What is it?"

"I don't know," he replies. "We found it in one of Rene's labs. All I know is it's important to him, and I want to exploit it."

He's either stupid, reckless or desperate, and I don't know which would be worse.

"You want me to make something you know nothing about; that you stole from the most dangerous man in the city?"

He runs a hand through his hair and paces across the room, his body twitching beneath his shirt as he clenches and flexes his fingers.

"We know it's some kind of drug, and vampire blood seems to be the key. As far as we can tell, he wants to start a whole new industry."

He doesn't sound confident.

"Do you have more information?" I ask. "More notes? Anything?"

"That's all we took before we torched the lab," he replies with a shake of his head. "Well, there's some stuff in a bag too, but we don't know much about it."

He's going to get me fucking killed. If he stole this from Rene, the bastard will want it back. He'll hunt Dominic down for it.

"So you brought me here for this?"

He rushes to my side and puts his hand on my cheek, eyes desperate and wild.

"I need you. We can't find anyone who will–"

"This is dangerous, not to mention stupid."

"I'll give you anything you want."

What I want is my life back. What I want is to go for a fucking walk outside without worrying about being torn to shreds. What I want is to walk into my son's bedroom and see him coloring at his little Fisher Price desk while his dad watches TV downstairs.

I want the chance to watch Charlie grow up, not stare at a picture of him frozen in time and wonder what could have been. But I can't have that. Everything I've ever known and loved has been ripped away from me, and all that's left is my club, Ruby, and this fucked up relationship with vampire I barely know.

"You can't give me what I want," I whisper.

Dominic's knuckles brush my cheek, the metal from his rings almost the same temperature as his skin. I look down at the formula in my hands, the tears in my eyes making it difficult to read it anymore.

"Look I– I need time to think about this."

He grows contemplative, a cloud of self-control obscuring his features as he brushes my hair behind my ear.

"We have all the time in the world, little dove."

SOFIE

DOMINIC'S LAB

"I HAVEN'T EVEN SAID yes yet, Dominic," I mutter as the elevator doors open.

"I know. I just wanted to show you where you might be working, given you make the right decision."

It only took a couple minutes for his more serious demeanor to melt away, and when he offered I couldn't deny the opportunity to see the lab. I'm nothing if not curious.

"What exactly is that supposed to mean?"

He's silent as I trail behind him, heading down a long, dark corridor. I can feel my anxiety spike as I take in my surroundings. It's nothing he's said or done, but something feels off.

"You're not going to murder me for saying maybe, are you?" I give another nervous laugh, but the possibility seems more real than it did a few minutes ago.

We stop in front of a set of double doors and he looks down at me, a smile on his face.

"Murder you, just for a maybe?" He whispers, grasping my hand. "I'd never be so ruthless. I just thought a little tour might push you in the right direction."

I'll admit, that vampire charm is working wonders.

What would be so bad about teaming up with him? Other than putting my club in danger, or the fact that I don't know what I'm *really* getting out of this deal. Well, aside from the sex. Still, I kind of want to see what he has to offer.

"Alright, fine. Show me what you've got, Duncan."

He pulls a key out of his pocket and unlocks the doors, swinging them open dramatically.

I'm *more* than impressed with what he's managed to scrounge up. It's a large room with multiple workstations filled with different implements and scientific paraphernalia. It's as if someone looked up 'lab' in an encyclopedia and just bought everything on the list. There's even a door that leads out to a large balcony overlooking the city, a feature both completely out of place but somehow entirely in-character. The moon seems to shine a little brighter in here, bouncing off of the walls and filling the entire room.

"Look around." He nudges me. "Feel free to play with anything you want."

Even in the few seconds we've been here, I can tell he's woefully unfamiliar with this space. If I accept the offer, it's very possible I'll be in charge of things – well, me or whoever else he's wrangled into this scheme. Either way, it's clear Dominic's not getting any of this done on his own.

Slowly, I meander around, brushing my fingertips against the tables and picking up equipment. This is some state-of-the-art shit, with big computers, safety equipment. There's even blood testing supplies and some boxes that are marked with the blood bank's logo.

I chuckle and shake my head.

"How long did it take you to put this together?"

"A few days." He winces a little. "Is it not good?"

"No, it's actually impressive." I pick up a box of test tubes, also with the bank's label on them. "I'm just shocked that Avery let you guys take this shit."

He stuffs his hands in his pockets and offers a bashful smile.

"I was very charming."

"*You* were?" I ask with a raised brow. "Because *you've* been spending an awful lot of time at the club. I don't know how you found the time to be charming, especially with Avery."

Dominic ignores my question, moving quickly toward me and grasping my waist. He pulls me in close, dragging his mouth up my neck while he slips his hand between my thighs. I gasp at the pressure. His eyes are the warmest I've seen them, golden and shimmering in the darkness.

"Say yes," he pleads.

I shake my head. I need time to think, to talk to Ruby, and to figure this out.

"Aren't we supposed to be eating dinner?"

"I want something else," he whispers.

"Dominic, you said you would give me time, I–"

He dips his head to kiss me. It's slow, passionate, and intense. I claw at his chest, popping open a few buttons on his dress shirt. Dominic chuckles against my mouth as he backs off a bit.

"When was the last time you really looked at the moon?"

I blink, confused.

"Why?"

"I just want to know."

"You mean, when was the last time I had the chance to appreciate it? Without a pane of glass and some bars in the way?"

There's sadness in his eyes.

"Do you live in a cage, little dove?"

He takes my hand and leads me toward a set of beautiful french doors that open onto the large balcony. The moon hangs high in the sky, giving off a vibrant silver glow. Sometimes I catch it in the daylight, or in the midst of the odd run to the Blood Bank. Rarely do I spot its reflection in the window during a shift. It's like a ghost in my life, always in the corner of my eye. I wonder if Dominic feels the same about the sun.

I lean up against the massive stone wall and look out at a landscape that's long since lost its warm familiarity. There used to be beach parties with massive bonfires and dancing. People wandered around with portable radios at night, and there was always laughter in the air. The Santa Cruz of today is a hollowed out husk of its former self.

Dominic's arm wraps around my waist, his free hand pushing my hair to the side, pulling the strap of my dress down as he lays kisses along my back.

"What do you think?" He asks.

"It really is beautiful."

He sucks on the side of my neck, surely leaving a dark bruise behind as his hand travels upward to cup my breast.

"When's the last time you saw the sun?" I ask.

"October 25th, 1851. I was 34."

He didn't even hesitate.

"Do you miss it?"

Everything comes to a stop, and he nods. His hands linger on my body, unmoving, holding me like I'm all the warmth he's lost over the years. I look back to see him staring up at the moon, sadness eclipsing his eyes.

"I don't know how much you can miss something you barely remember."

He's reliving nearly three lifetimes right in front of me. I wonder what he's seen, how many people he's lost, how many he's loved over his 170 years on the earth.

"Who... who turned you?"

I think I know the answer, but I need to know for sure.

"I'd been working for him since I was a teenager." His hands move up and down my body again, almost absentmindedly. "I was so happy the day he turned me. I was dying."

"Of what?"

"Cancer. Rene gave me a gift."

"Is that what it is? A gift?"

"Yes," he breathes. "And you get a hell of a lot from it."

"Like what?"

He groans against me, and I can feel him smile against my skin, followed by the gentle nick of a razor-sharp fang.

"Life. Power in the palm of your hand." His hands glide over my breasts and I shiver. "I think it must be what God feels like."

Fire burns deep and low in my belly, and my knees are shaking as I hold onto the concrete wall with everything I have.

"I need to fuck you," he begs.

One of his hands slides down, pushing my dress up my thigh as he grinds his cock into my ass. A soft growl ripples through me as his fingers glide along the hem of my panties. I spread my legs a little wider, arching my back as he flicks his tongue along my neck.

Suddenly, the knife attached to my thigh is dangling in front of me. Panic surges through my body; I got so caught up in the moment I didn't even notice him remove it from its hiding place.

"You still don't trust me." He mutters, kissing my shoulder gently.

"Why should I?" I breathe. "You're not just a criminal, you're a literal predator."

Dominic hums, dragging the tip of the blade across my throat and down my sternum. A small, warm trickle of blood runs down my chest and a half-nervous smile spreads across my face.

"You just can't help yourself, can you?" I try to keep my voice steady.

"Not when it comes to you," he rumbles.

My pulse races as beads of sweat form on my upper lip, but something keeps me from running, holding me in place.

"You know why I like you so much, Sofie? Because you're always so prepared."

I feel warm air brush against my skin as he takes a step back.

When I turn around, he hands the knife to me before he unbuttons his shirt and looks down at his heaving chest. His finger traces a blank spot of skin underneath his collarbone that his tattoos haven't touched.

"Is that silver?" He asks, flicking his head toward the knife.

His eyes grow wilder with each passing second, and I'm clenching every muscle in my body.

"Yes."

Dominic snatches my wrist and pulls me close to him, forcing me to press the tip of the blade into his skin. It sizzles and I smell burning flesh as he snarls in pain and forces me to drive it deeper. It's hurting him, but he likes it. I think I do too.

"You're going to use this knife the way I tell you to." He pushes it deeper and smiles at me.

I can only nod. There's something about seeing him on the razor's edge that puts me right back in the feeding room, watching him crawl toward me.

He rips the knife out of my grasp and drags the blade across his palm before thrusting it back into my hand. I blink, standing on wobbly legs as he holds his hand inches from my face, opening it to reveal a deep cut in his palm. He lowers it slowly, intently, until he reaches his cock. He begins to stroke himself, slowly and methodically covering it in blood. Heat floods my body, and my nerves are on fire. Dominic glances down at his cock, smearing blood and precum around as it drips from the tip.

"Kneel. And clean me off," he orders, his voice so gentle I'm almost shocked by it.

Vampire blood alone won't turn a human. You have to be on the verge of death for it to work. Still, fear gathers at the base of my throat.

I drop to my knees, tasting metal as I swirl my tongue around the tip. A soft, sultry rumble fills my ears as my eyes slide shut. He grabs my hair and forces his cock deeper down my throat, a buzzing sensation gathering at the back of my skull as he snarls above me.

He hits the back of my throat as his hips buck. I'm choking, tears pricking my eyes and then rolling down my face. I can feel blood and saliva leaking out of my mouth and dribbling down my chin as he uses me like a toy. Each thrust is more brutal than the last and the noises he's making are glorious, better than any music I've ever heard.

"Fuck yourself with the knife," he orders. "Be my good girl."

My eyes meet his, and he smiles, malicious intent painting his features. The look on his face makes me ache for his cock; for the power he has over me. I spread my legs a little wider, teasing my clit with the knife handle as he drives his cock deeper down my throat. He's got me right where he wants me, my hair clutched in his fist, completely at his mercy.

I slide the handle into my pussy and thrust it deep inside of me, gripping the blade. I don't care about anything other than how good this feels. The sharp edges slice into my palm and fingers, but I feel nothing but pleasure as I hit my G-spot over and over again, pushing me to the brink faster than I thought.

Dominic purrs when I let out a choked whine, holding my face against his pelvis as his cock pulses in my throat. I can't get enough air, but I don't give a shit. Waves of pleasure threaten to knock me over and I'm driving the handle harder and harder; faster and faster until I'm teetering on the edge.

Heat creeps down my neck, down my shoulders, flooding my chest and I gaze up at him, watching a smile eclipse his face.

"Come for me," he breathes.

It's all the permission I need, and my pussy flutters around the handle as I'm rocked by an overwhelming climax. Dominic doesn't wait for me to come down from my high. He pulls me back by the hair, relishing my gasps for breath as the knife clatters to the ground.

He tugs me to my feet, and I stumble backward the second he releases me. I lift my head and check the wound on my palm, compelled in a moment of pique to taste myself. I can't taste any of the notes he'd mentioned, but there's something so compelling in how disgusting the act is. We match now. Just like in the alleyway, I stick my tongue out, offering him blood like communion wine. This time, he gives in, his movements so desperate that his fang knicks my tongue and I wince.

Dominic pulls back slightly, an appreciative smile on his face, and I take the moment to dip my head and clean the wound he made in his own chest. My throat tightens as I lap at his wound. I haven't given myself enough time to recover and my lungs are barely able to get the air that they need, but I don't care. I feel like his little apprentice, relishing my newfound bestial nature.

"You're perfect," he whispers.

When I look up, his eyes have lost their golden hue, all soft and calm again. He's back in the driver's seat. I stifle a laugh and lift my head, his blood smeared on my mouth.

"Perfect?"

He hums, sliding a finger beneath my chin and kissing me.

"Beautiful, soft, obedient." He runs his thumb across my bottom lip. "You're going to take my cock exactly the way I tell you to, aren't you?"

I feel emboldened. He could have killed me and he didn't. Instead, he trained me.

"And if I don't? What's the big, *bad* Dominic Duncan going to do if his perfect girl doesn't live up to expectations?"

He reaches down and teases my clit again, tearing a whimper from my lips in the middle of my retort. He drinks it in, and as my mouth opens, he licks the blood from my chin and spits it back onto my tongue.

"I'd have to tie you to my bed and teach you a lesson."

"Maybe I'd like that."

"Christ, where have you been all my life?" He groans, moving in to taste the blood on my lips.

I wrap one leg around his waist, desperate for more friction as he grinds up against me and pulls me as close to him as he can. All the air feels like it's being pulled from my lungs and the harder I fight it, the more it hurts to breathe. But I need him. I need this. He makes me feel so alive after sleepwalking for so long.

Suddenly, he breaks away and turns me back around, smacking my ass hard as I shift my hips. I swallow a yelp, letting out a jagged moan instead. Dominic's hand wraps around my throat again, pushing hard against my windpipe. I whine and hear the unmistakable clink of his belt buckle.

The tip of his cock pushes against me and he lets out a feral growl, as though his voice is being dragged across broken glass. The sensation is sharp and electric, torturing me as he pulls all the way out before slamming every inch of his cock back inside me.

"Scream for me," he snarls. "I want everyone to hear who you belong to."

"You!" I cry, tears stinging my eyes as I relish that familiar stretching sensation. "I belong to you!"

Dominic rewards me by smacking my ass one more time as he moves his hips, filling me to the brim every time our bodies meet.

"That's a good girl. Louder for me."

"Oh my god!"

"You can do better than that," he snarls. "I want them to hear you from *all* the way down there."

Vampires really do like to play with their food.

I bite down on the inside of my cheek as he reaches around in front of me, rubbing my clit in tight circles until it's pulsing beneath his touch. The only thing that soothes the growing heat inside of me is the icy hand around my throat, squeezing tighter and tighter with each passing second.

Every muscle in my body trembles as I hear snarls and growls behind me. One of his thrusts is particularly brutal and sends a shock wave of pain through my body that quickly twists into something pleasurable. The scream that leaves my body echoes through the air like a clap of thunder. Dominic's laughter ripples through me as he fucks me harder and deeper.

"*That's* a good girl. I knew you would do as you were fuckin' told."

My back arches and I tilt my head, moaning at the moonlit sky. I want it all, everything he can give me and maybe more. Every day. But I'm terrified to say it, to admit it to him or myself. I barely know this man, and our relationship seems to depend on my willingness to help him screw over Rene. Something that could be life-threatening.

I have to play my cards right.

"Bite me," I say, sounding more desperate than I intend. The edge of my vision is fading black, but I don't care. "Please, Dominic. Do it."

When he releases my throat, a flood of oxygenated bliss hits me all at once, and he wraps his arm around my torso, bringing our bodies closer.

He feels like a brick wall at my back, holding me tight against him as his fangs slowly pierce my skin. I scream again, this time feeling nothing but pure euphoria. It's better than any drink or drug I've ever taken. His gruff moans somehow sound sweeter as they rumble through my bones. I take over teasing my clit, pushing myself closer and closer to the edge as he continues to drink from me.

He's perfect. This is all perfect.

There's blood pouring down my breast, slipping beneath his thick tattooed arm that's covering my torso. My head is hazy, but my body feels more alert than it's ever been. I rub my clit harder and faster, quivering and whimpering until finally he dislodges his fangs.

The viciousness of his thrusts become more and more intense. The tip of his cock strokes my G-spot as unwanted tears sting the corners of my eyes, but I never let them fall. I squeeze them shut as hard as I can and try to calm my ragged breathing. God, my heart feels like it's going to burst out of my fucking chest. I can't even tell if I'm about to come or have a panic attack, but there's nothing to do but ride the wave.

"Come for me, Sofie. I know how close you are."

"It hurts," I sob.

"Do you want me to stop?"

His tone is mocking, condescending, and he knows it makes me angry. A wave of rebellious fury pulses through me and I grit my teeth.

"Don't you fucking *dare*."

His harsh laughter only spurs me on, my fingers clumsily circling my clit.

"Good girl."

It only takes a few more thrusts before I'm coming so hard my ears ring. The sound of my fingernails dragging across concrete underlines the desperate wail that erupts from the depths of my chest. It's primal, carrying everything I've been holding in for so long.

"That's what I wanna hear."

A few more brutal thrusts and his body stills, shuddering against mine. A whimper fills my ears. It's almost sweet, and he buries his head in my shoulder, moving his hips languidly as he pushes through the last dregs of his climax.

After a few moments united in our shared silence, Dominic pulls out of me and turns me around. His long fingers wrap around the hand that's now glistening with my slick. He examines it in the moonlight before popping each finger into his mouth one at a time and licking them clean. My nerves are only a little more than frayed wires, unsure if I'm still coming or just in the afterglow. Little aftershocks hit me every time I shift my weight, and my clit is practically rubbed raw. But if he asked me to go again, I'd agree in a heartbeat.

He pulls my last finger out of his mouth, kissing me sweetly. I can taste myself – different fluids mixed together into a sharp and sweet metallic slick on his tongue. When he pulls away, his eyes are that natural softer gold again, warm like the sun.

"Come on, let's head back up. I'll get you a robe, and we can finish dinner."

I nod and try to take a step forward, but nearly topple over in my heels. Immediately, he drops to the ground next to me and taps my calf.

"Lift your leg."

"I'm fine," I insist. "I just need a second."

He gazes up at me, tilting his head to the side and giving me a look that says he doesn't believe a word that's coming out of my mouth.

"Don't be stubborn."

I lift my leg and Dominic slides off one heel, and then the other, plucking them off of the ground as he stands up and takes my hand. Our relationship is reciprocal. We both need something from the other, but I have a feeling that the more I come to depend on him for sex, money, or protection, the more dangerous this is going to be. Just the way he wants it. But here, now, he's being so sweet and supportive, and I can't help but revel in it.

As he helps me inside, my legs wobble again, making it hard to even walk with his help.

And my head spins.

How hard did he fuck me? My hand squeezes his, and he glances back at me. My vision is hazy, but I can still make out a smile.

But this time, it doesn't bring comfort.

"What is it, little dove?"

There's something in his voice.

Something's wrong.

The walls feel like they're shifting and turning around me, and the look on his face fills me with dread. My eyelids get heavy, fluttering as my heart pounds in my ears.

And in an instant, I know I was right from the start. Something *was* wrong. It's been wrong the whole time.

I snarl and try to swipe at him, but he's too fast, dipping out of the way as I tumble to the ground. He swoops back just in time to catch me, barely stopping my head from slamming against the floor.

He cradles me in his arms, so softly, close and tight.

I feel the light caress of his hand on my cheek, and the warmth of his breath on my neck, just as everything goes black.

DOMINIC

Duncan Towers

I DIDN'T WANT TO do it this way, but I had a feeling she would ask for more. Conditions. Freedom. She'd want time, everything to be under her control, and I can't give any of that to her.

Not until Rene is dead.

He forced my hand. *Technically*, this is all his fault.

But thankfully she's here, she's safe, and she's mine. That's what matters. We can focus on our relationship when she wakes up, and fix all the little issues.

I sigh, kissing her on the cheek. She's beautiful when she sleeps, even if she drools a little. Her hair is like silk, rich coppery strands spilling all over my pillow. I see her eyelids flutter as an imperceptible sound escapes her lips.

I wonder what she dreams about. Is it me?

Jury's still out on whether she trusts me, but we'll get there. I brush her hair away from her face, watching her groan in her sleep. I'm not worried about her bindings coming loose, even if she wakes up, but I'm still anxious. All day I've been falling in and out of consciousness, fighting sleep for the chance to look at her, and to be there when she wakes up. I hold out for about half an hour before passing out, snap awake again, and the cycle repeats itself. I don't know what time it is, or how long I've been doing this for, but it's okay.

We have all the time in the world.

I nuzzle up against her, closing my eyes at the sensation of her warm skin against my cheek. She's like a furnace, and it's been so long since I've actually shared a bed with a human that I forgot how hot they can run. My legs tangle with hers, and each touch sends a jolt of bliss through my veins. It's almost better than drinking blood. She lets out the sweetest sigh, and I feel a little giddy. It seems like the only time she's not trying to fight how she feels about me is when she's unconscious.

Go figure.

I can't trust her if she won't trust me, that's what makes all this necessary, but over time I can convince her I'm doing this for her own good. With me in control, the humans can have free rein over their own affairs. Hell, we could even work together and build the population back up. We could live in the kind of harmony they hoped for back when Rene fed them all that bullshit about equality before putting them under his boot.

My mind is running wild with one key question: do I turn her? The selfish part of me says yes, but the cautious and more paranoid part says not yet.

Wait it out.

Neither Rene nor I make new vampires often. Mateo and Luke were the exception to my own personal rule because I needed numbers after the last clash, and even they were a risky call. So many vampires think they can just drain a human entirely and leave them to fade away. Some rip them to shreds. I know better. We need to keep our numbers stable. The more vampires there are, the more competition there is for food, and the less likely it is we can keep the wildcards in line. The only real regulations are imposed by Rene and I, and for the fear of running out of food.

Nobody wants to hunt rats in the sewer.

Not again.

Rene's motivations are a little different than mine, as he stopped making more vamps after what happened between the two of us. Betrayal bit him hard, and I keep biting every chance I get. Me though... My secret is I just don't really like to share. Besides, who needs an army of idiots when you have a real solid crew?

I almost slip back into sleep, but jolt awake just before I go under. Turning Sofie might be the endgame, but for now, I need her under my thumb. She's going to be hungry when she wakes up, and I've still got more steak in the fridge. She seemed to like it last night. Even said it was amazing.

That I'm amazing.

I place a kiss on her cheek, and she groans in her sleep.

"I'll be back in a bit, and you and I can hash this out."

I look like shit, feel like shit, and I need to feed. Not the fun, playful kind I do with Sofie, but for real. No matter how rough I feel, though, there's this manic energy that's infected me.

This whole dinner kidnapping thing was desperation more than anything. But it's working. Everything's going perfectly. Why plan if you get it all right on the first try, right?

I leave the bedroom and head straight for my record collection. I need some music while I cook. It clears my head, helps me think. So, something to fit the mood. I feel good – great, actually.

Rene's going to be dead in no time, and I'll rule Santa Cruz.

I find an old Temptations record and flip it over in my hands, scanning it. I slip the vinyl out of the cover and examine it for cracks and dust before sliding over to the record player when I find nothing amiss. Music booms through the speakers and I close my eyes, letting out a gentle exhale.

Ain't Too Proud to Beg. Maybe it'll make Sofie laugh.

I dance toward the kitchen and start fixing up dinner as I sing along to the music. I wonder if she likes to dance. I should have asked her. We could have had some fun.

But it's fine. We'll have time.

She's probably starving. She barely got to eat anything at all. Needs a bath, too. It's important that I take care of her. It's been so long since I've done this, I almost don't know where to start.

A sigh leaves my body, and I smile, glancing back toward the bedroom door. This feels like a honeymoon.

Then the apartment buzzer rings, dragging me from my thoughts. I curse and toss the vegetables in the pan a few times more before wiping my hands and heading for the front door.

"Who the fuck is it?."

"Dom, let me up!" Theo barks.

"You were supposed to be here *before* she got here last night! What the fuck happened?"

"I got held up!"

"Doing what?"

"I'll tell you in a minute. Just... let me up!"

I buzz him in and head back to the kitchen. Whatever it is, he can tell me while I'm working. Sofie comes first. Within a couple minutes, I hear the elevator door open, followed by the quick patter of Theo's footsteps. He paces a room or two before narrowing me down to the kitchen.

"Jesus Dom, there you are. We gotta talk."

"You get her stuff?"

Theo points at the dining room table. There are two large suitcases resting on it, and I give him a nod of approval before turning the heat down on the stove and heading over to them. Makeup, hair products, clothes, shampoo, perfume, jewelry. He got everything. I can't help the smile on my face as I glance back up at him.

"This is great."

"Yeah, sure, it's awesome," Theo replies flatly. "Listen, that thing we were gonna talk about? I got to thinking– you got the formula up here, right?"

"In the drawer."

I pull the key out of my pocket and toss it to him.

He nods and walks into the living room, returning with the piece of paper, his thick accent rising up as he mutters to himself.

"Yeah, see, I remember this... See this?"

Theo points to some numbers and letters that are all squished together with a bunch of lines underneath them. He might as well be asking me to read another language. I just nod and let him talk.

"This sequence here, whatever it is, ends up almost as pure as real vampire blood, but it's all mixed with some kind of new barbiturate that *only* works on humans. For us, it's a food source, maybe gets us a little fucked up, but for them...

It totally rewires the brain, makes them compliant, desperate for more. Maybe permanently." He looks up at me as I blink. "He's making a fucking bio weapon, Dom."

"Why the fuck...?"

Theo pinches the bridge of his nose.

"I swear to god, man, did Luke and Mateo's pea brains rub off on you?" He turns, furious, as his jaw ticks. "Jesus, can you *turn that music the fuck down*?!"

"Chill, Theo. God, make yourself a fucking drink."

Theo sighs and heads for the liquor cabinet while I check on the food. The steak is cooking nicely, and I flip it once before I hear a glass clink on the counter behind me. When I turn around, he's guzzling my Johnny Walker Blue right out of the bottle.

"Put that in a glass, you fuckin' animal!" I bark.

"Think about it," he tells me as he sets the bottle down, ignoring me. "Whatever's in that formula, it's coming out like vamp blood, and what do humans need our blood for?"

"Inoculations. Well, that and better sex," I reply.

"Exactly, and we need *blood* to survive, but it doesn't need to be human. We only go for them because it's dangerous to go after each other. This drug, whatever it is, It's a double-whammy!"

He paces around the room, waving his hands wildly.

"Look, if Rene gets them all hooked on it, says it's a substitute to start, or just distributes it as the real thing, they're done. He can keep whoever he wants completely hooked on this stuff and he can just kill the rest of them. He can produce however much of this shit he wants and *we* never go hungry. Think about it, he wants to remove them from the equation!"

"Slow down Theo, you–"

"It's even more important than we thought. Whoever controls that shit has *all* the power. If we have it, if we can actually synthesize it before he gets to us, you can force him out, completely take control of the city. You think his vamps won't flock to our side if you tell them they'll never go hungry?

I lean against the counter, crossing my arms over my chest. The inoculations are crucial to keeping humans alive. It's the key to our little balancing act, along with the blood bank.

Our system works, but it's taken years to perfect. Rene's looking for absolute control, squeezing the last ounce of power the humans still have. He's obsessed with it.

"So what you're saying is if he gets his hands on it again, it's an open buffet, right?"

Theo nods.

"You think he *likes* making deals with humans? He wants them to know their place. They already can't do anything without a meeting with him or his goons, but he wants to take even more."

"What's his endgame?"

"If he can disrupt the balance that *we've* created, he can round them all up and treat them like fucking pets. Remember, he talked about that shit back when everything first went down? You know how many rich vampires would jump at the chance for their own personal juice box right in their homes? Keep a few of 'em like fine fucking wine in a cellar and kill the rest."

"He's insane."

"Sure, he's nuts, but with that formula it won't matter. He'll be able to do it." Theo's bright eyes dig into mine. "It might as well be a fucking nuke, Dom, and if you hadn't burned down the entire goddamn lab, we might have had a chance in hell of figuring it out fast enough. Honestly, I can't believe we haven't been hit yet."

"What if it's all bullshit?" I ask. "You said it yourself, you can't really read it–"

"I said I couldn't *make* it, asshole, but that little redhead you kidnapped? She can. I found all this medical shit at her place. She even used to work at the bank. Give her a fuckin' mansion or something to keep her quiet, promise her endless blood for her bar, whatever you have to do to get what you want." He leans over the counter, his big sky-blue eyes glistening with hope. "It'll be you and me, all the way to the top."

It's what we always dreamed of, and now we have a way to do it.

It also means I am out of time when it comes to Sofie.

"I didn't kidnap her," I say softly. "I invited her for dinner and just didn't let her leave."

"That *is* kidnapping!"

"Tomato, tomahto." I wave him off with one hand. "And I'll get there with her, I just need a bit more time."

"It's not–" He takes a breath. "Look, just get her on board. Rene is hunting you, man. And the rest of us, too. I had to waste one of his men on the way here. *Make her* do what you want."

"It takes time."

"Time that you don't have, Dom. Shit's ramping up. You've crossed a line, like it or not."

I glare at him but he stares right back, not giving an inch. He's the only person I trust enough to call me on my shit, but what the fuck is he talking about me crossing a line? Rene wants to enslave what's left of humanity and *I've* crossed a line?

"Whose side are you on?" I ask.

"Yours," Theo snorts. "Fucking obviously. I just think that you've been…"

"Rash," I mutter.

"Stupid is what I was going to say," he counters. "You're obsessed with that girl, and now you've brought her into this."

"Because she can help."

"Yeah, and thank God she can, but you didn't know that when this all started. Besides, even if she couldn't, you'd still keep her here."

He's got my number, and we both know it.

"Look, man. You don't want anything to happen to her, right?"

"That's right."

"Then you have to get this shit moving and shut down whatever Rene's doing. Or he's going to deliver on those threats and do to Sofie what he did to Selene. He's angry, Dominic. He's setting up to slaughter us."

"I'll talk to her."

"Don't talk, *convince* her. Lie to her, tell her Rene knows everything, use the weapon angle, anything."

I scoff, and Theo raises a brow.

"Look, you can't just pull her teeth out, no matter how much you like doing that shit."

I know he's right, and I hate it. I wanted to give her a few days, take her back down to the lab and ease her into it, but we're on the clock now.

He perks up, but I'm not in the mood for another speech.

"The steaks..."

"I fucking get it, Theo, the stakes are high and we don't have time, but can you just–"

He points behind me.

"No, Dom, you're burning your steaks."

I whip around and see smoke wafting up from the pan, rushing toward it as I grab the spatula and turn down the heat.

"Goddammit!"

How the fuck did I miss the smell? I must be more exhausted than I thought.

"I'm heading back out," Theo calls as I salvage the non-charred pieces of steak.

"Where?" I shout back at him as I struggle to salvage the meal.

"I'm gonna figure out what Rene's next step is. Help us stay ahead of him. You just get her to make that shit!"

I sigh as he steps into the elevator and disappears.

Trying to forge a genuine relationship with Sofie is a luxury I can no longer afford. I'm going to have to convince her.

Tonight.

SOFIE

DUNCAN TOWERS

IT FEELS LIKE SOMEONE took a sledgehammer to my head.

No, that's not quite right.

It feels like someone beat me with a bat, and then ran my skull over with a fucking tractor.

A chill rushes down my spine as I struggle to force my eyes open. I can't see a thing. All I hear is music.

"Is that the fucking Temptations?" I groan to no one in particular.

This isn't how I wanted to experience their greatest hits.

Every one of my new aches and pains slowly make themselves known, dull pangs traveling all across my hips, down my spine, and all the way to my toes.

What the hell happened to me?

I know three things: I hurt so badly I want to throw up, I'm on my back, and I'm bound with the least comfortable rope I've ever felt.

Slowly, I try to lift my head. The dull ache turns into searing pain and I stifle a scream, which only causes *more* pain to shoot through my body. My heartbeat picks up, and I look around the pitch black room, eyes wide open as I struggle to see *something*. Anything.

I strain against the ropes again, but my arms and legs barely move, save for my heels slipping against sheets.

Silk.

I haven't touched silk sheets in years.

This doesn't smell like my musty room; this doesn't feel like my bed.

I'm not in my clothes. I'm not in *any* clothes.

Panic sets in and my breath comes out in ragged wheezes. This is all wrong. A wave of confusion washes over me. Where the fuck am I? And why am I tied to the goddamn bedposts?

Suddenly, the door swings open and I recoil as much as I can. Through a sliver of moonlight, he comes into focus.

Dominic.

I'd recognize that Cheshire grin anywhere.

"You're awake."

His voice is low and raspy, and I can see his pearly white fangs and yellow eyes glowing in the dark as he shuts the door. Some of the night's memories rush back to me, jumbled out of order, and Ice water floods my veins. He took my knife, I have no way to defend myself. Is he going to kill me? Is that why he brought me here?

A bloodcurdling scream rips through my body and echoes off of the walls, piercing my own eardrums. His yellow eyes remain still and empty as I flail against the bed, hoping against hope that I can somehow break my restraints and take a swing at this motherfucker. But every time I try to move, the ropes around my wrists dig and rip into my skin.

Another memory floods back to me: the terrace. Dominic fucking me. I couldn't walk in my heels. He took them off, and then everything went dark. He must have put something in my food, or maybe the wine? I never saw him do it, but I was so transfixed by the apartment that I let my guard down.

A wave of nausea hits me and vomit creeps up the back of my throat, but I swallow it in favor of letting out another, ear-piercing wail.

My chest is in a vice, and every part of my body is tender. Even the silk sheets against my bare legs send little shockwaves of pain rippling through me. I sob, gasping for air. The muscles between my ribs clench, like they're clamping down on my lungs and I weep harder. Through the tears, I can barely hear Dominic trying to talk to me, stroking my face.

Sofie, my love. Listen...

Sofie...

"SOFIE!"

I freeze, shaking like a leaf as sweat drips down my forehead. My palms are clammy and cold. I'm going to pass out, and all I can do is stare into those golden eyes that float above me, beautiful but empty.

There's a soft *click* and the light next to the bed turns on, bathing the room in a gentle yellow glow that's far too bright. I turn my head to the side, jamming my eyes shut to block out the brutal reality I've woken up in.

"Sofie, look at me."

"Fuck you!" I yell, burying my face in the sheets.

He laughs. *Laughs.*

The grip on my chin is so tender that it brings tears back to my eyes. He tips my head upward and presses his lips to my forehead. I wrench my body in retaliation, nearly ripping my arm out of the socket as I fight to get free. The pain is instantaneous and overwhelming, shooting all down my arm as muscles and tendons almost tear away from the shoulder joint. My spine arches and a pained sob spills out of me.

"Shh... shh," he soothes. "Calm down. You're hurting yourself."

I open my eyes, slowly at first. He's right there, smiling back at me, his expression almost love-struck. Quiet sobs continue to pulse through me like a current. I want to be brave. I want to spit in his face and tell him to let me the fuck go.

"There you are." He leans in and kisses me. I swallow the fury that's stuck in my throat. "My beautiful little dove."

Slowly, my breathing calms, and hysteria gives way to rationality. He's calm right now, but I've seen his temper. If I keep freaking out, if I make him too upset, he might just kill me. Slowly, he sits up, straddling me. Rough denim scrapes against my skin, making me wince as the warm smile on his face does little to comfort me.

Everything's changed.

"See? It's okay. You're with me. You're safe."

"What the *fuck*– you said one night. You were supposed to take me back to Nox, and instead you fucking *drug* me?"

To my surprise, he winces, his eyes sympathetic. I hate him for that.

"Well, it turns out I sort of lied. But it was for your own protection, Sofie." He pauses. "And you have something I want."

"I don't have anything! Let me go!"

Dominic shakes his head, shushing me as he leans forward and strokes my face.

"Hey, hey... yes, you do. You have that big, beautiful brain of yours that can make me rich — You'll get a cut, of course. I'll give you everything you could ask for."

How many times has he said that to me now?

"I just want you to let me go."

His expression darkens immediately at my words, and he lets out a sigh.

"I can't do that."

"Please, Dominic, just–"

"I. *Can't.* Do. That." He repeats each word so they sink in. "But it's for your own protection. You're too valuable, Sofie. Your skill set, your relationship with the blood bank... Rene knows about all of it. He wants to hurt you to get to me! To stop me. That's why I had to do all this."

"That's not true."

He's lying. Rene only knows I'm fucking him.

"It is. He told me. Called me up out of the blue."

My breathing is getting more and more rapid as panic takes me again. It's hard to reason with a madman.

"People are going to wonder where I am. We have a system. They know where I went."

"Of course. You're with me," he whispers. "Safe."

What happened to him? He was so charming last night, so sweet with that edge of brutality that made it even more exciting and raw. Now he's fucking unhinged, staring at me like I'm a puppy he just took home from the pet store. He leans in, and I recoil as much as I can until the back of my head slams up against the headboard. I wince, but try not to show the pain in my face.

"Ruby is expecting me at work."

"Don't worry about that. It'll be *fine.* You won't be stuck here forever. I just need you to make my–"

"I'm not fucking making *anything!*" I scream, trying to thrash under his weight like somehow I'm going to magically break my restraints and throw him off of me. "Get off! Let me go!"

Dominic sighs, gripping my throat with one hand and nearly cutting off my air.

"You *will.* You don't really have a choice."

When his other hand passes close to my mouth, I try to bite him, but he's too fast. He snatches a dark bottle off of the nightstand and holds it up in front of me as I continue to thrash and struggle beneath him.

"This is chloroform. You scream again, and you're taking another fucking nap."

This time, the warm look in his eyes has been replaced with pure malice. His anger is infectious, wafting off of him like heat from a forest fire.

"Suck my dick," I spit.

The vein in his forehead looks like it's about to pop.

"You want Rene's men to hear you from the street? Keep screaming. They're all over the place. They broke in here once, and they'll do it again. And they *know you.*"

More lies. All of that shit he told me at dinner about working with humans and the delicate balance that we have… it's all bullshit.

"Fuck you."

"I could just kill you, you know."

"And then who would make your stupid little formula?" I snap. "Unless you want to break into the bank and take someone from there, but that place would turn you into a rotisserie chicken and you know it."

The second I told him what I used to do before I owned the bar I saw something in his eyes that made me feel a pang of unease, one which stayed with me the whole night. I should have listened to that instinct. What the fuck was I thinking agreeing to have dinner with him? Ruby's got to be freaking out by now. The entire *bar* has got to be wondering where I am.

He leans in close.

"Make my formula."

"Walk into the fucking sun."

Dominic's lip curls and a growl rumbles in his chest.

"I save your life, and this is how you repay me?"

All of that charm he showed me at dinner has burned away. Now, he's panicked, desperate, and full of rage. I can't believe a single word that comes out of his mouth.

"You don't understand the danger you're in. You've never seen how fucking twisted Rene can be."

"If he's anything like you, then I guess I'm in for a real treat."

The hand around my throat squeezes tighter, crushing my windpipe as he leans in close, his fangs bared.

"It would do you well, little dove, to *never* make those kinds of comparisons. You don't know what he's capable of, or what he did to–"

He cuts himself off, loosening his grip.

"To who?" I choke through gasps of air.

"No one."

He lets me go, turning away.

Vampires aren't necessarily soulless creatures. They can feel love, just like anyone else. It's all just twisted with years of monstrous acts. If I appeal to what's left of his humanity, maybe that'll help.

I try to make myself look as pitiful as possible. It's not an arduous task considering how sorry I feel for myself right now.

"Dominic, if you care for me at all, you'll let me go. We can forget about all of this and start over, just–"

"It's not about me, Sofie. If I let you go, Rene's going to take you for himself. You think I'm lying? That he's not going to swoop in on you the second you leave here?"

"I talked to him twice, and the only thing he seemed to know about me is that you and I had fucked."

"He has eyes *everywhere*."

"And you don't? You play the underdog, but you both have more power than any of us could get in our lifetimes, and you choose to waste it on all of this Montague and Capulet *bullshit*?"

Dominic glowers at me, the harsh light making his features stand out that much more.

"You don't know how deep this goes." He climbs off of me, opening the nightstand and producing a small bottle. "I'll let you calm down for a bit, but you'll need painkillers."

"How do I know those are actually painkillers?" I snipe. "I thought you were feeding me a regular meal last night, but it turns out I can't trust anything you say."

"I'd like you to," he says softly, taking out two white tablets and handing them to me. "I hope you'll be able to again."

"You can't be serious."

"I am. This wasn't what I wanted. Rene forced my hand."

"You hold me hostage like I'm fucking Rapunzel and you still have the balls to look me in the eye and say you want me to *trust you*?"

"Look, Sofie. We're doing this either way, hard or easy. It's your choice."

I stay silent, glaring straight ahead.

"I'm not going to drug you."

"Again." I can't help but spit venom at him. "You're not going to drug me *again*."

He sighs.

"I didn't want to, but there was no other way to make you say yes."

"I said I wanted to think about it," I whisper. "You couldn't even give me that."

"And I would have loved to give you the time you needed, I even thought I might be able to, but that's not a luxury we can afford anymore."

I can practically feel the lines forming on my face as I scowl at him.

"Now, be a good girl. Open."

The phrasing rings against my brain white hot, and I remember those sweet words in my ear. He was just buttering me up, but I enjoyed hearing them all the same.

Slowly, my lips part and he places the pills inside of my mouth, grabbing a glass of water and lifting it to my lips. I guzzle it, my eyes closing as the cool rush of liquid spreads through every part of my body.

I'd say I've never felt so helpless, but that would be a lie. For some reason, my last memory of Charlie comes rushing back to me, of watching him through the clear plastic curtain as he took his final breaths. His eyes were locked with mine, and all I wanted to do was hold him. He didn't even have the strength to call out to me. There were so many tubes inside of him, pumping things in and out of his little body, but nothing helped. I felt as helpless then as I do now.

My throat clenches, and I choke on the water. Dominic removes the glass as I weep, staring at me with a helpless expression. He seems uncomfortable with emotion. I sensed it last night, too. My eyes squeeze shut, and I cry harder. All the grief and anguish that I've buried for the past five years is coming out now that I'm tied to this fucking bed and a prisoner to some sociopath with a vendetta.

"I'll be back with your dinner," he whispers.

Through my sobs I can hear him suck in another breath, as though he's going to make an addendum, but instead I only hear his shoes click against the floor as the door creaks shut.

At least he's left the light on for me. That'll make things easier.

I sit up straight, immediately stifling my tears.

I'm getting the fuck out of here.

SOFIE

DUNCAN TOWERS

I'VE BEEN FIGHTING AGAINST my restraints for what feels like hours, trying to figure out a way to loosen the knots so I can get beyond step one of my escape plan. Sure, so far it only really has two steps, but you have to start somewhere.

If Dominic had given me the time that I asked for in the first place, I wouldn't be strapped to a goddamn bed like I'm waiting for a priest to walk through the door and give me an exorcism. Hell, maybe we'd be in the middle of another wild fucking session. I'd take anything over this.

Still, while I've been trying to figure out a way to escape this hellhole, I *have* pinned down a weakness I can exploit.

He said this building was empty, that he *intended* to fill it with vampires and make it an apartment complex, but that it's currently just used for storage. That means that this building has security flaws. It's structured for individual private homes and not built like an impenetrable fortress. He bragged about his state-of-the-art security system, but I didn't see him reset an alarm when we reached the penthouse. There weren't more than the normal amount of locks. There didn't even seem to be any cameras.

Dominic Duncan is full of shit, and I'm going to use that to my advantage. I just have to turn this around and make him think that I'm falling in love with him all over again. It's got to be quick enough that he doesn't escalate his plan, but not so quick that he sees through it.

As if on cue, the door opens, and he steps in with two plates of food balanced on one arm. I smell steak mingling with charcoal. I think this might be all he knows how to cook. It's a lot less romantic than the first time.

"Are you going to behave and keep your voice down?" Dominic asks.

"Oh, I'm sorry," I snipe. "Is my current predicament a pain in your ass?"

Shit. This whole being sweet and complacent thing might be harder than I thought.

"I'm going to untie your hands so you can eat, alright?"

"Oh, what a shame. I was hoping you'd feed me each piece and make this a little romantic getaway."

Dominic glowers at me, his brows scrunched together. Is that guilt on his face? I swear I can see it, smell it permeating the room like a stench he's desperate to get rid of.

"Sofie, I didn't have a choice."

"Yes, you did, and we both know it."

"I don't want to fight."

Is this asshole seriously treating this like we're a married couple getting into a spat before bed? I want to go another round, but unfortunately the smell of food hits my nostrils again and my stomach betrays me, rumbling like an impatient lion. Dominic smirks.

"You're hungry."

"No shit," I spit back.

He sets the plates down on the nightstand and sits next to me, reaching over to brush my hair away from my face. It's hard to resist the urge to bite at him, but I let him have the moment.

"You've got a cut on your forehead," he murmurs, biting into his thumb and pressing it to my skin. I wince.

"I think that's probably your fault."

"It's like I said. I didn't have a choice."

My stomach is clenching, twisting in frustration, but I say nothing. No retort, no clever comeback. Right now, I just want to fucking eat. I stare up at him, a helpless look on my face.

"I thought you were going to untie my arms."

He tips my chin upward, brushing my bottom lip with the pad of his finger.

"Promise me you'll be good."

"I promise."

The words hit him just right, his eyes flickering.

"What else?"

Ugh. I'm not in the mood for this shit, not right now. But it could work to my advantage. Maybe he likes this whole Stockholm Syndrome thing. I let my face soften and watch his expression shift.

"I promise *sir*."

He smiles.

"That's my girl."

It's a small comfort when he unties my wrists, fluffing my pillows up for me before handing me a plate. He's careful to sit on the edge of the bed, far away from me in case I try anything. I snort.

"What, you think I'm gonna stab you with a dull fork?"

"I'm not sure." He looks so sad. I guess he wanted this all to just... work? To be fine? He's more deluded than I thought.

"Look, I'm not an idiot. If I stab you you'll just tie me back onto the bed, and I'll probably get steak and asparagus all over the floor. It's a lose-lose for me."

Dominic nods and moves closer. He's dressed more casually today, in a dark blue sweater and a pair of baggy black dress pants. I've never seen him look this domestic before.

I sit up a little, balancing the plate on a leg as I immediately start shoveling food into my face like it's the last chance I'll get. The meat is a little charred, but still flavorful enough. More than enough.

He looks up at the sound of my animalistic gorging as he swirls his own piece of steak around on his plate.

"Good?"

I don't know if it's just because I'm starving, or if he actually is a good cook, but the food is even better than it was last night. Looking down at the burned meat, I feel like it must be the former.

"Yes." I pause for a moment. "Thank you. You didn't have to do this."

Dominic blinks and flashes me a little smile. "Well, you'd be useless to me if I starved you."

Great, he thinks we're getting somewhere.

Another long silence works its way between us, only interrupted by the sound of my fork and knife against ceramic. Dominic watches me, having put his plate aside after only a few bites. Meanwhile, I'm hoovering this shit down as fast as I can.

Once I clear off my meal, I look over at his plate with envy. The juice from the steak drips down my chin, and Dominic wipes it away with his thumb.

"Still hungry?"

I nod. I wonder if this is how they feel all the time, starving for more while it's sitting right there, close enough to tear into if they only gave in?

He slides me his plate and I'm on it in seconds, moving my empty one to the nightstand.

"I think you could be happy here, Sofie. That's what I want most."

That's rich coming from him. I want to say it, but I bite my tongue. Instead, I lean into the plan: Convince him I'm coming around, just enough to get him to leave me untied, and get the fuck out of here once he falls asleep. He *has* to sleep sometime.

"Is it?" I ask, with significantly less venom than I'd like.

Dominic's eyes are bright, that manic look still swirling behind them.

"I can take care of you, just like I'm doing now."

I flash him a bashful smile and bite my lip. There's a flicker of confusion in his eyes, like he's expecting me to bite back. I have to stick to the plan if this is going to work. He thinks I don't trust him, and I have to start to build up from that fast. But I can fake Stockholm Syndrome, I've faked worse before.

How hard could it be?

"Thank you," I whisper.

He looks bewildered, his eyes scanning my face for any sense that I'm lying. I stare right back, keeping my whole demeanor soft. I was shit in the school play, but now I've bullshitted my fair share of idiots who think they're in love. The kicker is deep down, there's a part of me that still wants him. That's the part of me that wishes none of this shit happened and we were still in the feeding room, or back in his little lab.

I hate that part of me right now.

"That's it?" He asks.

"What do you want me to say, Dominic?" I put my knife and fork down onto my nearly empty plate. "Do you want me to fight you? You're a hundred times stronger than me, and you've got my feet tied to the bedposts."

I have to cut myself off before the anger seeps back into my voice. He needs to think I'm giving in, that I'm defeated at the very least.

His eyes fall, his entire body slumping like he's trying to get me to feel sorry for him. We're each playing the other, but he doesn't have anything on me.

I clear my throat and hang my head in return.

"I'm sorry."

He picks up the fork, stabbing one of the last pieces of steak and bringing it to my mouth. With his other hand, he tips my chin upward, forcing my eyes to meet his.

"Open."

My lips part and I let him feed me, knowing I don't have a choice.

"You're so beautiful, Sofie."

I want to scoff, but I hold it back as he continues to feed me what remains of dinner. His eyes are warm, but lonely. Pity creeps into my chest and as hard as I try, I can't push it away.

Once the plate is cleared, he sets it aside and sighs, glancing back over at me.

"I'm going to draw you a bath, but you have to promise not to act up."

"Yes, sir."

I'll play along for now. Tonight, I'm getting the fuck out of here.

He carefully unties my legs and I try to memorize the knot. If I can convince him to leave my hands untied tonight, that only leaves a couple of major road-blocks. There are deep bruises on my wrists from where I've struggled against my ropes, and I might just be able to tug at his heartstrings. Before I have time to check the state of my ankles, he scoops me up and carries me to the bathroom, placing me right on top of the counter. The lights are dim and the marble is freezing. I wince at the cold, and in an instant Dominic cups my face in his hands.

"Are you okay?"

I say nothing. I don't want this man's care or his pity.

His eyes search mine, and he smiles.

"You'll understand one day."

Soft lips press against my forehead, and I struggle to stay composed. I can't take this constant personality whiplash. He's so sweet one minute, but then there's a 50/50 chance the second I resist or fight back he'll catch me by the throat. I can't predict him.

Before he can fully turn away, I snatch his wrist and pull him back. I need to soften him up a little more, make him weak like I did back in the feeding room. A tiny part of me feels guilty for exploiting his... kindness? Obsession? There's clearly something wrong with him, but even now I'm the one who still wants to fuck him, so there must be something wrong with me, as well.

He looks a little dazed. Exhausted. The dark circles under his eyes are more prominent now than ever before, making the blue of his iris even brighter. I wet my lips slowly, and his eyes follow my sultry tongue with laser-like precision. A small fire erupts in the pit of my stomach, completely unbidden, and that tingling sensation rushes all the way down to my toes.

"Kiss me," I whisper. For a second he hesitates, but I pull him closer. "Please."

It's sweet, like a quiet apology, and it's all that it takes. He sighs softly as I run my fingers down his arms and slide them beneath his sweater, feeling his muscles tighten as I brush over them. His skin is cool and smooth, but I don't waste any time, dragging my fingernails through the small tuft of hair that leads right to his cock. He presses into me, going in for a kiss, and that's when I let him take control. My legs twist around his waist and I roll my hips, aching for more friction.

Dominic tears his mouth away from mine and ghosts his lips down my neck, nipping at me with his fangs. I groan and part my legs for him as his knuckles brush against me.

"You're wet," he groans. "So quickly."

My head falls back as he teases me, playfully dancing around my newly swollen clit with deliberate feather-light strokes. A deep ache thrums in my belly as the fire inside me burns more violent by the second.

"Whose fault is that?"

"I'm not really sure," he mumbles. "I thought you hated me."

He slides his fingers inside of me, quickly hitting the spot that makes me cling to him for dear life. When he hears the moan slip from my lips, he thrusts his fingers deeper.

"But this doesn't look like hate."

"Keep doing that and you might convert me."

He sighs.

"I still have to run you a bath."

"Fuck me first," I beg, letting my voice rise in pitch as his teasing strokes speed up.

If I'm going to escape, I might as well get laid beforehand. It'll be easier to convince myself to hate this asshole if I'm not aching for his cock.

"Say it again."

"Please, Dominic," I beg, tugging at his sweater. "Fuck me."

He pulls his fingers out of me and steps back as he drags his sweater off. No matter how many times I see it, my heart always skips a few beats at the sight of his bare, chiseled torso, and those tattoos that make him look even more intimidating than he already is.

But not around me. Not today.

Dominic sinks to his knees, staring up at me as he grabs one of my legs, taking care to be as gentle as possible with the bruises that wrap around my ankle. With each kiss, he works his way further up, refusing to take his eyes off of me. I catch a glimpse of his fangs as he sticks out his tongue and lets it trail along my skin.

"Always such a tease," I rasp.

He grips my hips and pulls me toward the edge of the counter.

"I want to taste as much of you as I can."

Warm breath fans my aching clit, and my body is so wired that even that's enough to almost make me come. My back arches and I grip his hair tight, pushing his face against me. Dominic's chuckle ripples through me as he lets the flat part of his tongue glide between my folds. I grab a breast, teasing my nipple as moans spill from me like wine.

At the very least, I'm going to miss this. The man eats pussy like a starving artist.

His tongue dips inside of me, curling ever so slightly. It doesn't have the same reach, but when his nose grinds against my clit I lose it, my eyes rolling back as my moans get louder and louder. I'm already so close, tidal waves of pleasure rocking my body.

My thighs clamp down on his head to keep him from pulling away. As I'm right on the edge, he slides two fingers inside of me, pushing against my G-spot. I cry out and come so hard I feel like I might see stars.

"I'm coming! Oh god, don't stop!"

Dominic fingers me right through my dizzying climax, but quickly gets to his feet and pulls me off of the bathroom counter. He spins me around and pushes my face into the cool marble, my limbs feeling like rubber as the aftershock continues to ripple through me. Not giving me a moment to recover, he pushes himself deep inside of me, pleasure folding over pain as my pussy clenches around his cock.

"That's it," he groans through languid thrusts. One hand buries in my hair and I feel his claws extend, grazing my scalp. "You like it like this, don't you?"

The goal was to make him feel confident that he owns me, so I guess my plan is working.

"You're gonna take all of me," he grunts. "Every inch."

"Yes, yes!"

"I know you're clever, little dove," he whispers in my ear.

My heart feels like it's completely stopped. Was I too obvious? Has he figured out what I'm planning? I begin to panic, but hold myself together just long enough for him to finish the thought.

"It won't take you long to finish that formula for me, and when you're done, we'll both get everything we want."

I can feel my whole body relax. Thankfully, it's just more grandstanding. Sure, it would have sounded tempting a day ago, but Dominic's proven he's the kind of man who talks a big game, but either can't or won't deliver. What I want now is the power to stop men like Rene, and even him. I'll never have it as a human, and I doubt he'll ever turn me. That plan went out the window about four and a half seconds after waking up tied to that bed.

My relaxation is short-lived as his thrusts become more and more vicious, stretching me open. Pleasure shoots through me again and again as my fingers curl, nails scraping against the countertop. A cool hand slips around my throat and forces my head up, turning me to face the bathroom mirror, and the image I see shocks me a little: a tear-stained face, mascara smeared underneath the eyes, and raw red lips cracked and bloody. I meet Dominic's reflected gaze as he squeezes, cutting off my air.

"I want you to see how beautiful you look when you come," he groans. "Just for me."

"Yes, sir," I groan.

He beams, his head tipping back a little as he thrusts deeper.

"There's my girl."

Dominic pulls me all the way up so that my body is nearly flush with his, my fingertips are just barely managing to touch the counter. He lets out a low hiss and bares his fangs, his eyes still locked with mine in the mirror. I'm already anticipating the pleasure of the bite as I tumble toward the edge. It always gives my climax that extra kick. God, I must be fucking delirious after being tied to that bed. He's made me crazy.

"Do it," I growl.

I cry out as he sinks his teeth into my neck. I can feel him draining me slowly, pain rushing to the site of the wound, but it's so quickly wrapped up in pleasure that I can't help but be swallowed up in this twisted bliss. Dominic lets out another deep snarl, rattling my bones before he tears his fangs away and finishes with a sinful moan.

Blood drips down my neck as his hips slow to a more languid pace, cock pulsing inside of me as he fills me up. His hand brushes affectionately against the small of my back, saying nothing as I slowly come back down to earth. A groan slips past my lips as he pulls out of me, and I'm immediately struck by the feeling of emptiness without him.

I fucking hate it.

I can hear the water crash into the tub as he starts the bath, and I manage to find the strength to push myself up and see my reflection once again, a rivulet of dark red blood running down my pale skin. The tattoos on my chest are smeared with it, crimson briefly obscuring Charlie's name before I lick my fingers and wipe it away. I stare at myself, feeling like I'm looking at a complete stranger as I recall what Dominic had said last night. I put my finger to my lips, tasting my own blood. He had said I was sweet, like a strawberry popsicle.

All I taste is rusted metal left out in the rain.

He watches me with fascination, and I wonder what it would be like to be in his position. To be him.

I want what he has: the power, strength, speed.

All of it.

If I were one of them, this never would have happened. I could have put him down before he hurt me. I could have slaughtered Rene for disrespecting me. I could protect everyone at Nox.

Dominic slips out of his pants and kicks them aside, his body on display for me as he holds out a hand. The hand of a captor, desperate to be my savior.

So I take it.

It'll be the first thing of many.

DOMINIC

DUNCAN TOWERS

I SIT ON THE bed, watching Sofie the same way I used to watch Selene go through her nightly routine. She pulls a nightgown over her shoulders as her long copper hair cascades down her back. There's a part of me that's been reliving my old life together, but Sofie's got sharper edges. There are more glares, which is fair considering what I've done.

"Have you reconsidered?" I ask.

"Reconsidered?" She echoes.

"Making the formula."

She turns to me and grabs a brush off of the dresser. It's an ivory handle with little gold flowers decorating it. My mother's hairbrush, and the only thing I have left of her. It must be well over a hundred years old by now, passed down through the family.

Sofie runs it through her hair, little flecks of water dripping onto the floor.

"I want something from you."

My eyes fly up and down her body, admiring the way the silk clings to her curves. She's close enough to reach out and touch, but I keep my hands to myself. Watching her. Her demeanor has changed since our romp in the bathroom. I figured she was planning something, and now I get to find out what.

"And that is?"

"I want you to leave me untied tonight."

"No."

I don't even have to think about it.

She huffs, folding her arms across her chest, and I remember what Theo told me. Give her more freedom. Convince her any way you can. In theory, the more I slacken the rope, the more she might cooperate with me. Everything I know about Sofie, however, defies theory.

"You're not negotiating your way out of these ropes," I tell her.

"I'd like to sleep comfortably."

"And I'd love to let you, but I need to trust you first. You made your feelings extremely clear."

"You're an asshole," she spits.

I grin.

"Proving my point."

I stand up and take a step toward her, gently grasping her bruised wrist and bringing it to my lips. Her cheeks flush, and I can feel that strange affection creeping back into me.

"You've been far too sweet."

"I'm being a good girl," she whispers. "Just like you want me to."

We're at an impasse, each of us staring straight through the other. My skin bristles as she gently pulls her arm away, forcing me to relinquish my grip on her. Her hands caress my face, nails scraping at the stubble on my chin.

"Just my wrists," she whispers. "And not above my head. How's that for negotiation?"

"Not bad, little dove."

"You can even watch me sleep."

I narrow my eyes and tilt my head.

"What are you planning?"

"Nothing. Why are you always so suspicious?"

"It's in my nature."

She trails a fingertip down my bare chest, tracing my tattoos.

"I think that's just something you tell yourself."

"Oh, do you? You get a minor in psychology along with that PhD?"

"Just an educated guess."

Her arms slide around my waist. Even if this is fake, I'm content to let myself fall into the comfort of the gesture. The humanity of it. As much as I spend my time mocking and tormenting humans, part of me is afraid that I've lost what makes them feel so alive. I take pleasure in death, crave it. But they can still get their hooks in me, even now.

My arms wrap around her, and I close my eyes, just for a moment. I'm transported to quiet mornings with Selene, smelling her skin and hearing her silky sweet voice.

I've missed these moments. Holding someone, feeling a heartbeat against my body.

The thought of turning Sofie has occurred to me more than once, but it'll have to wait. I have to monitor her, ensure I have her trust and can trust her in return, then we can move forward. That was the mistake that Rene made, after all. He was arrogant, desperate for progeny he could mold in his image. So desperate, in fact, that he created his greatest enemy.

I look down at her and smile.

"How's this, I'll tie your wrists to the bottom of the bedposts and leave your ankles free."

She gives me the sweetest smile, one I'm so desperate to trust.

"Thank you."

I nod.

"Let's make up your bed. You need fresh sheets."

I grab new linens out of the bottom drawer of the dresser, and to my surprise, she helps me make up her little prison. Wordlessly, we strip the bedding and I toss the old stuff into a pile on the floor. We tuck the fresh sheets under each corner of the bed and I take the time to fluff up her pillows as she lingers by the dresser, holding one of her wrists.

I raise a brow.

"Does it hurt?"

She shakes her head.

"I was just wondering something."

"What?"

"You're gonna keep me here, right?"

"Until Rene is dead and the formula is made, yes."

She stares at me and I wait for more questions, or at least an acknowledgement. I'm met with bitter silence and a furtive glance. I want to tell her about how dangerous it all is, that Rene has a weapon he can turn on every single human, but that's a conversation for tomorrow. Once we've both had a decent sleep, we can sit down and hash this thing out.

"There's something I need. It would help me feel a little more at home."

Every word feels measured and meticulously chosen.

"Name it."

Sofie chews on her bottom lip.

"At Nox, there's a picture on my desk of Charlie. My son. You bring me that picture and I'll do it." She has tears in her eyes and my heart just about cracks. "I have to be able to see him. I won't work without him."

I won't fight her on this. I can't imagine a world where a picture of her son will be a key part of some plan to work against me. Besides, even if it was, I can have Theo scour the frame just to be sure.

"I'll send someone to get it for you right away."

"Thank you. And please tell Ruby that I'm here and that I'm okay. She's probably going fucking nuts."

I shake my head.

"*That* I can't do."

"Why?" She snaps. "You think my best friend is going to sell me out to your little rival?"

"Nobody but Theo, Mateo, and myself know that you're here. We keep it that way, and we keep you safe."

She scoffs and leans against the dresser, all of that sweetness sucked out of her like the air deflating from a balloon.

"Okay, then tell Theo good luck getting into my office because if she sees him back there, she's going to put a bullet between his eyes. You wanna lose your best pal, then be my guest, Mr. Duncan."

It's funny, Theo would probably tell me the same thing. There's not a single part of me that's used to any of this shit. You'd think kidnapping would be in my repertoire, but to be honest, I can't even remember the last time I pulled a stunt like this.

"Fine, fine. He'll let her know."

She smiles.

"Okay.." She moves toward the bed and lies down flat on her back, arms spread out in preparation. "So, you gonna tie me up?"

It's supposed to be a joke, but I can't help the pang of regret that echoes in my chest. I don't want to do this, so I'm gentle with her wrists, making sure not to tie the knots too tight.

"Thank you," she breathes.

I smile at her and catch a flicker of warmth in her eyes.

"You're welcome."

Once she's secured, I brush a few strands of hair away from her face.

"I'll be back when you wake up with breakfast."

"Real breakfast?"

"Would you believe me if I told you I could make pancakes from scratch?"

"Absolutely not." Her eyes shine and another smile tugs at the corners of her mouth. "But I didn't believe you'd kidnap me either."

It's been a while since I've felt shame like this. I lean down and kiss her forehead.

"Goodnight, Sofie."

"You're not sleeping here?" She asks as I put my hand on the door handle.

I turn to her and shake my head. She's still fragile, processing this new future that I've already planned in my head.

"Not tonight."

With that, I step into the hall, letting the door shut behind me. There's no key. I never designed the bedroom with locks in mind. I always thought whoever was in there with me would be a willing participant, or dead long before anything like this could happen.

———◦❈◦———

I've shifted the couch so that I can watch the bedroom door, my eyes flicking up to it every half-minute or so. I haven't heard a sound in a few hours beyond her heartbeat. It varies between calm and erratic, but whenever I go to check on her, she's asleep, her head turned to the side. Nightmares.

Whiskey burns my throat and the sound of rich classical music fills the room as I rifle through Sofie's purse. She has a wallet with all of her ID cards in it, and punch cards for her inoculations.

"Sofie Fournier. Born July 25th, 1958 in Los Angeles, California."

I toss the ID onto the coffee table and keep flipping through the wallet, finding a birth certificate. The ink has faded from years of being folded up. I take another sip of whiskey.

"Charles Jonathan Fournier. Born October 31st, 1977. Parents, Sofie and Samuel Fournier."

No death certificate. Of course, there was no more government to hand them out. All of the bodies were burned or devoured by us.

By the worst of us.

There's nothing else in her purse except for a gun and a tube of lipstick. Nothing else to know that I can't just ask her, that she probably won't tell me. My search of her purse has yielded no insight into who she is other than what she's told me. I can't shake this paranoia.

She's not secretly a vampire, and she's not secretly working for Rene. That's a plus, I guess. I take the bullets out of her gun, hissing through my teeth the second they drop into my hand. They clatter onto the coffee table and I smirk as the smoke rises off my lightly charred skin. I place the gun in the drawer beside the couch, locking it up along with the formula, and slip the key into my pocket.

I love the fact that she's clever. Sometimes, I'm even turned on by some of our sparring, but I miss when she trusted me. Maybe that's what's feeding my paranoia — that and the fact that I haven't slept a goddamn wink since she's been here. God knows I've tried, but this whole thing with Rene is eating at me, and this couch is a hell of a lot less comfortable when you're not working off a wild bender. The floor is even worse, but I continue to resist the urge to head back to the bedroom and join her. It's still hard to tell if she hates me or not, but I'm still leaning toward yes. I'd probably hate me too.

I'll earn her trust, and I've already started. The clothes, the negotiations, the picture—

Fuck, I almost forgot.

I grab the phone and dial Theo's number. There's still a few hours until the sun goes down.

It rings. And rings. And rings.

I tap my foot incessantly against the tile. I'll let it ring until this son of a bitch picks up. He's home. He always is around this time. Theo has never would never risk being caught in the sunlight, and he'd never go out without a mission. He's far too meticulous..

Finally, the line clicks in, and I hear the muffled sounds of a woman moaning. I can't help but break out in a smile.

"Yeah?" He sounds worn out, but there's a twinge of irritation there, too. *"What do you want, Dom?"*

"How the fuck did you know it was me?"

"You're the only guy who calls before my bedtime, asshole. Now hurry up, I'm busy."

I wonder who the woman is, but I know better than to ask.

"I need you to do something for me."

"Like I said, I'm busy," he grunts, followed by a slap and a muffled, *"Shut the fuck up."*

"Are you finally getting some pussy?" I ask with a grin.

"Uh-huh, sure. So what do you need?"

"Tomorrow night, I want you to go to Nox and tell Ruby where Sofie is."

"Okay, but why?"

I frown. Things are a lot less funny when he pushes back.

"Because I'm telling you to. Is there a fucking problem?"

He sighs and I can picture his extremely exaggerated eye-roll.

"Dom, the more people who know where she is—"

"Then threaten her to keep her quiet, I don't give a shit. We get this done and she'll work on the formula." I pause for a moment. "Speaking of, I need you to get something from Sofie's office and bring it to me while you're there."

"What?"

"A picture of her son. It's on her desk."

There's silence on the other end of the line. I examine my claws and click my tongue as the seconds tick by.

"It was your advice, sunshine. Do whatever it takes to get her to do the work, right? Well, this is what it's gonna take, so get your ass out there and bring it here."

"Fine. Fine. You're right. I'll see you tomorrow night."

The last thing I hear as the line goes dead is the start of a long, drawn-out moan.

"Good for him."

I finish my drink, abandoning the empty glass beside me on the sofa cushion. My body sinks into the couch and I close my eyes, completely exhausted. It's all hitting me at once, and I can practically feel the weight of the sun press down on me as it rises.

Just a couple of minutes. That's all I need.

Besides, soon we'll have all the time in the world.

SOFIE

DUNCAN TOWERS

SOMEHOW, I'VE KEPT MY heart rate mostly under control as I wait for him to fuck off. He's been outside my door for what feels like hours now, and he's almost caught me a couple times, coming in to check when he senses some shit or another. He has a tremendous advantage here. Those senses, his speed... But I have some perks too. The main one? I'm not a fucking idiot.

Luckily for me, he used far looser knots this time. He probably felt bad about the bruises. Good, he fucking should. With a little more work, I'll be able to slip them, but it's taking a *while*.

They make this shit look so easy on TV. I guess that's what I get for basing the first part of my plan on shitty cop shows.

I keep wiggling my wrists, ignoring the burning sensation building up against my skin. My left hand is faring better than my right, so that's the one I'm going with first.

When he was tying me up I was able to position myself so that I'd have enough slack to bend my elbows. Dominic didn't seem to notice. He was too busy making doe eyes at me and laying little kisses on my forehead. He's so fucking delusional.

I hear a brief and muffled conversation on the other side of the door, spiking my heart rate as I drag the rope up and down the bedpost, but thankfully he doesn't come to check in on me.

I'm not even sure how long I've been here anymore. It feels like at least two nights now, but it could have been more depending on how long he kept me drugged. He doesn't keep clocks in this room, and there aren't any windows, so I have no clue if I'm escaping into the sunlight or not. A massive wave of exhaustion washes over me and I have to take a break.

I close my eyes for just a moment and already feel myself slipping into unconsciousness, not quite asleep but not quite awake. I want to cry and scream and thrash, but all of that takes energy. Loosening the ropes is taking all that I have. I can't imagine being able to make it back to Nox in this state during the night, so I hope beyond hope that I'm escaping into the brightest fucking sun I've seen in years.

My mind runs through scenarios, the visions dreamlike and hazy as they blend with the nightmarish images that flood my head. In one, Dominic is chasing me through the streets, the moon high in the night sky. Glass and rocks dig into my bare feet, and the sensation is so real that I wince from ethereal cuts. Unfortunately, the smell of my blood only makes him more feral.

I make it a few blocks, almost to the doors of the blood bank, but in the end, he catches me, bashing my head against the wall over and over. All I can hear is him screaming that he did this for me.

All for me.

In another I don't even make it out of the tower. He slashes my throat with a steak knife as I claw at the elevator door. He's telling me he's sorry. That he loves me.

I gasp, sitting straight up as I'm shocked awake, only halted by the sharp burning sensation from my bindings. Anxiety vibrates against my nerves, and a strange buzzing sensation lingers in my skull as I run through a slightly less depressing outcome. First, I get out of the building, which should be easy if I can make it to that elevator undetected. He has to sleep sometime, and if I can take advantage of that I'll have an easy ride to the lobby, and then it's just another quick dash to the blood bank.

I have to be careful, keep it quiet, and find Jesse without getting too much attention from the other guards. I'm tempted to ask Avery for help, but she's made a lot of deals with Rene over the years. Who knows who she really works for. Jesse, though... I know I can trust him. And if I can't, I'm dead anyway, so I may as well try. If I make it that far, it's a clean shot to Nox by car. Even Dominic wouldn't try anything there.

My little nap, combined with my at least half-decent plan, gives me a surprising burst of energy. This time it's only a few minutes of wiggling my wrists before my hand finally begins to slip loose, my heart soaring as I feel the first rope give way. It looks like positivity pays off sometimes after all.

With my eyes locked on the door, I reach over and work the other knot with my newly freed hand. It's not nearly as easy as I thought it would be; I'm shaking so much that I keep fumbling the rope. My fingers are tingling from the new rush of blood flow, but I force myself to take calming breaths, making sure not to make too much noise.

After another few minutes, the knot finally loosens enough for me to slip my fingers inside, and I have to hold back an excited yelp as the loop slackens and falls away. I don't waste time resting or rubbing my wrists, no matter how much they ache. I'm on my feet in a second, searching for my purse. My gun is in there, and if I find it, I'm putting a bullet through his head on my way out. The drawers next to the bed are empty, save for a set of keys to a Jaguar.

I snatch them up with a smile and keep looking, padding swiftly to the closet and opening it up as quietly as I can.

I'm met with clothes from all different decades, like some sort of eclectic exhibit at a museum. I rifle through them, finding leather jackets, bell bottoms from the '60s, platform shoes and so much more.

It's hard not to get distracted in here. But there's nothing to use as a weapon save for shoes and belts. I'd have to be dangerously close to wrap one of those around his neck. Besides, the fucker would probably be into it.

I abandon the closet, leaving it open as I search the rest of the room to find... nothing.

He really prepared for this. Ensured there was no risk in leaving me here alone. Maybe that's it though, he prepped for me to be in *here*. There has to be something outside that I can use.

My stomach starts to swirl as I head for the door, my heart thumping loud enough I worry I might have already tipped him off. Still, I can't stay in here forever. He's going to come back soon, and there's no way I can put those ropes back into place correctly. When he sees I've gotten out, he'll punish me, hurt me, and tie me back up. Maybe for good. And that's the best-case scenario.

I've seen him mad before.

My trembling fingers wrap around the doorknob and I purse my lips, pushing out a quiet breath as I crack the door ever so slightly. My entire body clenches like a fist, muscles wound so tightly I feel like I might collapse in on myself. Adrenaline rockets through me, my fight or flight instincts kicking in as I have no idea which one to embrace.

And then I'm met with silence.

Darkness.

The large window from before is completely covered with massive blackout curtains. If I'm lucky, it's daytime, but I don't dare risk bringing attention to myself by checking.

I take one step, muscles already screaming at me to give up.

Go back.

Collapse.

Despite the warning, I take another step, the cool tile keeping me light on my toes.

Quiet.

Careful.

Can he hear my heart beating?

Shh.

How could he not?

The tension in the room is so thick, it strangles me. My fingers tingle and I feel as though I'm watching myself from above, like a movie.

As I take another step forward, the elevator finally in view, I suddenly freeze. I glance down and there he is, splayed out on a couch he's dragged into the middle of the room. I almost walked right fucking into it.

But I didn't. Thank fucking God.

I hold my breath, trying not to move as I take in the whole situation. His head is tipped back, his mouth hanging open. I think he's sleeping, but it's impossible to tell if his eyes are closed in the low light. It could be a trick, part of some sick game he's playing with me. Maybe if I turn back now he'll forgive me. The moment of panic almost convinces me, but that would be it. There'd be no coming back.

My hand rests on my chest and I close my eyes, willing myself to calm down. I'm no good to anyone if I have a heart attack and die on his floor.

I glance to the right, where I vaguely recall the kitchen is.

Knives. He has knives. He was flipping one last night — was it last night?

I creep into the kitchen, slipping past the counter where I sat drinking wine as he charmed me. There was a moment, then, when I thought we might make something of the spark between us, but now a heavy bitterness floods my chest in its place. It creeps down into my guts and quickly festers into a seething rage.

I set the keys down and scour the room for anything I can use as a weapon, but drawer after drawer reveal absolutely nothing: no knives, no scissors, nothing to stab him through his shriveled little heart. Maybe he had them all removed, just in case. He might be smarter than I thought after all, or maybe he's just really goddamn paranoid.

In the end, I settle on a lone meat tenderizer, snatching it up in an instant and testing the weight in my hand. It's heavy, maybe enough to put a real dent in his skull given the chance. Not enough to kill him, but enough to slow him down.

I want to look for more, something that'll actually make me feel safe, but Dominic could wake up at any moment, and the less noise I make the better.

More details come into focus as I make my way back toward the elevator, and past my resting captor. The texture of the couch, the stubble on his face... and my *fucking purse*, like a glowing red beacon in a storm.

There's just one problem.

It's resting right on his goddamn chest.

I stand at the edge of the couch, watching him. No pulse to speak of, no rising and falling chest. He doesn't need to breathe, he only does it when he's conscious, probably leftover physical conditioning from his humanity. His eyes are closed, his eyelids twitching.

What the fuck could he be dreaming about? Can vampires even dream?

His lips press together, and then more into a smile. I swallow hard and something shiny pulls my focus away. The bullets from my gun are scattered all across the coffee table.

Suddenly Dominic shifts and I drop to my knees, crouching behind the arm of the couch. I don't know how deep vampires sleep, and I'm not about to find out. He pulls my bag tighter to his chest, like he's cuddling a fucking teddy bear. My throat is burning, dry and desperate, and every muscle feels like it's one moment away from betraying me.

I don't have time to look for the gun. The tenderizer will have to do.

I push myself to my feet and head for the elevator, and I hear him grunt behind me. I freeze in place, turning my head as carefully as I can, a ragged breath held still in my chest.

But it's alright. He's still asleep.

For now.

I have to go. Now. I have to run.

My hand reaches out for the button on the elevator before logic takes over, and I pull back just in time.

Elevators make noise. It dinged when we arrived the other night. The doors grind as they open. There's no fucking way he sleeps through it, not with hearing like that.

Fuck, that can't be it.

There has to be another way out of here.

I stifle a cough, my throat screaming for water. With the meat tenderizer in one hand, I press myself against the wall, creeping forward step by step, desperate for something, but with no idea what I'm looking for.

Until my fingers bump up against a small slit in the wall.

I turn my body to the side, keeping one eye on Dominic as I trace my fingers along the crack. It feels cool. Maybe that means airflow? My eyes strain in the dark as I feel around with my hands, searching for anything that could force it open. I sink to my knees and run my fingers along the seam down to the floor, before I finally bump against something tiny sticking out at the very bottom. A switch?

There's a soft click, and there it is. Of course he has a secret fucking exit.

It's then that I realize I left the keys to the Jaguar on the counter. I look back at Dominic, and then to the kitchen. It may as well be miles away from here. I've gotten this far on luck, I can't risk another minute in this place.

Hopefully, I get out long before he realizes what's happened, but I'm only focused on my freedom as I slip into the darkness of the passage.

I'll kill him to get it, if I have to.

DOMINIC

DUNCAN TOWERS

I WAKE UP WITH a harsh gasp, blinking furiously as my eyes scan the darkness.

Fuck.

How long was I out?

I sit up and glance at my watch.

Two hours to sunrise.

Something falls onto the ground and I groan, seeing the contents of Sofie's purse scatter all over the floor. I meant to close my eyes for a second, not a goddamn hour.

I glance over at her door, more as a reflex than anything, and stare at it for a moment in complete shock. It's wide open. I leap to my feet and rush to the bedroom, greeted only by emptiness, her scent still lingering in the air. Panic leads to rage. She fucking tricked me. She played me, used my kindness and threw it back in my fucking face.

Never again.

I dash back into the living room, heading straight for the elevator before I see something move ever so slightly from the corner of my eye. The hidden door, swinging ever so slightly as cool air slips past it. She must have realized the elevator would wake me, but she'd have to walk right past me to find the switch. How did I not hear her?

I scan the rest of the penthouse and spot my car keys sitting on the kitchen counter.

Clever little bitch. She's brave all right, but she must have panicked.

If she makes it to the lobby, there's no way she makes it out the front door. It's locked from the outside, all the glass is reinforced... but maybe she could find a way. If anyone could, it'd be her. Fuck, why can't she realize that the safest place in Santa Cruz is right here with me?

Well, it was an hour ago.

I head for the door she escaped from, peering down into darkness. I can just make out the sound of her heightened heartbeat in the distance, her feet squeaking against the tile as a door slams. My face twists into a wicked grin. She's still about 10 floors from the bottom. More than enough time.

I peel off my shirt and kick off my shoes. I always prefer to hunt barefoot, to feel the earth beneath my feet – or the marble floor, I suppose. The thrill of the chase courses through me as I let my instincts take over, leaping five or six stairs each at a time as I race to catch up to my prey. I can see everything like it's daylight, every heightened sense pushing me forward as I leap down another flight of stairs. Darkness has always embraced me like a brother.

In another instant, I can smell terror mixed with something else... the faintest scent of arousal? Even in the midst of this betrayal, I can't help but long for her. She's so sweet, and her fear will make her even sweeter.

More footfalls, and another slamming door, all much closer now. I've bounded down so many flights she has to be only another floor away.

I swing open the door to the next floor, the sound of her blood roaring like a raging river in my ears. My fists clench at my sides and I take a step forward, my foot meeting the cool stonework. I can hear her breathing, smell the sweat that clings to her skin.

I've missed this.

I know exactly what room she's in, not completely trapped, but with no actual way to make it outside. Impressive that she made it this far, only a few floors away from the lobby. I slow to a meandering stroll, inhaling the fear in the air that gets me harder by the second. Maybe I should turn her after all. She'd be able to handle my strength, my urges. It really is such a shame that I always have to hold back. I want to show her everything I can do to her. With her.

I stop in front of the door and click my tongue, raking my claws across the surrounding wall. There's nothing but this glorified plank of wood between us; I can hear her toes curl, sliding against the floor. Her heartbeat is like a hummingbird's wings as I turn the doorknob, standing in the threshold of a nearly empty room.

I take a deep breath, sniffing the air. Her pussy might as well be right in front of my mouth, taunting me. I turn my head to the side, seeing the door shift just a little. She's right behind it, struggling to control her breathing. She doesn't know how loud she's screaming her location to me.

"Come out, come out, Sofiieee," I sing. "We'll forget this whole thing ever happened, I promise. I won't even rip you apart. Not completely."

Suddenly, a deafening crack echoes through the room, accompanied by a dull pain that crushes its way into me. I can feel bone fracture in the back of my skull as I stumble forward, and can already taste blood as I reach back to feel a large gaping wound. The echoing sound of a violent scream pierces my ears. I have no clue if it's mine or hers.

I don't even get a moment, my face crumpling as I turn straight into another blow. I feel a wet heat pouring out of me.

By the time I get my bearings, she's already sprinted from the room, and with a rumbling growl, I give chase. When I make it out into the hall, she's halfway to the staircase, straight for the lobby. There's no other option.

Thank God I ate today. Healing won't take too long.

And then she's *mine.*

My feet pound against the floor and I leap forward, clearing half the hallway and just barely missing her as she rushes into the stairwell with a panicked scream. I'm right on her tail as she makes her descent, a vicious sneer on my face as blood pours down my torso from the wounds she made, already half-knit. Is this what she wanted? To see me at my most brutal? I hope she knows what she's done, because all I want right now is to fuck her raw, until she's begging me to let her rest. Until she's completely broken.

Her fiery hair trails behind as she flies down the stairs, skipping steps and hopping the railing to hit the landing twice as fast as I expected. Fuck, I love this.

I feel free, like a wild beast let out of a cage. As angry as I was that she's tried to escape, I should thank her. If she lives, at least.

Even after I leap down one of the final flights of stairs, landing just a few paces behind her, she still doesn't look back. I slow myself down, prolonging these last moments of the chase. Every so often I reach out to brush my fingers against her hair, or leg, or arm, barely missing just to tease her. Each time she shrieks and speeds up, but I can tell her legs are growing sluggish, her breathing becoming more and more ragged.

The smell of sweat and desperation hangs thick in the air.

On the second floor landing she slips through the door ahead of me, turning and slamming it down my fingers with a brutality I don't quite expect. I yelp, feeling the crunch of bone as they break. Before I have a chance to pull them away, she smashes them again, this time with that goddamn mallet. I let out another sharp scream as I hear her feet slam down the hallway. This isn't just fear and panic. She wants me to hurt. Wants me to suffer.

I swallow the pain, using my mangled fingers to tear the door open just in time to see her dash inside of a waiting elevator. She roars, smashing the button over and over, but it doesn't light up.

Of course it doesn't. Does she really think I'm that stupid?

I stride toward her, my slow and methodical footsteps echoing through the hall as I spread my arms.

"Come on, Sofie. I shut it all down. You had to know I would."

She turns to me, her wild eyes struggling to see in the dark hallway as she brandishes her shockingly effective weapon.

I smile.

"This is what you want, is it? To play hard to get?"

"I want to leave, you piece of shit!"

I stop, maintaining the distance between us. She snarls.

"I told you, little dove. You're here for your own protection. That, and to give me what I want. You're not going anywhere."

She's white-knuckling the handle of the mallet as she draws herself up to her full height, her copper hair like angry flames licking the air. As much as she professes to hate me, there must be a part of her that's just as enraptured as I am with her. The scent of her arousal is heavy on my tongue, and the jackhammer of her heartbeat drives me even wilder. Still, I hold myself back for the treat that's still to come; the realization that soon eclipses her angelic face. That there's no escape.

But that's the best part.

She's going to try anyway.

There was something about her that first night I saw her, a darkness in her eyes that seemed to permeate her entire being. It's the thing that draws me to her, regardless of how much she pushes me away.

I take a step toward her and she breaks into a dash, straight for the door at the end of the hall. A door that leads straight down to the lobby. This time I don't rush, I don't chase. I merely saunter after her.

The game is almost over.

No way to win.

No escape.

DOMINIC

DUNCAN TOWERS

BY THE TIME I step into the lobby, she's already using the mallet in a feeble attempt to smash the glass. Grunts of effort bounce off of the walls as she gets nowhere, barely making a dent, yet even in all her chaotic flailing, she manages to look stunning.

"It's vampire-proof glass." I flex my still-healing fingers, the bones sliding back into place with a series of satisfying pops. "Which is just a fun way to say shatter-proof. I must have told you that."

She turns to me, panting, eyes wide and rabid. Her body is taut, fully primed for a fight.

"No more bullshit. You let me *go!*"

"Bullshit?" I ask, taking a step forward. "You think this is all bullshit?"

She backs up and raises the tenderizer above her head.

"Get back!"

"I think you're the one who's bullshitting. I can smell you from here, Sofie. You like to be chased, don't you?"

She spits at me, pressed up against the glass. I can see condensation forming in an outline around her body, like a halo. I chuckle and take another step forward.

"I said *back!*" She shouts, her voice trembling.

This is getting exhausting for the both of us. She should stop kidding herself and just give in.

"See, we were having so much fun, but now you're starting to piss me off again. You run, you smash me in the fucking head, you break my goddamn hand, and all I'm trying to do is protect you!"

"You're a fucking monster!"

She charges at me, her eyes wild with frenzy. She takes another swing at my head, teeth bared. I put my hands up, and the weapon connects with my forearm, cracking straight through my bone. A pained grunt tumbles from my lips and I stumble backward, raising my good hand to block another. There's a horrible cracking sound, and two of my rings slip off of my mangled fingers and clatter to the ground.

Her strikes are primal and vicious. It makes me so fucking hard.

I pull my arm back just in time for her to smash me in the side of the head again. That's it. I can't just keep letting her get away with this. *That* was the final fucking straw.

In an instant, I have her up against the window, my good hand around her throat. She grunts and gasps, taking another swing at the side of my head. I grin, blood pouring down my face as I snatch her arm and squeeze until I hear bone splinter. The weapon falls to the floor and I kick it across the room, leaning right up to her with a snarl.

"You want the monster? You've got him."

She laughs, her beautiful green eyes wide.

"What's so fucking funny?" I ask.

"You are. You're so fucking desperate for control."

She's breathing hard, her throat bobbing beneath my grasp as exhaustion finally takes hold of her. I can feel her arms go limp as I run my lips along her jaw. She doesn't know it yet, but I'm going to ruin her.

"You don't have to live in a cage forever, little dove. This is all temporary."

"I fucking hate you," she rasps. "You and your pathetic little empire."

Her eyes are black, her pupils so dilated from the dark that all I can see is a thin green ring around the edges. I'm torn between wanting to be soft, and wanting to punish her for even thinking she could outsmart me. I'm leaning toward the second one.

"I'm going to fucking *shatter you*."

I spin her around and slam her face first against the front window, tearing at the beautiful nightgown that I paid for until it's falling to her feet.

"That's another dress you owe me." Her tone is still mocking, even in all her exhausted desperation.

I knot her hair around my knuckles and she groans, spittle flying from her lips as I pull hard.

"You think you're so fucking clever."

She slams her hand against the front window, her fingernails clawing at the glass like she's fighting something within herself.

"I am clever," she grunts as I drag my fangs across her skin. "At least compared to you."

Even the foreshadowing of my bite sends a wave of goosebumps across her skin, and she pushes back against me.

"I think you wanted me to catch you."

With my other hand, I reach between her legs to test my little theory. Even from this angle, I can see her bite down on her lip, her eyes rolling back as my fingers slip inside her.

"I know every nook and cranny of this building. Do you really think you could have gotten out?"

"I think you're too fucking arrogant for your own good. Falling asleep on the job's pretty fucking pathetic. Five more minutes and I'd have–"

I yank her head further back, and she yelps as she's forced to grind her ass against my cock.

"You're going to take everything I give you. My fangs, my cock, and in the end, you'll be begging for me to make you come, just like you always do."

Just then, I catch movement from across the street. A pack of four young vampires snicker at us as they suck on their cigarettes. I lock eyes with the leader, a young blond with a patchwork leather jacket and shredded jeans. There's blood on his face and he licks his lips at the sight of Sofie's bare tits pressed up against the glass.

They're young. Bikers. I've seen them around a couple times before, always trying to get their footing in the city. We push them back every time, but they always swarm back like cockroaches.

"They're watching us," she whispers.

I lick the smeared blood off of the side of her face.

"So you're the kind of girl who likes an audience?"

"Maybe they're here to watch me kill you," she replies, struggling against my grasp. She makes it look really convincing, but I can feel her shiver as every little movement pushes my fingers deeper.

I chuckle as I slip my fingers out, roughly flicking her clit and enjoying her little shriek.

"No, my love. They're going to watch me break you."

I unzip my pants, unable to control myself anymore. She wants the monster, she's going to fucking get him. I slide my cock between her legs, resting it against her pussy for just long enough for it to register before I grab her hips and slam her back against me, forcing my way inside her in a single stroke.

"Now be a good little whore and *take it*."

With her hair wound tightly around my knuckles, Sofie screams, swallowing me up. Her pussy flutters around me, squeezing me and soaking my cock as she makes some of the most sinful sounds I've ever heard. In the midst of it all, though, she somehow holds her own.

"Is that all?" She taunts. "Come on. Show me what you really are, Dominic. Rip me to shreds in front of those little dogs outside."

She's a fucking animal.

"They want a show." Her voice is like a knife, tearing into me without her ever having to lift a finger. "Is this all you can give them?"

She's ruthless, with almost nothing left of the softness that used to flutter in her eyes. I've crushed it into dust.

She's almost ready to be my Queen.

The vamps across the street are still watching us, so I decide to escalate things a bit. My teeth sink my teeth into her shoulder and I bear down even harder, making the bite messy and painful. Sofie lets out a desperate and pained howl. Her fist pounds against the glass as my pace becomes more and more brutal.

I only want to punish her; make her hurt a little, and then maybe a little more. She can take it. She's a good fucking girl.

As her blood pours down my throat, I'm rewarded with the most beautiful pulsing sensation around my cock. I close my eyes, imagining us bathed in crimson while she rides me all the way through her own dark transformation.

"Fuck!" She screams. "More!"

I dislodge my fangs, pulling out with a jolt as Sofie lets out a cry of protest, but she won't be complaining for long. I need to look her in the eye when I make her bleed for me.

When I turn her around, she leaps up, wrapping her legs around my waist. I capture her lips in a messy kiss, forcing her to taste her own blood on my tongue all over again.

My claws sink into her supple skin as I grip her hips, and she wiggles desperately to find my cock.

"They're still watching, Dominic. I thought you were going to break me."

With a sneer, I push myself inside of her and she trembles against my weight.

"Hard," she begs between sloppy kisses. "Fuck, just bite me again already."

My eyelids flutter as I bottom out. She's so fucking warm, and my body gives in instantly. I bite down near the same mark I left near the back of her shoulder, and in seconds her hips match my frantic rhythm, one hand bracing her against the glass as I drain her, right on the edge between control and frenzy.

I groan into her shoulder, my hips colliding with hers, hard enough they're sure to leave bruises. I've always craved this kind of brutality. It's so much more intense than anything we'd done before, but somehow everything feels off – it's all wrong. The way she touches me cuts straight to my core; it makes me want to fucking cry.

All we have is this strange connection, these violent outbursts and antagonism that draws us back together over and over again. It makes it impossible for me to stay away. The formula, destroying Rene, the city... somehow it's all become secondary. It's become an excuse. Even if she knew nothing, if she had nothing to offer to my grand scheme, I'd still want her.

I'd want her to love me.

Sofie feels like a rag doll in my arms as I feed on her. The deep clawing scratches she was inflicting upon me have slowed into a soft caress as her head rolls back, her cunt clenching down on my cock. I buck my hips faster and faster until I finish with a howl, pressing my forehead into the crook of her neck.

It takes a few moments, but as my senses return I feel her slow, steady heartbeat against my chest. We've collapsed on the floor, her on top of me. She's not struggling, not trying to fight or flee. She's staring at me with a renewed sense of vigor, despite her dangerously pale complexion.

She's hatched another plan.

"Turn me," she whispers. "Turn me and I'll stay. I'll make your formula."

I dip my head to lick her wound, nicking my tongue to close the violent bite marks for her. The bruises remain, physical and otherwise, as silence unfurls around us.

The inky-black of the sky has faded, replaced with the slightest orange glow, and our audience has gone along with it. We need to get upstairs before sunrise.

I swallow hard and pick her up, cradling her in my arms as I head back to the penthouse.

"Dominic?" She frowns. "Did you hear me?"

"Back upstairs," I mutter. "We'll talk when I know you're safe."

SOFIE

Santa Cruz Boardwalk

When we got back upstairs, he gave me a quick bath before locking me back in the bedroom. I waited hours for him to come back in, worried that he might just leave me in there, but eventually I lost out to the exhaustion.

He woke me up with the sunset, apologizing for leaving me alone. He said he needed time to think, but he'd figured things out. Now, after a short drive, we're out by the old boardwalk, sitting as the waves crash into the shore, dredging up old memories.

Dominic looks out at the water, ignoring me, his brow furrowed in concentration. It's strange how much he can change in so little time. Far from the feral beast chasing me last night, now he looks deflated, his face only half-healed from my earlier assault.

I hear a distant scream across the water that makes my blood run cold.

This isn't the same Boardwalk I brought Charlie to years ago. The sound of laughter has been stripped away, the smell of cotton candy and stale donuts replaced by rotting wood and washed-up debris.

But if I close my eyes, I can shut all of that out. I can see my son in my mind, waddling through the sand in his little bucket hat and a big plastic shovel in his hand, frustrated by the sunblock smeared across his nose. I'm on a sunny beach surrounded by smiling people and crashing waves, watching Sam scoop Charlie up as he squeals with delight.

My chin quivers and tears rush down my face.

"Sofie?" Dominic's voice is a scalpel, carving the memory right out and forcing me back to this shithole.

He tightens his grip on my waist.

"Are you okay?"

I laugh. What a stupid fucking question.

"I haven't been okay in a long time." I wipe my nose on the back of my hand. "Now why did you bring me here?"

"To talk." He pauses, choosing his words carefully. "If you're afraid–"

"I'm not afraid," I choke.

Nothing could be further from the truth, but it's not in the way he thinks. I'm terrified of losing what I have left of Charlie if I'm turned; of slowly letting myself drift away if I'm not.

"Are you sure you–"

"Dominic, stop wasting time. You brought me to talk, so let's talk."

He nods, standing and taking my hand before gently tugging me toward the water.

"Before I turn you, I want to make a deal."

Jesus, this fucking guy.

"There's always something, huh?"

"We'll both be getting something we want, I just—"

"First off, asshole, you never gave me that money you promised. I don't know how much of anything you say actually carries any weight."

He chuckles.

"It's in my dresser, payment upon your return to Nox, like I said. I keep my promises, Sofie."

I sneer up at him.

"That's the most bullshit thing you've said the entire time I've known you."

He sighs, leading me down some stairs and onto the beach itself.

"I need to know that I can trust you. That you're not just going to flip on me after I turn you."

"Because of what you did to Rene?"

Everyone knows they used to work together, and Rene was clearly the one at the head of the ship. There's a natural conclusion: betrayal.

"It's not that simple."

I expect him to lash out at the accusation, fly into a rage like he did last night, but he's managed to keep completely composed.

"He took someone from me. He brutalized her, and now he's planning to do it again. With you. Like I've always said, I took you to protect you. You won't be safe until he's dead, and I need you to help with that." He stops and smiles. "You're important to me."

Oh god, has he convinced himself that what we have is love? Love and obsession can look nearly identical after a life as twisted and raw as his. I doubt he can tell the difference anymore.

"That's what it comes down to, Sofie. We're out of time, and I need you to make that formula. Once it's done, we'll have him right where we want him."

"You haven't even let me look at that piece of paper for longer than a few seconds. If you want me to help you with this, with any of it, you need to be honest with me. How can I trust you if you've never really trusted me?"

He sighs.

"Theo says it's... it's like some kind of biological weapon."

My heart pounds. I knew he was leading me into something fucking dangerous. If he had been honest from the beginning, I would have– Well, I would have told him to fuck off, but he still should have told me the truth.

"What do you mean a weapon?"

"For humans, it's... well, it'd seem fantastic at first blush. He's perfected synthetic blood, mimicking our strain rather than yours. Vampires won't need to drink from humans anymore, at least as long as he can produce enough of this stuff. Humans won't need our blood to inoculate themselves. He's solved all of our biggest problems, all with a single little vial, but here's the trick: it's all blended in with some other shit. Extremely addictive to your kind, completely fucks with your brains; makes you compliant."

He shakes his head, glaring out at the moon as he continues.

"If we have a new, *renewable* food source, then humans can be harvested. He can round you all up, keep the best of you, and cull the rest like cattle. All he has to do is get this shit out, pitch it as a replacement for your inoculations, or just force it down your throats, and it's all over. No more balance of power. No more freedom."

I think I'm going to be sick.

"Rene used to go on these insane fucking rants about how it was our time; that humanity had wasted its gift, and the virus was the perfect opportunity to take control. I never thought he'd get this far, but I think it's always been his plan. It would be open season for vampires to hunt, kill, and do everything and anything Rene wants them to. Santa Cruz would be his playground, your bar would be gone, your friends would be dead, or worse. I don't even know what he'd do with you."

I can imagine it all too vividly.

"And you agreed with him?" I rasp as that pain in my stomach knots itself tighter and tighter. "Back when he said we wasted our gift, you were on his side?"

Dominic shakes his head.

"Everything in nature has a balance, and if something tries to overpower that, it throws the whole thing off. What we have it's... well, it's precarious, but it works."

"It works *for you*. You have all the power, you control almost all the territory, the money, everything."

He sighs.

"I know. Some things will need to change. That's all part of the plan."

"What fucking plan, Dominic? What are you even trying to do here?"

"My goal, what I want the most, is to repair the relationship between us. Find a better balance. Make it work."

Is he talking about humans, or just *me*?

"I think we can live together. I want to create some kind of... I don't know, council or something. Humans and vampires side by side."

"But you'd run it, right?"

I can see a small smile creep across his lips, reveling in the idea.

"Well naturally. I'm making it all happen, it seems only fair that I'm the one in charge when the dust clears."

There's always a catch with this guy. I think he enjoys the power and control just as much as Rene does, it's why they butted heads so much. The thing is, at the very least Dominic seems to care about a future that's at least somewhat sustainable. He's happy with the status quo we've created, and content to let the human population balance out.

Rene only works with us because he has to. He thinks of us as a food source, and nothing more. We're a means to an end. With Dominic, at least there's a chance at something more.

"Show me the formula."

He seems taken aback, worried at how quickly I've folded.

"Now?"

"Dom, I saw you slip it into your pocket before you left. If you want me to do this for you, I have to be able to trust that you're not just doing this to fuck me over and keep me as your own personal sex toy. I need to know this thing is real."

He's reluctant to give me even an ounce of freedom, no matter how reasonable the request. Even this little trip to the Boardwalk was his plan, completely under his supervision. This isn't a man who'd be willing to cede any significant amount of power on his own. It has to be negotiated step by step.

He digs into his pocket and hands me the formula. I barely got to look at this thing the other night, but it only takes a couple more minutes to confirm he's right about the mix. There's some sort of barbiturate, impossible to miss once you know it's there. The issue is in the measurements. There's not enough data for me to fully understand how the blood itself was synthesized, but the barbiturate? There's a real chance it'd just kill the subject instead of hooking them. The worst part is extremely clear one half of the formula could never work without the other, at least not the way they've been laid out here. They're bound together at the base level, one likely activating the other in some important way. That means no blood without the drug, no drug without the blood.

"Well, your friend... Theo, was it?"

"Yeah."

"I think he's right. It may not be literally a weapon, but it'll certainly cause some serious damage to our brain chemistry. Problem is even if we could use it ourselves, it would take multiple trials to get this thing to actually work. I'm not even sure how practical it is in its current form, even for the fucked up shit Rene wants to use it for."

"Trials? Plural?"

"Yeah, see, that's the thing people don't really understand about drugs. They're delicate. One wrong measurement and suddenly they either don't work right anymore, or you've got a real fucking monster on your hands."

I pause, a little issue that's been nagging at me for a while finally digging its way to the surface.

"Theo must be pretty smart. That whole speech of yours, it was all just what he told you, huh?"

Dominic's eyes shift to the side, clearly a little annoyed I saw through him so easily.

"Look, don't worry, you convinced me. I just want to know how your friend knew all of this. There's a lot going on here and your crew doesn't strike me as the scientific type."

"You're not the only one who went to school. He's got a degree in chemistry."

I raise a brow. He can't be this dense.

"And... what year did he get that degree? I'm assuming he wasn't in night school."

Dominic's eyes narrow.

"What are you implying?"

"That figuring out what's on this page is complicated enough for me. I think I can assume my own studies are based on a significantly more modern set of textbooks. I'm surprised he can even read some of this shit."

"Isn't math just... math?" Dominic scoffs.

I let out a frustrated sigh.

"Math *is* a universal language, sure. But these chemical formulas are a lot more complicated. They're modern. Half of this shorthand wouldn't even have made sense 20 years ago, let alone when you two were young enough to getting an education."

"Couldn't he have just looked it up?"

"It's possible," I reply. "Or maybe he talked to one of Rene's men and tortured it out of him, I'm not sure. All I know is this is pretty hard to parse, even for me."

I hand him back the formula and he stuffs it into his pocket. I can't get what I want without giving him the thing he needs the most in the world, and that's my loyalty. Right now, what that looks like is sitting in a lab and cooking up a drug that has the potential to blow up in my face in more ways than one.

Once again, he's given me the wonderful choice of not having any choice at all.

Back at his apartment, I realized there may not be a way out of this dynamic, that I would always be inferior to him. While he had me up against that wall; while he was threatening to rip me apart, I had an epiphany. I need the power that he has.

And then suddenly it wasn't about beating him at his own game, it was about doing what he wanted, but on *my* fucking terms. Dominic isn't willing to give up complete control, but he's willing to move goalposts so long as I string him along a little. I got him to beg in the feeding rooms, and I'll get him to turn me. Soon.

Over the years, I've thought about what it would be like to be one of them, to live for hundreds of years, to have their strength and their cruelty. I could walk the streets at night and I wouldn't have to be afraid anymore. Humans have rearranged our entire lives — our sleep schedules, our jobs, our friendships — all for survival. It's not living, not really.

"I'll make your formula, but you have to follow through with your end of the bargain when this is all over. Make me a vampire, and I want half of Rene's territory–"

"How about we rule together, as a team?"

He doesn't even miss a beat.

"I want my own territory," I seethe through clenched teeth. "Nothing more, nothing less."

He scowls.

"What for? We'll be working together."

"Because I'm worried about you running this entire city into the ground, and me getting me nothing for my efforts. We haven't known each other for that long, Dom, and I might hate Rene Deschamps enough to sign up for your batshit plan, but I want some kind of guarantee that this is going to go down the way you promised."

"I'll give you loyalty," Dominic whispers. "And power, money–"

I poke him in the chest with one finger.

"And you'll turn me *and* give me half the territory. No bite, no land, no deal. You get me, Duncan?"

His jaw ticks.

"You're tenacious."

I grin.

"Have to be in my line of work."

He takes my hand, squeezing it gently.

"We have a deal, Miss Fournier."

"Glad to hear it. Oh, and I also want Ruby on board or there's no deal."

He blinks and shakes his head.

"What? No. We just shook on it, you can't just add new terms."

"Yes, I can. I want to get her looped in *tonight*."

"I said no, Sofie."

If he can negotiate, so can I, and if he wants this done, he's going to do it my way. He's been fumbling in the dark this whole time, and I'm confident that I can get him to bend. He might be charming, but I actually know what the fuck I'm doing.

"Look, Dominic, I can't make the formula alone. I know blood, but I'll need some extra hands. You want your power? Earn it. Learn to cooperate for once in your fucking life. You can start by driving me to Nox and getting Ruby on board."

He blinks, standing completely still. He doesn't seem to know how to react. "Why her?"

"She was a nurse, and she knows pharmaceuticals. She'd be a hell of a lot more valuable than me for something like this. Honestly, if you had any idea what you were doing you'd have kidnapped *her*."

He pinches the bridge of his nose, and I pat him on the shoulder.

"Okay. Alright, you win. Let's go to Nox."

I'm beaming as he looks up, and he catches my eye instantly, his mouth curling into a warm smile. So long as he doesn't fuck me over, this could be the start of something good between us. An actual partnership.

I bring his knuckles to my lips and kiss the skull ring that adorns his index finger.

"Thank you, Mr. Duncan."

SOFIE

Nox Nightclub

It's all business on the ride over. Dominic grips the steering wheel with one hand while the other drums out a nervous rhythm on his thigh. The silence between us makes my skin itch, and I lean forward, fiddling with the radio out of necessity. I know there's nothing on it, but I try anyway, and we're greeted with static.

"I think I have a Bauhaus tape in the glove box," Dominic offers.

"Let me guess, it's got Bela Lugosi's dead on it?" I scoff.

He shrugs.

"I'm a simple man, my dear."

I sigh and switch the radio off, leaning back in my seat. I can feel him watching me out of the corner of his eye.

"You're agitated."

I shake my head. I'm worried about how Ruby is going to react when we walk in there. No doubt I'm going to have to step in front of Dominic to keep her from killing him.

The rest of the drive is silent, and when he pulls up in front of Nox, I feel like my limbs are suddenly made of concrete. Dominic gets out first, his head on a swivel as he glances around. He opens my door.

"You ready?"

"Not really," I confess.

He takes my hand as he helps me out of the car, and we head toward the club. Bobby has a particular look on his face, but he lets us in without argument, merely moving aside and pushing the door open.

The second we step inside, it feels like everything stops. Heads turn and humans and vampires alike stare at us. I forgot how strange we must look, Dominic's wounds still knitting up, and my body covered in cuts and bruises. Fuck, half the clothes I'm wearing are completely wrecked. We should have picked a busier night.

"Sofie!" Kirby shouts from the bar. "Ruby, loo–"

"Duncan, you *motherfucker*!" Ruby roars as she leaps over the bar, rushing him with her gun already aimed at his head.

Dominic raises his hands, but it's too late. She fires a bullet that whizzes past him, embedding itself into the far wall as patrons scatter.

"Jesus Christ, Ruby!" I yelp. "We're–"

She's already on him, pistol whipping him in the head. I can see his muscles twitching as he's trying to keep his temper in check. The veins in his neck and forehead pulse as Ruby just keeps hitting him.

"You. Fucking. Promised!" She bellows.

I have to step in, grabbing her by the shoulders to pull her away.

"Ruby, stop!"

She turns to me abruptly, tears in her eyes.

"Where the fuck were you?! What happened? Why do you have bruises all over your face?"

She lurches back around to Dominic and raises her gun again, aiming it right at his forehead. Her face morphs into that *'I'm going to fucking destroy you'* look at only Ruby can give.

"You hurt her, Duncan. You're done."

"Ruby, look I'm okay. It's okay." I put my hands over her gun, lowering it down as I attempt to calm her down. "I'll explain everything, but we have to talk to you. In the office. I promise it'll all make sense."

Dominic's eyes flick around the room, humiliation clouding his expression. Everyone is looking at us, and no matter how much he might want to, he can't lash out. Ruby might as well be castrating him right now.

"We really need to talk to you." I motion to the back office. "Please?"

She takes a breath and stares at the two of us, her gun still half-raised.

"You walk him there, I follow."

I avoid Ares' judgmental gaze as we head to the back, through a small crowd of vampires that seem intent to follow us until Ruby turns around and waves her gun at them.

"Employees only, motherfuckers."

She ushers us through the back and into the office, lingering by the door, her gun still in-hand as she slides the deadbolt into place.

"Ruby, you can put the gun down," I sigh. "He's not gonna try anything in here. He knows he'd never make it out."

She shakes her head, her cheeks flaming and her eyes full of ice, piercing Dominic's skull. He stares back at her with an amused expression.

"You know, Ruby, if I wanted I could just snap your–"

"Nobody's snapping anything!" I spit, glaring at him. "Dominic, you shut your fucking mouth, and Ruby, put the gun *down*."

"What makes you think I can trust you — either of you?!" She shouts. "You were gone for three fucking days, Sofie! He promised to bring you back! *You* promised you'd be back."

"Well, he kidnapped me Ruby, it's not like I had a way to get back here much faster"

"I didn't kidnap, I just didn't let you–"

"Shut up!" The two of us shout in unison.

I cross my arms over my chest and lean against the desk, trying to show Ruby that I'm not a threat. Her eyes bounce between the two of us.

"What, so he kidnapped you, beat this shit out of you, and you're just working together?"

"We came to an arrangement," Dominic sighs. "After a couple of minor setbacks."

He winks at me and I flip him off. This isn't my ideal scenario, but I've given him my terms. He's proven he's not willing or able to kill me, and if he doesn't follow through with our deal, it'll be easy enough to take advantage of that after Rene's gone. Then, with them out of the picture, we can declare open season on all vampires and we'll drag them all out into the fucking sunlight. Go to war.

Of course, that's not the ideal scenario. Even if we won, we'd eventually lose our inoculations, no matter how much vampire blood in reserve. If the human population expanded again, we probably wouldn't be able to keep them all from getting sick and spreading the plague all over again. Not unless we succeed in synthesizing their blood, but that could take years to get right.

"So what you're telling me his dick is so good you just stuck with him?" Ruby asks. "That's not like you, Sof."

"I appreciate the compliment, though," Dominic mutters under his breath.

She takes a step toward him and presses the gun to his forehead.

"I swear to god, Duncan. Give me one more fuckin' reason and I'll paint the wall with your brains."

Her voice is a deep rumbling growl that even gives Dominic pause for a moment. It's rare that I see Ruby like this. She's all sunshine and rainbows until someone fucks with her or someone she loves.

"Deschamps is planning something, and it's big. I wouldn't be asking for your help if we didn't need it."

She looks from Dominic, to me, and back again before slowly lowering her gun and setting it on the desk. Dominic heaves a sigh of relief and puts his hands down. Ruby's body is coiled extremely tight, tears pooling in her eyes. I can't ignore the feeling of guilt that wells up inside me. She didn't deserve any of this.

"My help? What did you tell him about me?" Ruby growls.

"Nothing, just the medical stuff. Rene is making some kind of... synthetic drug, laced in with some new kind of blood. He's going to use it to tip the scales, take the rest of what we have away from us." I sigh. "I don't like the idea of being some vamp's fucking pet–"

"Clearly, you do," she retorts.

Dominic covers his laughter with a cough, and I snap up Ruby's gun, aiming for his head. I'm completely calm, my eyes dead-set on his.

"Dominic, keep your fucking mouth shut. You've got me one step away from finishing what Ruby started."

His eyes light up, the same as they do in his most passionate moments.

"I didn't say anything," he murmurs, his voice low and raspy.

I sneer.

"We still need each other right now, so no reason to fuck things up any more than they already are, right?"

"I love it when you talk dirty," he rumbles, a grin spreading across his face.

"Shoot him, Sofie."

"Yeah, Sofie, do it," he urges. "Pull the trigger."

As much as it might feel great in the moment, I can't. I want to see this promise through to the end. There's something broken in Dominic, fragments that he's shown me. Not to put back together, but to understand. I know he's obsessed with me, maybe even thinks that he loves me, but he can only show it through delusion and violence.

Slowly, I put the gun on the desk and Dominic beams at me, flicking his bottom lip with his tongue. He thinks he's called my bluff. He'll find out how wrong he is if he tries to fuck with me.

Ever since he walked into my life, my entire world's been turned upside down, and there's no going back. Me, Ruby, and everyone in Nox have been roped into this, and none of us will be free until Rene Deschamps is dead and gone.

"Look, Ruby, you studied pharmaceuticals. We can't make this formula on our own. We need you."

"You want to make the drug that's part of the big evil fucking plan?!" Ruby exclaims. "What for?"

"Because we still don't know if Theo's theory is legit. All we have is a formula," Dominic tells her. "If we can test a small sample, we'll know what we're dealing with. Maybe we can even figure out a way to make it benefit the lot of us."

"And how do I know you're not just going to use it on Sofie and I, turn us into your fucking playthings?"

"Because, unlike my counterpart, I'm not interested in fucking brain-dead zombies. I like you with a little bite."

Ruby glances at me, and I nod.

"I'll sign my half of Nox over to you when this is all over. It'll be under the full protection of myself and Dominic, but not controlled. It'll still be neutral ground, no strings attached."

"So you're gonna kill Rene and go into business together?" Ruby asks.

Dominic shrugs.

"That was the plan."

"It's a good deal, Ruby," I mutter. "I'll be able to get you more resources for this place. More money. You'll never have to do a late-night blood run again. Protected deliveries, protected servers... hell, some of you could even have a day off once in a while."

Ruby runs a hand through her hair and sighs, staring up at the ceiling.

"This might be the dumbest fucking thing I've ever done," she groans. "Okay, I'll do it. We make *one* sample, test it, and then destroy it. And Duncan, if I get even a whiff that you're planning to use this stuff for yourself–"

A sharp pounding on the door tears us from the moment. I reach for the gun, but Dominic holds out a hand, pressing it against my chest. He creeps toward the door, prepping for some kind of attack as he moves to open it.

"Dom? Dom, open up, I know you're back there!"

More knocking.

"Luke?"

"Who the fuck is Luke?" Ruby asks.

Dominic wrenches the door open. The dark-haired vampire from his first night at Nox stands in front of him, looking completely terrified.

"How did you know I was in here?" He growls.

"What do you– Your car's parked out front, and you're always here!" There's panic in his eyes, and he keeps glancing back behind him. "Look, it's bad, man. I've been trying to find you for hours."

"What are you talking about?" Dom asks.

"It's Theo, Dom. He's... he's dead."

For a moment, Dominic looks completely broken, his entire body shattered by the shock, but in a flash he's returned to a more stony disposition, grabbing Luke by the jacket.

"When? Where?"

"Rene's house in the mountains. I saw some guys tossing the body into a car just outside of your building after they got him. Tailed them until they hit the highway. There's nothing else out that way, it's gotta be where they went."

Dominic draws himself up to full height, his jaw clenched tight, as he wordlessly makes his way toward the front. My heart is in my throat as I trail behind him. This isn't even about the formula anymore.

I have to wonder if it was really ever more than an excuse.

DOMINIC

SANTA CRUZ MOUNTAINS

THERE'S A LUMP IN my throat, choking me as I try not to scream, and focus instead on white-knuckling the steering wheel. Luke's car trails behind us as we drive further into the mountains. He was a little reluctant at first, terrified to end up just like Theo, but he knows better than most how hard it is to turn me down when I'm set on something.

My grief has teeth, and I can feel the sharp and jagged edges as it tears away at me. It's gnawing at the back of my neck, like a hungry beast that just won't go away. I reach back and claw at the skin, hoping there's simply something physically wrong with me, but the sensation only grows more intense.

"You didn't have to come," Sofie breaks the silence from the other seat, looking over her shoulder at Ruby.

"Babe, I'm the one with a bag full of weapons and ammo. You're going to need all the help you can get."

Sofie shifts in her seat, glancing sidelong at me for only a moment before turning to stare out the window. She didn't know Theo. I can't expect her to understand what I'm feeling. I keep hoping she'll try to comfort me, to show me the tiniest bit of tenderness, but it's too much to ask. I burned that bridge with a single match, along with all the kerosene in the city.

All I can really hope for now is revenge.

Every passing minute is agonizing, double-long as our cars crawl toward the villa. Ruby sighs in the back. The sound of her loading a gun bullet by bullet is chipping away at my patience. Sofie's jaw twitches, her eyes intense and focused on the road ahead, each quiet breath another needle in my sense of calm.

I'm gripping the steering wheel so hard I can feel it bend.

I clear my throat.

"Ruby, did you happen to see Theo the other night?"

The memory of his final job hit me suddenly. I wonder if she was the last person who saw him before he died. Maybe she saw who took him.

"Duncan, I have no fucking clue who any of your goons are. How should I know if any of them were at the club?"

"You'd have known. He was supposed to tell you about Sofie."

He never even made it. They probably found him on his way to the club, chased him down. Luke said he saw them stuff him into a trunk outside the tower. He was probably trying to get in while I was busy with Sofie. Fuck, I could have saved him.

My foot presses on the gas, as if by instinct, as Rene's mansion rises into view. Not a single window is illuminated, the dark of the night consuming everything beyond our headlights.

Maybe they weren't expecting a full-on attack. Maybe we got the jump on Rene after all.

All at once I hear engines revving, and the windshield explodes, glass raining down on us as gunshots ring out ahead. The car fishtails and we nearly careen into a tree.

Maybe not.

Ruby and Sofie are both fine, but my relief is short-lived as something smashes into the side of the car, pushing us back onto the road. I look back just in time to spot Luke slip by us; the gunshots slowing to nothing as he makes his way to the house. It only takes me a moment to realize what's going on. Our car smokes, sitting in Rene Deschamps' long driveway, illuminated by the headlights of three vehicles as Luke joins them as their fourth. A vaguely familiar voice rings out across the open air.

"Damn, Dom, you made good time. You must be really motivated these days!"

I squint against the light, but have little trouble placing the drivers.

Gabriel. I plucked out chunks of his eyes for days, letting them regrow each time before starting again. And then I let him run back to Rene like a good little lapdog, the souvenirs I'd taken placed like prizes on my mantle.

Malachi, who I left burning alive, hanging by a silver chain around his ankle after I took the wharf.

And poor Silas. I blew off his progeny's head right in front of him. What a fucking mess.

Theo always said I left too many loose ends.

Luke exits his vehicle, joining the other men. His stride is confident, and he seems completely different from the sniveling worm I'm so used to kicking around. He beckons me over with one finger, a grin plastered over his smug fucking face. The icy dread of my worst fears confirmed makes me feel sick. Theo is dead because of me, because I couldn't keep my men in line, and now here we are, staring down a hit squad.

I throw the car into reverse, smashing what's left of the windshield out of the way, and swerving to the side as more bullets pound into the car.

They're all fucking dead.

Rene said the clock was ticking. He warned me. I should have taken the threat more seriously. I don't even know if I have anyone left I can trust outside of the people in this car. I keep us moving, trying my best to keep them from getting any clean shots as I shout back to Ruby.

"You got anything in that bag that'll make a bigger dent than a pistol?"

"Fuck yeah I do!" She grins, the adrenaline riling her up. She roots around, retrieving a couple of hand grenades that look like they might be at least a decade old. "How's that for making a dent?"

"Perfect, now listen: I'm gonna head straight for them, and swerve at the last second. That'll give you a tiny window to get one close enough to light them up, got it?"

"Dominic, this is insane!" Sofie shouts. "We need to get out of here, we can't–"

I turn and lock eyes with her, bullets still screaming past the car as I shift gears.

"You help me kill Rene and you can have it all. Fucking all of it, Sofie. I just need that fucker dead!"

The moment of panic in her eyes is replaced by determination as she nods, bracing herself behind the dashboard as more gunshots ring out.

I still don't know if I believe what I'm saying to her, but right now I need all the allies I can get. Behind me, Ruby readies her grenade, cranking the window down with her free hand.

"Sof, remember what we did to city hall back in the day?"

"Yup," Sofie murmurs as she flips the safety off on her gun. "I guess we're fucking doing this shit all over again."

Vampire or not, nobody survives a fucking grenade. It's hard to regenerate when you've been blown to smithereens. I grin grimly as I rev the engine, slamming my foot on the gas again. Sofie acts as a mild distraction, firing blindly out her window while I barrel toward the four vamps at full speed. The engine roars in front of me, tires screaming as we tear forward into the hail of bullets.

"Ruby, now!" I bellow, cranking the wheel to the left.

The tires squeal against the pavement and the back end of the car skids wildly as Ruby tosses the grenade right at the cluster of cars. It's possible a couple of them noticed, and it's possible they didn't, but it doesn't matter either way. I spin the car to face the end of the driveway and pound on the gas pedal with everything I have.

The last thing I see of Rene's men in the rear-view mirror is Luke's shit-eating grin as he lines up a shot, and then all that's left of them is an eruption of flaming metal as meat and gore rains down on the pavement.

I turn the car a final time before bringing us to a screeching halt. From the end of the expansive driveway, we watch as the flames spit and lick at what's left of the cars, masses of charred flesh scattered all around.

Sofie leans against the dash, breathing hard, her gun resting in her lap. Ruby is in hysterics, cackling in the backseat.

"Holy fucking shit!"

I shake my head. Rene isn't here. No one is safe for those four assholes. There's something wrong.

"Don't celebrate yet," I warn. "We're going in there."

These guys were small potatoes. I want the man who gave the call to pull the trigger. I want some real fucking revenge.

I open the car door and motion for the two of them to follow. A wave of heat from the smoldering cars hits me right in the face, and I wince as I make my way toward the front of the building. Sofie and Ruby are close behind, guns at the ready. I feel like I should be doing more to protect them, to prepare them for something as dangerous as this, but it's too late for that. All safe houses could be compromised. My other men haven't been around in days, maybe weeks. I've let things slip, been... preoccupied. We're weak, but hopefully so is he. This is our best shot, it's now or never.

As we approach the house, I'm amused to find a good chunk of the front entrance in pieces from the explosion. As I move through some rubble, kicking away some errant metal and glass, I can't help but think back to the lab. Here I am, wrecking another one of Rene's beloved holdings with no sort of plan. We've come full fucking circle.

As I step through the threshold, my heart sinks. Rene's left me a gift: Mateo's corpse pinned up against a massive wooden door that leads into the foyer. He's a mangled mess, two large silver stakes smashed through his wrists and another in his throat. I can still see the agony in his brutalized face.

Ruby retches, the sight a bit too much for her, but Sofie stands completely still, unaffected.

As I walk toward him, I notice the note pinned to his jacket, written in blood.

Dom, come and play.

Sofie's breath is shallow, the gun in her hand trembling despite her cold demeanor. Maybe she's taking it harder than I thought.

"Someone's waiting for us," she mutters. "Was this his plan? He knew we'd make it past those fuckers outside?"

She's right, but if Rene knew we were coming, there should be vampires crawling over this whole fucking place. Why is it empty?

I want to pull her in close, to kiss and comfort her. This is the world that I'm used to, and she's stumbled into it because of me. But it's the world she wants to be a part of now that she's demanded space in it. I guess she's learning the hard way.

"You two ready?" I ask.

"No, but we don't have a choice, do we?" Ruby shoots back, adjusting the duffle bag on her shoulder.

I sigh.

"At this point? Even if we all left, he'd just—"

"We know," Sofie murmurs. "We're finishing this, one way or the other."

I can see the wheels in her head spinning, worrying about the bar, about the future, about what lies ahead of us. I can't help but wonder if there's even going to be an us when it's all said and done, or if I'm gonna have a new rival, one to fight for power every step of the way.

But it doesn't matter.

I lean back and kick the door open, the three of us moving past Mateo's corpse. My head is filled with the sound of beating hearts, rushes of breath, and blood flowing through their veins. I have to remind myself to keep calm, to manage my senses, but this entire situation feels like a powder keg I've chosen to light it with no plan of escape.

As we step into the foyer, the depth of the darkness slows my two companions to a crawl. I can see everything in sharp detail, but to them it's pitch black. I move around, looking for a light fixture before finally finding one beside the spiral staircase that leads to the rest of the house.

I flip the switch, turning at the sound of a creaking floorboard behind me.

A man lounges in a door frame, smoking a cigarette, his mouth curled into a wide, devious grin.

"Evening, sunshine," he calls, in that soft Irish lilt. "It's been a wild few nights."

DOMINIC

RENE'S MANSION

RAGE, WHITE HOT, EXPLODES through my body like a bomb. I feel everything all at once – betrayal, shame, and guilt, all covering the tiny sliver of relief I'm holding onto, despite the circumstances.

Theo clicks his tongue and takes a drag of his cigarette.

"Oh, Dominic, it was so nice of you to bring Sofie and her little friend out to play. Rene can thank you for that personally before he rips you to pieces, but... running straight into his big scary house without a plan? Have you learned nothi–"

Sofie barely hesitates, raising her gun and taking the shot before he even has the chance to finish his speech. The bullet whizzes past his head as he leaps to the side. He doesn't advance, though, remaining near the doorway as his face contorts and he lets out a vicious snarl.

"Keep your bitch on a fucking leash," he snaps.

I cock my gun and move in front of Sofie.

"We're going to have words, you and I."

"Hey, I'm just playing the game, boss. You taught me everything I could possibly want to know about a well-timed coup." He chuckles. "Well, how not to do one at least."

"How long have you been working for him?"

He takes another long drag, absolutely fearless in the face of all my fury.

"Not too long after you blew up that lab," Theo replies. "I was trying to do things your way, I really was! I went out to find you someone to make that formula and, lo and behold, who do I run into but the man himself? Honestly, not the best meeting I've ever had. Took some convincing to stop him from torturing me until I begged for death, but we get along just fine now."

"Why all this bullshit? Why not just bring him the formula?"

"Unfortunately, that's the one thing I wasn't lying about. Remember that night in the lab way back? You killed the only person who was even close to making that shit a reality. Rene was furious at first. I was so sure I was done for, but..." He laughs, shrugging a little. "Well, you know I'm a real fast talker when I need to be. I slipped him a real fuckin' good idea, cracked him right up. *'What if we let Dominic do all the hard work? Find someone to do the heavy lifting, and then make him bring it right to you?'*"

"He's gonna turn on you, Theo," I rasp.

"Not this time. He's already given me territory, and a nice little spot right next to this. Real generous of him, you know? That's the difference between you two. You both make promises, but he's the one that delivered. Everything would have been fine if you just cooperated with him and didn't fight it–"

"Fuck you!" I growl. "You know what he did to Selene!"

"Oh my God," Theo sighs, rolling his eyes. "Get over it, will ya?! It was four fuckin' years ago now! Besides, how many families do you think you've destroyed since then?"

He walked me right into this, every step of the way. Any time I stumbled, he pointed me back on track; all to finding someone to finish what we burned to the ground.

"Haven't you noticed how easy everything has been? How no one's come after you? How you've been free to traipse around and play house with your new little toy?"

"Rene threatened her! He was going to torture her, kill her."

"And you fell for that? What about when I showed up and spoon fed that shit about the drug to you? You didn't even wonder for half a second how I knew all that? He's played you like a fiddle, Dom. And you know what? He didn't even need you to do it. We could have found someone on our own, stolen the formula back from you, and rebuilt things from scratch. This whole thing is about humiliating you, making you do the grunt work and then laying it at his feet. You're so fucking drunk on the very *idea* of power that you didn't even see it!"

"Why?"

Theo scoffs.

"Jesus Christ, haven't you been listening at all?"

"No, him I understand. He's a power-hungry freak with a god complex. It's you I don't get. Why do this to me? We could have run this city together."

He blinks, his face contorting as if I've just asked him the stupidest question in the world.

"Because after these years, Dom, you still don't know your own weaknesses. You're arrogant, selfish, and you never deliver. You're so afraid of ever ending up as someone's lackey again that you never let anyone up to your level. No matter what you promised, ever since we came up together, it's always been all about you."

I shake my head. I've always seen Theo as an equal, as someone I can depend on, even in my darkest moments. He was there when Rene killed Selene, consoling me and vowing revenge in turn.

He used to be my brother.

Now he's in my way.

"Theo, I'm giving you one chance. Walk away."

"See, this is exactly what I'm talking about! You undermine every single god-damn thing I say, and you're so fucking *stupid!* You went chasing after this cunt like a dog in heat when we were supposed to be stealing an empire from a tyrant! What do you even want? Power or pussy?!" He roars. "What was it you said? '*Give me five years, Theo. Five years, and I'll give you everything you could possibly want.*'" He raises a brow. "Do you even remember?"

Sofie's eyes are on me, and her breathing quickens. Maybe I do make more promises than I can keep.

"So I did what I had to do," Theo continues. "Deschamps gets to keep running the city, you'll be in the fucking ground, and I'll be beside him the whole way. The devil's right-hand man."

"Where is he?" I growl.

"On his way. He said he wanted to face you alone. He's taking his time, building up all of that anticipation, you know? But hey, I figure if you somehow didn't make it, what's the harm?"

My gaze rests on him.

"I won't need long to take you out, Tierney."

"Then do it," he taunts, stepping toward me with his arms wide. "Come on, Dom! Where's all that confidence?"

I hear the crack of gunfire as a bullet grazes his cheek, and I glance back to see Ruby readying a second shot. Theo takes advantage of my moment of distraction and charges her, and I'm forced to move to intercept him. Another shot rings out as we leap into the air, this one hitting him right in the arm. He doesn't even flinch as blood soaks through his suit.

We collide like boulders and smash against the wall. A mirror shatters during the chaos and I hiss as I'm pushed onto the ground, cutting myself on a shard of glass. Theo gets the upper hand, rolling me onto my back as he raises his fist. I didn't even notice him slip on the brass knuckles. He wants me to hurt.

He brings his fist down hard, hitting me square in the jaw, and then again in the chest, like he's trying to punch right through my ribcage. I dodge the last strike just in time, the marble beneath me exploding into dust as he readies another blow.

Before I can get my bearings, I hear him let out a frustrated howl; Sofie and Ruby are trying to haul him off of me, both of them struggling against his strength.

He knocks Ruby back first, her body making a wet thunk as she hits the corner of the staircase. By the time I try to get back on my feet, he's already on to Sofie, grabbing her by the throat and pinning her to the wall a few feet away. Veins pop in her forehead as he squeezes, tighter and tighter until her head looks like it's going to burst.

"You're in over your head, princess," he snickers, kicking out at me as I try to reach for his leg. I let out a yelp of pain as his shoe smashes against my nose. "Down, boy. If you're good, maybe I'll only paralyze her for you."

She chokes and gags, her hands flailing as she tries to work her way beneath his grip, but it's ironclad.

My hand fumbles along the ground blindly until it bumps into a large shard of broken glass. In the few moments Theo looks away to revel in Sofie's torment, I'm on my feet, rushing him and driving the shard straight into his left eye. He releases her, stumbling back as he brings his hands up to claw at his face.

"You mother*fucker*!"

Sofie instantly moves for the crumpled Ruby, who is still slumped on the ground, blood pooling around her head. I can tell she's still breathing, but barely, and I grasp her arm to hold her back.

"Don't," I hiss.

Theo turns, blood pouring out of his eye and running down his face. He's finally got his hands on the shard, yanking it out in a single motion. He's not even bothered that his eyeball's still on the tip, attached only by the optic nerve.

"You should listen to him," he murmurs, examining his own eyeball before ripping the entire thing out with a twitch.

His fangs are bared, but he surprises me as he turns, pacing slowly toward Ruby instead of us.

"She's fading," he taunts as he kneels down beside her, dipping his fingers into the pool of blood gathering all around her. "Look at that head wound. Ooh, she might even have a broken neck. Bad luck."

He turns to us, a crimson waterfall rushing from his now vacant eye socket as he pops his blood-soaked fingers into his mouth and licks them clean.

"Should I turn her? Or maybe just let you watch while she bleeds out?"

He bends down for more and licks the blood off her forehead.

Sofie charges toward him, taking wild shots as she runs. Theo laughs, leaping into the air and tackling her, not caring that a couple of bullets make their way into his chest before the gun hits the ground beside her.

He picks her up by the hair and wrenches her head to the side, his fangs glittering like knives. I let out a roar and rush him, and he breaks his grasp just too late to stop me from flinging him across the room.

Theo slams against the wall, putting a brutal dent in it before he crumples to the floor. His eyelids flutter as I sprint over to him, the sound of Sofie struggling toward Ruby in the background of my mind.

I grab Theo by the scruff of his shirt, my fist connecting with his face before he can recover, over and over again without taking a single moment's pause. His skin is torn and pulpy, his remaining eye rolling back in his head as his skull crumbles beneath my fists. Fury pulses through me as I hear him try to speak, only managing a pathetic gurgle as I continue, each and every blow brutalizing him even more. With every strike he twitches less and less, and soon my anger gives way to overwhelming grief.

I'm losing the one final constant in my life, the single thing I've depended on since we were children. My mind flashes with images of the two of us growing up together, playing in the fields in County Clare, drinking until we were howling with laughter in between vomiting fits, chasing girls, and then coming to America to chase even *more girls*. And then money. And power. But always together.

Always.

We could have built an empire.

Finally, Theo's body lays still, and I grab what's left of his head. I press my cheek against it, tears streaming down my face as I can already feel him start to move again, his body slowly knitting back together.

"Brothers," I whisper.

Twisting as hard as I can, I tear his head right off his body with an agonizing and sickening wail. I almost think I heard him try to say something one last time, but it was too late. It always is.

My chest heaves from the effort, but I have no time to rest, turning to see Sofie cradling Ruby in her arms and trembling like a leaf. Her chest is stained with blood and she lets out a wretched sob.

"She's dying."

When I don't move fast enough, she loses control, slamming one hand on the floor as she shrieks at me.

"Dominic, fucking *do something*!"

The grief in her voice makes me nauseous. I toss Theo's severed head to the floor and crouch down to check Ruby's pulse. It's faded to nearly nothing.

"I can't live without her, Dominic. I've lost everyone I love." She lifts her chin, suddenly defiant. "I won't do it again."

"I'll turn you both," I choke out. "But you'll have to die before I can."

"Ruby first, and then me," she whispers.

I roll up my sleeve and drag my claw down my wrist, opening the vein like a canyon. A rivulet of crimson comes to the surface, and I press it to Ruby's lips as Sofie strokes her head.

"Come on, babe. Drink."

Ruby lets out a moan, her eyelids fluttering. I can only see the whites of them, but her lips latch on to my wrist and she begins to feed. The sickening silence is filled by the sound of Sofie's heavy breathing.

"We can help with Rene." Her voice is raw, but still full of hope. "With the three of us we can—"

"You won't have the strength to take him on. He'll do the same thing to you that I did to Theo." I pause, letting out a long sigh. "And he'll enjoy it."

Ruby moans as she feeds, her body twisting as her grip on my arm tightens. Normally, this is an extremely intimate process, but time is of the essence. Sofie and I stare at her in a silent plea for her to keep drinking. Seconds feel like hours, and the weight of my anxiety crushes me.

Finally, it feels like enough, and I check Ruby's pulse again. Her heart has slowed, and she lets out one final wheezing breath before her body goes limp.

"Did she get enough?" She chokes out through tears.

Ruby's body seizes up and her eyes shoot open, one still blue and the other fading to a midnight black. She lets out a panicked gasp, and Sofie clutches her to her chest.

"What's happening?!"

"She's coming back. It's okay."

Ruby's body seizes violently, her broken neck straightening out as the bones snap and crack back into place. Her pupils widen, eyes now fully black as she stares at the ceiling with parted lips. A low howl pours out of her, filling the room as she shakes. The veins in her forehead and neck are engorged with blood, and she foams at the mouth, letting out another gurgling wail.

And then a car door slams outside, and I hear him whistling.

Put on a Happy Face.

Fuck, we're out of time.

I shove Ruby aside and grab Sofie by the hair, pulling her neck to the side as I sink my fangs into her. She chokes and claws at me in a panicked desperation. I drink deeply, hearing Ruby moving and whimpering in the background before she leans in, newly yellow irises vibrant and piercing as she lets out a little hiss.

Sofie grabs her and brings her to the other side of her throat, pressing Ruby's mouth to her skin almost as if by instinct. This has to be done delicately. Ruby could kill her before I have the chance to step in. A human can't be drained for too long before we bring them back or the change isn't always guaranteed.

Sofie moans and I can hear her flesh tear as Ruby drinks from her, the two of us feeding until her heart finally comes to a complete stop. Ruby lets out a growl and tries to go further, but I grab her and throw her off to the side. Blood-drunk, she flops against the wall and sobs.

"More."

"Shut up."

I can hear his steps getting closer and the panic sets in.

I make another deep cut in my arm and force Sofie's mouth onto it, pulling her into my lap to protect her as Ruby pushes herself back onto her knees. She's weak and unsteady, like a newborn foal.

More soft footsteps, and his whistling gets louder and louder.

Blood trickles down her chin and I pray she's actually ingested some of it. There's a very limited window.

Suddenly, the door to the foyer swings open and Rene stands on the threshold, casually looking around at the carnage. He clicks his tongue and takes a few steps toward what's left of Theo's head.

"First you blow up my front door, then you kill my new best friend..." He looks up at me. "And now, just look at you, trying to make yourself a little army."

Ruby scrambles to her feet, her instinctual loyalty to her sire kicking in. She tries to run at Rene, but she's far too weak, falling on her hands and knees and scrambling toward him on all fours instead. Rene grins, meeting her halfway with a long stride, kicking her straight on the chin, and sending her flying backward. She breaks a bookshelf into pieces while I struggle to rise, Sofie convulsing beneath me as she begins the change. The veins in her forehead and neck protrude just like Ruby's.

Rene grins.

"Kind of a little cunt, don't you think? I thought you liked them obedient."

I glare at him.

"I think that's you, asshole."

He heaves a dramatic sigh.

"Oh, Dominic. When are you going to give this up?"

"When you're in the fucking ground," I growl.

Rene smooths out his dark suit jacket as he shakes his head. His black snakeskin boots have a pearlescent sheen to them. He has tattoos scattered across his knuckles, along with rings that adorn every single finger. One of them is mine. I left it for him when I turned on him.

"You've been promising to kill me for years!" He exclaims. "All you do is concoct these little schemes to *ruin* my empire, but you barely ever even make a dent! Do you think that last grab for territory hurt me? I've got more money and power now than ever. I've even expanded, little one! I've got territory in other cities. Just think, if you just joined me again we could—"

I draw my gun and fire in a single motion. The bullet skims past his skull, searing the flesh on the side of his head. He hisses as he brings his hand up to the wound, a look of amusement taking over his face.

"You missed? I'm standing here talking right at you and you missed?!"

"Think of it as a warning."

He scoffs.

"You know, I've changed my mind. You can't do anything right. I thought you'd have finished my formula by now, but you're so pathetic you can't even do that!"

"The formula's gone, Rene. We destroyed it."

"You know, you really are a terrible liar."

He walks toward me lazily, taking in the surroundings.

"I have to say, despite how terrible a leader you are, I was surprised how easy it was to turn your men against you. You know how much shit they talk behind your back?"

I swallow my rage as he smirks.

"You're a loser, kiddo. The only one who was foolish enough to stay loyal was Mateo. And I gut him like a fucking pig."

Instinctively, I step in front of Sofie, leveling my gun again. He doesn't bat an eyelash, gazing down at her with a grin as he chews on his lip.

"What are you gonna do with her, hmm? Do you think she'll love you? Do you think she'll be loyal after you break promise after promise? One way or another, somebody's going to take you out. If not me, it could be her, or maybe even the one dying against the wall."

"Fuck you!" I roar, taking another shot and watching him absorb the impact like it's nothing.

He's just fucking smiling at me.

"Fuck!"

I try to shoot again, but he's too quick, already rushing at me.

I sprint to meet him, both of us crashing into each other in the air and scattering across the floor. I try to scramble to my feet, but in the blink of an eye, he's grappling me on the floor. I swing my arm up and my fist connects with his chin, the bone making a thunderous crunching noise as it shatters, rocking his head to the side. He grunts as he snaps his neck back toward me, his jaw loose and hanging open. He looks like a broken toy.

I wrap my legs around his waist and violently twist my body, flipping him over and pinning him to the ground. I manage to reach the gun and aim it at his head. But when I pull the trigger, the hollow clicking sound spurns me on to pistol whip him instead as a roar erupts from my throat. All the grief and anger I've pushed down for so long finally comes bubbling to the surface.

I have to make it out of here alive. Sofie has to make it out of here alive. I will not let this *monster* begin his true reign of terror over this city.

I'm hitting mindlessly, without any real purpose beyond causing pain, sending blood and viscera flying into the air. Letting go feels amazing, and I lean into every single strike to make him hurt as much as I do, but that's what gives him the window he needs.

My empty gun is knocked out of my hand as Rene snaps my arm in a heartbeat, following it up by shattering my nose with his palm. I collapse backward, grabbing my face as blood pours out of the wound.

I try to cry out to her, but that single moment of weakness is all he needs, and he scoops me over his head, rising to his feet and hurling me against the far wall with absurd force. So many of my bones crack and snap that I lose track, but I'm almost certain there's a piece of my rib puncturing my lung.

"You're pathetic, Dominic!" He calls from across the room. "How hard is it to shoot someone in the fucking head?"

I pull myself forward with one good arm, struggling to reach the other gun in the middle of the room In a desperate hope it's still loaded, only to see Rene's snakeskin boots slide in front of me as my vision blurs. He kicks it out of my reach as I catch sight of Sofie's limp body splayed halfway across the floor, barely moving. When he reaches me, he crouches down, tipping my chin upward. There's pain in his eyes, but I can't tell if it's mockery or real. He's really kind of fucked up like that.

"See, the thing about loyalty, Dominic, is that even after someone as smarmy and weak as you betrays me, I still *feel* something for you." Rene strokes my cheek. "I want you to know, that when this is all done, I'm going to tie your pretty little girlfriend to your own bed and fuck her until she's nothing but a broken little doll." He lets out a satisfied sigh. "It's been such a long time since I've had a redhead. Maybe I should make you watch this time."

I try to struggle, choking on the blood pouring down my face.

"You didn't get to see what I did to Selene, did you? I sent you a tape, but you never watched it. I thought I was being considerate. Thought you might want to see her final moments."

"I'm gonna fucking kill you," I sputter, blood drooling from my mouth.

"Shame." He shakes his head as he grips both sides of my skull. "At least you'll look exquisite mounted on my wall."

I can feel him pulling, my vertebrae snapping and muscles tearing as I face death once and for all. The worst part is knowing that the last thing I'll see is Rene's hideous yellow eyes.

SOFIE

RENE'S MANSION

THERE'S NOTHING AFTER DEATH. No "other side", no bright light, no angels.

Nobody is waiting for me with open arms.

No Charlie, no Sam.

Only emptiness.

I feel a deep sadness staring into the black, like something has been hollowed out of me as the light dims, and all I want to do is fade into stardust.

Like so many others before me.

And then come the memories: days on the beach with Charlie, wrapping him in my arms and listening to the sound of his laughter. Moments at the dinner table as I watched the dimples form in his cheeks.

He was always smiling.

I can feel Sam's arms around my pregnant belly while I fix myself breakfast, his warm breath on the back of my neck. I see all the days we laid in bed and stared at each other until one of us started to laugh.

None of this hurt to remember, not like it did before. It's just laid out behind me, a testament to the fact that I lived, that I was here. That I loved and was loved in return.

But that was all before, and all that's left of me now is bleeding out on the ground.

A violent heat.

Iron on the tongue.

What...?

There's so much sound, and the brightest light burns my eyes as the room comes into focus with an earth-shaking roar.

Thrashing shapes.

And the screams. They're all around me.

My whole body is hollowed out and raw, desperately broken.

Is this what he promised me?

A violent shape slams into the wall, and another follows quickly after.

I know them. Him.

He's screaming.

He needs help.

And I don't care.

Every part of me is wailing, screaming for something so much louder than he ever could. I can't stop it.

The air is full of blood and sweat, and I'm starving.

The new hunger creeps through every inch of my bones. My skin bristles; my jaw hangs slack. In the brief moments when my eyes can stay focused, I see one shape crash into the other again and again.

Rene is killing him.

And still, I don't care.

Across the room, another shape lies crumpled against the wall.

Blood and sweat, but not just in the air.

It's all over her. Dripping red.

Ruby.

I'm already halfway across the room before I know it. Dragging myself. Clawing at the floor.

New, sharp sounds.

A different kind of violence.

Brilliantly cruel.

I strain my neck to the side to meet the sound as I pull myself towards her. Teeth smile back at me.

Rene.

Panic takes over as I claw my way toward the edge of the room, but he only gives me one quick glance and some words before he goes back to work.

Dominic crumples further under each strike.

And I just can't seem to care.

I'm almost on top of her.

Still breathing, drooling blood.

She's sleeping.

She has everything I need.

I can almost feel it rushing through her body, reaching out to me.

It can be mine.

It *is* mine.

But then there's a shout, panicked.

I hear something clatter across the floor. My leg brushes against it as I drag myself those final few feet. Rene's voice fills the room again, along with so many other sounds.

I don't even look, but it wouldn't matter if I did. Everything is a blur of color, out of focus and twisted. Everything except Ruby. She's practically pulsing with new life.

My new life.

I run my tongue absentmindedly across my teeth, tracing the new shape of my fangs. They're so sharp I feel like I could tear through anything. Or anyone.

She whimpers as I pull myself on top of her, barely able to struggle as I lean in toward her neck. But then something breaks through the haze.

"I'm going to tie your pretty little girlfriend to your bed and fuck her until she's nothing but a broken little doll."

Every part of me freezes, stuck in place as my instincts scream at me to tear everything Ruby has away. To make it mine.

But I'm not an animal, and I'm not a toy.

I'm not going to be a fucking prisoner.

I'm not playing this fucking game all over again.

I feel the entire world come into focus as I turn. Rene is crouched down in front of Dominic, who's covered in blood, one of his arms crushed like a squashed tube of toothpaste.

I look back down at Ruby and blink.

How did I get here?

Rene's hand rests just below Dominic's chin, tipping it upward, and that's when I see it: my gun, just a few feet away. Quietly, I slide down until I'm lying on my side, my fingertips stretching out further and further as I push myself along the floor, all while keeping my eyes on him. It's hard to move, and it's even harder to do it silently. Every muscle and bone in my body burns, each one feeling like I haven't used them in decades.

Dominic's screams fill the room and I panic, my whole body shaking as I give it one final push and my fingertips reach for the gun. I pull it toward me, checking the chamber as I hear Rene's words.

"At least you'll look exquisite mounted on my wall."

With both hands, I take aim, just as he grasps Dominic's head and begins to pull. The sound of bone cracking and muscle tearing fills the room, along with a vicious scream of pain. My arms are trembling, and I can barely hold myself together.

I squeeze the trigger and the gun goes off, the bullet whizzing into Rene's arm and leaving a large crimson gash in his sleeve. I smell iron and scorched flesh, gagging as I drop the gun. My senses are heightened. Colors are brighter, smells are more intense. I can hear the creaks in the building all the way down to the basement.

It's torturous.

Rene's head whips around, the sneer on his lips looking even more disgusting due to his half-ruined jaw. Dominic is slumped on the floor, head turned to face me. Staring. Anguished.

I'm sorry, he mouths.

Rene turns back to Dominic, leaning down and whispering something so soft that I can't make it out. He stands, towering over the carnage that he's inflicted.

Click. Click. Click.

His snakeskin boots, still shiny, glisten in the light with each step he takes. I don't think I have the courage to lift my head and meet my own grisly end, whatever form it takes.

I should have let Dominic kill me.

Begged for it.

Rene's boot heel squeaks against the floor, and suddenly he's crouched in front of me, his mouth bloodied and his eyes like wildfire, violent and scorching. Where I find a dangerous beauty in Dominic's feral side, Rene is only monstrous. His elongated fangs are yellowed with age, and his tongue thick with saliva darts out like a serpent, tasting the blood in the air. He's surely ready to feast tonight.

"Look at you, trying to be the hero," he hums, brushing the sticky hair away from my face.

I don't think there's an inch of my skin that's not covered in blood.

"You're mine, Sofie."

I snarl and hiss reflexively, nearly gagging on my own words.

"Go to hell."

He grins.

"Ah, so the heroine finally speaks! Not much bite left in you, though." He leans in closer. "That's okay, pet, I like my toys obedient. If you stay nice and quiet, I might not have to sew your mouth shut."

Tears roll down my face as a lifetime of torture flashes before my eyes, Rene's weight on top of me, taking whatever he wants. I mean nothing to him, not really. He'll use me to make his formula and keep me like a prize, locked away. I can't do it again. I'll die before that happens.

The only power I have left is to end this new life before it's even started. My arm juts out for the gun, but Rene snatches it first. He must think I'm still trying to kill him, wants to show me how weak I really am. I let out a shriek as he crushes the gun into my hand with his own, snapping my fingers as he forces me to press the barrel under his chin.

"Do it," he urges. "You didn't have the guts at the bar, and you won't do it here. You're a coward, just like your little boyfriend. Do you see him, Sofie? Dying on the floor? First you're going to watch, and then you're going to wish you were as lucky as him."

A happy sigh escapes his lips as I struggle against his incredible strength.

"I think I'll mount his skull in your bedroom, so that you can look at him every time I fuck you."

Rage begins to overtake my fear, building up in my chest, hot and volcanic. I won't end up like that, fading into nothingness as he keeps me like a toy, only taken out of my box when I'm useful.

From across the room, I see Dominic inching his way forward, dragging himself with one arm. Agony clouds his expression and veins pop out of the side of his neck as his exhausted body strains with effort. Rene glances over his shoulder and a dark chuckle ripples through the air, equally noxious and nauseating.

He turns back to me, his expression sick and twisted.

"Just look at him. It would be cute if it wasn't so pathetic."

I strain against his hand, trying to get any sort of real grip on the gun.

"Rene you fucking worm, I'm gonna–"

"You're not going to do a damn thing," he rasps, crushing the bones in my wrist beneath his grip as I let out a piercing scream. "You're all talk, all you humans are. You don't know what it means to have power, because you wasted every last bit of it you had. It's why we're here, now, just like this. All that's left of your kind are going to *bow* to me."

"I'm a fucking vampire, you pig."

He grins, studying me with soulless eyes.

"That's where you're wrong, pet. You might have some of our strength in your veins, but have to *earn* that title. If you can't even bring yourself to kill me, how are you ever going to feed on another living being?" He leans forward and spits in my face. "You're too pathetic to save yourself, let alone anyone else. Hell, a little birdie told me you couldn't even save your *son* when he needed you the most."

Suddenly, as my rage reaches a fever-pitch. I find the strength — my new strength, Charlie's strength — and I howl, the broken bones in my hand knitting together just enough for me to jam down on the trigger.

And in all of his arrogance, as he stares at me in his twisted, grinning, fucked up self-obsession, he doesn't even think to move aside.

Rene's head explodes like a water balloon hitting a wall. Blood, brains, and pieces of his skull rain down on me, smacking against the floor. His body collapses, its weight threatening to crush me, and I wriggle out from beneath him as blood drenches my clothes. It's everywhere, down my arms, smeared on my chest and already pooling beneath me.

I collapse and toss the gun aside, my eyes fluttering open and shut in pure exhaustion as I hear Dominic begin to drag himself across the room. We're not that far apart, but it seems like he takes a century to get to me. I reach out for him, tears streaming down my face as I struggle to stay conscious, until finally his arms wrap around me. Somehow I feel safe, for the first time since this all began.

Dominic is all tenderness as the two of us tangle on the floor, with Rene's bloodied corpse at our feet. When I finally open my eyes, I find him smiling at me, perhaps the first real smile I've seen him give.

"It's over."

I kiss him, not knowing what else to do as he holds me tight. I might be the only thing he has left.

"You need blood."

"I can–"

"No. Let me." He drags himself to his feet, one arm still hanging limp at his side. "Rene kept blood packs in the kitchen. I'll be back."

"You'd better keep that promise," I rasp.

My eyes slip closed again and I try to breathe slowly through the pain, but it's barely working. It would be so easy to fall asleep, to let go.

Suddenly, my mouth is filled with an explosion of flavor. It's different this time. It feels like cracking a beer in the dead of summer and guzzling it all in one go, or like a rainstorm after a week-long heat wave. I squeeze the blood bag, trying to get everything I can out of it while Dominic strokes my hair.

"Keep drinking," he whispers. "I have to feed Ruby."

I nod, my mouth still attached to the top of the bag. Everything is getting sharper by the second, each of my senses reaching their peak, and the hunger slowly subsides. Relief washes over me as I watch Dominic tend to Ruby, who takes to her own bag with even more ravenous hunger than me. He kisses her forehead as she drinks. It's paternal, a softness that melts me as he coaches her through her first real feeding.

"You're okay," he mutters. "I've got you."

She's still pale, makeup smeared under her eyes like paint, and blood staining her skin.

But she's alive. We all are.

Well, close enough.

Dominic pushes himself to his feet and stumbles back to where he left his own blood bag, collapsing onto his knees as he slices it open. I gaze over at him. He could have let me die. He could have fought Rene at full strength and he might have won. It would have been so much easier.

But he kept his promise, even if it meant risking it all, and rebuilding his empire from ashes.

"Hey, Duncan," Ruby coughs.

He tears his mouth away from the blood bag.

"Yeah?"

"You couldn't have killed that asshole five fuckin' years ago?"

Dominic laughs, and I crawl over to him, my body still trembling and exhausted. I'm still adjusting to how this whole vampire thing is going to work, and I really just need someone to fucking hold me.

He smiles as I lean against him.

"What do we do now?" I ask.

"We eat, we sleep, and we figure it out tomorrow night," he replies, reaching into his pocket and pulling out a crumpled piece of paper. "But first, I think I have one more promise to keep."

He flicks the lid off of his lighter, holding it out.

"You wanna do the honors?"

I shake my head.

"I think you've earned this," I whisper.

Dominic lets out a hollow laugh as he sparks it, the blue and gold flame licking the air as he holds it to the crinkled page. He keeps his hand steady the entire time as the formula is reduced to little more than smoldering ash.

It seems that even with his greatest enemy dead on the floor, feeling that final flicker of its fading light is the only way he can know for sure he's finally won.

DOMINIC

RENE'S MANSION

THEO'S HEADLESS BODY LIES next to Mateo in the courtyard as the dull orange hue of the sky just barely begins to creep over the mountains. I crouch down, unclasping the gold pendant from around my neck and placing it delicately in his hand. I wanted to give him something, to show him that I understood, and to tell him that even after all of this, he's still my brother.

A tear drips onto his bloodstained shirt as I move on to Mateo, kissing his forehead. He didn't deserve this. The only thing he did was try to be loyal to me.

Ruby and Sofie took care of Rene's body, cutting off what was left of his head and tying his corpse to the front of the building as a warning to anyone who dared drive up here. I wanted him far away from my brothers.

I glance back up at the sky. The sun is coming up in thirty minutes, and all I feel are waves of grief crashing into me, tossing me around like a buoy. I'm helpless against it. This is the last time I'll ever look at them. My progeny and my brother will vanish with the sunrise.

Years of memories twist into my chest like a knife. Theo knew me better than anyone, which meant he was the perfect choice to betray me. All he had to do was convince Luke and Mateo, and promise the same shit that I'd promised him.

I should have expected it, but Theo was so meticulous and secretive, and I was too trusting. I'm sure Luke fell for it instantly. He was just that kind of guy, but Mateo wouldn't budge, and he paid for it.

Tears roll down my face, and I'm startled as I feel Sofie's soft hand slip into mine.

"We have to get inside," she whispers.

"And then we have to figure out our next move," Ruby announces from the back door.

She's leaning up against it and smoking, with dark circles under her eyes, and her body covered in slowly healing cuts and bruises. She looks as worn down as I feel, and with a broken nose, a torn up face, and a hand that'll surely take more than a single night to heal, Sofie hasn't fared much better.

"I don't..." I glance between the only two people I have left, newly reborn and looking for guidance, and I sigh. "I don't know what to do."

I always thought I'd be able to take charge when the time came, but now that it's here, I feel lost.

What I *do* know is that the hard part is coming in the following days. News of Rene's death will spread like wildfire, which will help as much as hurt. There will be pathetic grasps for power, with some of his cronies thinking they're just the right person to fill his shoes. Others will fall under our rule immediately, not wanting to rock the boat before they see how we run things. And then there's the outskirts of the city...

Theo mentioned that Rene was expanding operations. If that's true, then it won't be long before some of them come knocking to see what's happened to their business partner.

No rest for the wicked, I suppose.

"First thing's first: We have to convince who we can of Rene's men to join us, and capture the ones that try to run." Sofie's tone is soft, but firm, and her voice doesn't waver in the slightest. "We'll need numbers if we want to hold power."

"Agreed," Ruby replies. "And if we want to get the rest of the humans on board, treat 'em right and make sure they know they have a say. That'll make this a whole lot easier. If Rene's goons try anything, we'll have more manpower to take them out, and having people on our side that can function during the day probably won't hurt our chances."

I nod solemnly. I know the storm that's coming, the resistance that Rene's men might put up, but it all feels so far away. Right now, all I want to do is watch Theo's body sink into the earth. He might be a traitor, but he deserves this goodbye.

Sofie brushes my cheek with her fingertips. The gesture makes me want to curl into a ball and weep.

"We take things one step at a time. We'll sleep, meet up at Nox, and go from there."

We all need to rest. My wounds have started to heal, but the arm that Rene crushed remains weak, tucked at my side in a makeshift sling.

"We've got twenty minutes," Ruby says as she flicks her cigarette into the ground, watching the cherry suffocate in a small puddle of rainwater. "I don't know about you two, but all that murder was exhausting."

Sofie turns me away from Theo and walks me inside, past the pieces of broken marble floor, splintered wood, and pools of blood that now adorn Rene's former home. All I can think about is how it could have been me.

"You really didn't know he was going to turn on you, did you?" Sofie asks.

"No."

"I'm sorry about your friend," Ruby offers, looking back at me with sympathy as we climb the stairs.

It's kind of her, and I'm a little surprised.

She's processing her own transformation right now, and she's been a bit hard to read. One minute there's a look of bitterness in her eyes, and the next she's all smiles and jokes. There's no going back now, and she knows it. She's just doing the best she can with what she has.

Sofie squeezes my hand, and we walk in silence until we hit the top floor where Rene's bedroom sits beyond a set of double-doors, along with a guest room on either side. Ruby has already picked out a place to sleep for the night, and pulls her door open.

"You comin', Sof?"

Her fingers interlace with mine.

"I think I'm going to stay with Dominic tonight."

Ruby grins as I turn to Sofie with a frown. In the short time since Rene's death, she's been distant. I didn't expect her to get down on her knees and thank me for all of this, but even this level of kindness is surprising. It's hard to figure out if it's pity or something more.

"Well, as long as you're sure."

Sofie smiles.

"I am."

"Alright, let's get some sleep, shower, and we'll head to Nox tomorrow night." I hold my head a little higher, fully aware I'm merely repeating the words of a woman who seems far more capable of leadership than I am. "We can meet in the back office and come up with a plan."

"Hostile takeover?" Ruby asks.

I grin.

"Anything's possible."

Sofie runs a hand through her hair.

"What the fuck are we going to tell the staff?" She asks.

Ruby shrugs.

"That they're going to have to adapt to a change in management style. It'll be the same old chaos, just with a little twist." She wiggles her eyebrows and gives us a little wave. "I'll see you lovebirds tomorrow night."

"Goodnight, Ruby," I whisper.

"Night, Dominic. Oh, and be good to my girl. Remember, I've still got Little Miss 9mm."

We walk into our room, completely pristine in contrast to the brutalized mess we left downstairs.

"Fuck, I'm exhausted."

"You're also covered in blood," she says matter-of-factly. "You need a shower. It'll make you feel better."

"I don't know about that."

It's not just the grief, the guilt is worse. It's all catching up with me. I should have seen the signs, should have planned everything better.

I should have done a lot of things.

My apology lodges itself in the back of my throat, drying it out as we step into the bathroom. Sofie closes the door and turns to me, unbuttoning my shirt and pushing it aside to check the wounds on my chest. She takes my broken arm out of the makeshift sling, gingerly inspecting it as our eyes meet. She smiles.

"You'll live, cowboy."

I grunt, trying to keep myself from falling apart.

"I really am sorry about Theo. I know he was like family."

This is where the tough guy act comes in. I swipe a hand through my hair and stare at her bloodied bare feet, holding all of that anguish inside. I'm afraid that if I open my mouth, I won't be able to stop screaming.

Sofie kisses my cheek and heads for the shower, checking the temperature before she disrobes. My eyes trail up her body, to the bruises that the fight has left behind. I grimace. They're healing, but they cover most of her back and legs.

She opens the shower door and turns to me, extending a hand.

"Come here."

How is she so sure of herself? How does she always know just what to do next? The last time I felt this helpless was with Selene, and that scares the shit out of me.

Well, at least we're on the same page when it comes to the city.

We're going to be able to run things the way I've always wanted. We can work more closely with the humans, to build trust and connections with them. We'll keep the vaccine clinics going, maybe even remake the synthetic blood from scratch without the barbiturate, and help the population grow.

We can do it right this time.

I try to take off my pants, but my fingers are still half-numb and clumsy. My teeth clamp down as I strain, trying to pop the button, and in an instant, Sofie is at my side.

"You can ask for help, you know."

"I can do it," I insist.

My fingers continue to fumble, trembling through grief and muscle that's repairing itself. Suddenly, I feel her hands on mine and look down into those beautiful green eyes.

"Don't be stubborn," she whispers.

I'm not in the mood for this shit right now. My shoulders slump and she kisses me on the cheek.

"Why are you being so nice to me?" I ask.

"Because you kept your promise, and you saved Ruby's life. I tend to value qualities like that."

Sofie pushes my pants down past my hips, helping me out of them before leading me into the shower. The scalding hot water feels exquisite, and so do her hands on my waist, even if they're just holding me up.

She washes me first, taking her time to clean the blood off of my skin with a cloth. When she brushes against bruises and over fractured bones, I hiss and bare my fangs, but she only shakes her head.

"Thought you were a tough guy."

It's a joke, but it's hard to laugh it off right now. I'm struggling with the weight of my guilt. I don't know how to tell her I'm sorry; it's so much more complicated than those two words now.

"I didn't mean for it to go down like this."

"What do you mean?"

I shake my head and blink away the threat of tears. What more can I possibly say?

"Turning Ruby, Theo almost killing you, it... it was supposed to be different."

"It's okay to grieve." She brushes her knuckles against my face. "And you saved Ruby's life. We're not going to fault you for that."

I feel so fucking useless. I thought that finally having control over this place would fill me with vigor and life, but I'm just empty.

Except for when I look at her.

Sofie is the closest thing I have to an anchor.

I grab her, kissing her as hard as I can. She tastes different now, feels different now. A gentle ache ricochets around my heart like a shattered bullet, knowing that I'll never feel the warmth of her skin again. Touching her used to feel like being out on a warm summer's day, and now she's only cold. My reflection.

But somehow she still carries that light.

"Stay with me," I beg through kisses. "Be my Queen."

I need her humanity, her softness. I need her to be graceful and patient, to balance out my cruelty. She's the best thing that's ever happened to me, and I can't let her go.

"What, you want us to get married or something?" She laughs, breaking away with a wry grin.

I don't know what I want. All I know is that when I'm touching her, when I'm kissing her, nothing hurts and everything feels possible.

I need her to love me, but I don't know how to ask for it.

"I want to be with you," I rasp. "In any way I can."

Her eyes fall, and suddenly all she can offer is a pained smile.

"We have a long way to go, and a lot of work ahead, Dominic."

The words are like poison seeping into my veins.

"You want to leave."

"And abandon the territory you promised me?" She laughs.

It's not what I mean, but it's a start. This time, I have to deliver on my promises. It can't end the same way as with Rene, or with Theo. I *want* to make her happy. I'd spend the rest of my life on my knees for her, without question or protest, if she only asked.

"You'll get it. All you want and more. You can control our relations with the humans, logistics, the blood bank... it's all yours if you'll stay."

I'm not certain, but I think her eyes are a little misty.

"You're always making a deal, aren't you?"

I drop to my knees, kissing her knuckles one by one as she stares down at me, her mouth curling into a tiny smile.

"Not a deal, a promise. Undying loyalty to you, and only you."

There's a mischievous glimmer in her eyes that lights my chest on fire. All the grief, the rage, the joy, it hits me at a dizzying pace, and my only comfort is her embrace.

Sofie lowers herself to the ground and her weight sinks into me as she runs her lips along my neck. I hold her tight, pressing even harder against her, craving this kind of permanence. She doesn't flinch in my arms, doesn't recoil or claw against me. I think this is the first time I've really seen her open. Free.

Maybe it'll work. Maybe it'll be just the two of us. For hundreds of years.

"Maybe we're better together than I thought," she murmurs.

Her fingertips trace a soft circle around the space above my heart.

"Do... you really think so?"

She nods, and I can feel my chest swell.

"I'm willing to try if you are."

I kiss her, living in this single moment, possessed only by my love.

Since I met her, my entire future has been wrapped up in this woman, and for the first time tonight, I have hope.

In us, and what we might become.

THE END

DOMINIC AND SOFIE WILL RETURN IN "BLACK MASS"

THANK YOU

My husband. Thank you for helping me plot this thing, listening to me while I went on different tangents, and encouraging me to *write everything down* even if it seems like a throwaway idea.

My editor, K. You saw this book at the very beginning and were *so* helpful in giving me the confidence I needed to write it.

My beta readers, Savanna, Grace, Tiffani, Nora, Jenni, Danielle, Alanna, Cassidy, Brooke, and Bianca for seeing this book in its very early stages and still giving it a shot. Your feedback was critical and I thank you so much for all of the hard work you put into beta reading.

To my ARC team. You were all absolutely essential to this book. Thank you for reading!

My street team. You hyped the hell out of this book and I'm so thankful. Thanks for sticking with me. You're amazing people!

ABOUT THE AUTHOR

THEA LAWRENCE IS A former PhD student and romance author currently living in Ontario, Canada with her partner of nine years. When she's not writing, she's watching horror movies or napping.

Made in United States
Orlando, FL
30 March 2024

45276597R00157